The Brightest Place in the World

The Brightest Place in the World

David Philip Mullins

UNIVERSITY OF NEVADA PRESS *Reno & Las Vegas*

University of Nevada Press | Reno, Nevada 89557 USA
www.unpress.nevada.edu
Copyright © 2020 by David Philip Mullins
All rights reserved
Cover image by OpenIcons from Pixabay.com.
Cover design by Iris Saltus

LIBRARY OF CONGRESS CATALOGING-IN-PUBLICATION DATA

Names: Mullins, David Philip, 1974– author.
Title: The brightest place in the world : a novel / David Philip Mullins.
Description: Reno ; Las Vegas : University of Nevada Press, [2020] |
   Summary: "Based on a true event, The Brightest Place in the World traces
   the lives and interactions of six Las Vegans in the wake of an
   industrial disaster. Grief and regret, disloyalty and atonement,
   infatuation and love—all are on display as the characters struggle to
   recover and adjust"—Provided by publisher.
Identifiers: LCCN 2019055458 (print) | LCCN 2019055459 (ebook) |
   ISBN 9781948908412 (cloth) | ISBN 9781948908559 (ebook)
Subjects: LCSH: Industrial accidents—Fiction. | Las Vegas (Nev.)—Fiction. |
   LCGFT: Novels.
Classification: LCC PS3613.U4536 B75 2020 (print) | LCC PS3613.U4536
   (ebook) | DDC 813/.6—dc23
LC record available at https://lccn.loc.gov/2019055458
LC ebook record available at https://lccn.loc.gov/2019055459

The paper used in this book meets the requirements of American National Standard
for Information Sciences—Permanence of Paper for Printed Library Materials,
ANSI/NISO Z39.48-1992 (R2002).

Although the opening sequence of this book was inspired by the PEPCON explosions
of May 4th, 1988, the book should be read as a work of fiction. All characters are products
of the author's imagination. In some instances, the author has taken liberties with geography,
and certain real places have been reimagined—sometimes for the sake of the narrative,
other times for the tempo of the prose.

FIRST PRINTING

Manufactured in the United States of America

for Zozo, Beezy, and Boods—
may the world be bright wherever you go

A little light is filtering from the water flowers.
Their leaves do not wish us to hurry:
They are round and flat and full of dark advice.

—Sylvia Plath, "Crossing the Water"

Russell

He spots the smoke off to the south, nine or ten miles away, maybe more. A dark cloud bellies out over the country clubs and subdivisions that have come to occupy the once-vacant periphery of the valley. He merges into the fast lane, lifts his glasses to his forehead, the better to see. The cloud moves swiftly, and he leans forward to follow its course, watching the interstate from the corner of his eye. High above the mountains to the east, a blue stretch of air is split horizontally by the chalk-line contrail of a jet plane. In no time at all the smoke erases the plane's condensation from the sky, making its broad, black way toward Lake Mead and the Arizona border.

Moments earlier the sound startled him, crashing like a wave, deep and resonant. It's quiet now, and Russell listens to a headwind push steadily at the windshield, to the hollow drone of tires against pavement. He wonders, in the stillness of the front seat, if some sort of bomb has gone off at one of the far-flung casinos of south Las Vegas. Ever since 9/11 there's been talk of potential attacks on the city, a few resorts on the Strip still searching backpacks and handbags on New Year's Eve and the Fourth of July, hampering their crowded entrances with metal detectors and armed guards. The glare of a mid-morning sun gives the interstate a kind of waxen luster that almost blinds him if he pays attention to it. An odor of exhaust permeates the atmosphere of his little sedan, charter buses and eighteen-wheelers making canyons of the lanes. Russell lowers the passenger-side window and squints out at the cloud of smoke, whose proportions suddenly double before his eyes. And then he hears it again, the very same sound—like a clap of thunder, like cannon fire at a football game—followed this time by a series of pops. They keep coming: *pop, pop, pop!* Each one louder, clearer, than the last.

He feels a throb of apprehension, then the guilty relief that comes whenever catastrophe strikes a remote region of the world, that unsavory sense of security brought about by the misfortunes of strangers: unlike those who might have already perished in the explosions or the ensuing fire, he is still alive. He raises the window and speeds up to seventy, tailgating an old Ford Mustang, reasoning that a terrorist's targets would be the MGM or Bellagio or the Venetian, Fremont Street or Nellis Air Force Base, places of size and prominence, not a little-known edge of the valley. It's ten thirty, a gusty Tuesday in May, and Russell is heading south on 515, on his way home from the All or Nothing after twelve straight hours tending bar—a shift and a half, because money's tight. He's a good deal stoned, as he often is during his drive back from the tavern. Weed calms him, and Russell needs to be calmed, each and every day. Sometimes, as a matter of course, it has the opposite effect, making him fearful. It seems to be doing so this morning, for he finds himself concerned about Emma, his wife, who's having brunch with a girlfriend downtown—many miles in the other direction. She's perfectly safe. The assumption appeases his fear, and he slows the Corolla and merges back into the middle lane.

He turned off the radio after the first explosion, and now Russell turns it back on, scanning the AM news stations until he hears mention of the fire. The exact location is unknown, a reporter explains in a slow, hardened voice. Somewhere in the desert southeast of Las Vegas, the man says, possibly a chemical plant, and before he can add another word, Russell feels a prickly tension across his forehead and around his ears, a crown of dread. Something in his stomach tautens like a cord. The WEPCO plant, where his friend Andrew works—it's out that way, just beyond the city.

He's known Andrew since middle school, where they shared a homeroom, their friendship a constant for the past thirty years. Russell, an only child, has always thought of him as a brother. He digs around in the console for a tissue, blinking as he steers the Corolla back into the fast lane. His left eye waters when he's anxious, and he lifts his glasses again and dabs at it, the reporter's voice turning soft and indistinct, held for Russell in some kind of abeyance—there and not there. The air conditioner whirs and the wind pushes harder at the windshield. Traffic zips along as if nothing has happened.

The smoke continues over the mountains, drifting higher into the sky. From the pocket of his shirt he fingers his lighter and the joint he rolled the day before, a half-smoked pinner containing the last of his supply. For as long as Russell can recall he's suffered from unpredictable panic attacks that not only start his eye watering but also cause his mouth to dry up and his hands to tremble furiously. His temples will grow slick with sweat, and for minutes on end he'll sit wheezing as though he's sucking air through a penny whistle. Cannabis, when it does its job, is both a neutralizer and a preventive. He toked the first half of the joint at work, on his way out of the parking lot. Now he lights the second half and inhales. He smokes it down to a roach and then stubs it out in the ashtray.

The plant produces a chemical called ammonium perchlorate—an oxidizer for rocket fuel—though Andrew has no background in chemistry or any other science. He's a maintenance technician and has been with WEPCO, the Western Engineering & Production Company, for the past seven or so years. It's among a handful of chemical plants in that part of the desert, with their turbines and storage tanks and great warrens of above-ground piping, slender smokestacks aimed like howitzers at the sky, white plumes mingling above. There's a marshmallow factory out there as well—a factory that manufactures an edible product right in the middle of a bunch of chemical plants. Russell can just imagine the range of hazardous substances stored within the confines of such places, what negligent or unscrupulous activity occurs, not that Andrew himself would ever be responsible. Who knows to what degree their secretions have contaminated the local ecosystem? It was a matter of time, Russell supposes, before something exploded.

•

He keeps south on the interstate, his thoughts turning to Andrew's house, which isn't very far from the plants. Russell wonders about Juliet, Andrew's wife, and about Maddie, their daughter. Are they in harm's way? Juliet—an art therapist—should be at her office by now. Maddie should be in class, her high school a safe-enough distance to the north.

Maybe he's overreacting. He's hopped up; his brain isn't right, isn't operating the way it's supposed to. *I'm panicked*, Russell thinks. *In a state. Jumping to conclusions.* He has no idea if the explosions have in fact taken place at WEPCO—or, despite the news station's hypothesis, at any of the plants at all.

Smoke has consumed much of the air above the mountains, bulking like an enormous rain cloud. Anyone in the vicinity, says the man on the radio, should take immediate shelter. No sooner has the reporter concluded his warning than Russell hears five or six more pops, accompanied by another crash of sound. He feels this one in his seat, a hard double-jouncing, as if the car has passed too quickly over a speed bump.

"Andrew," he says, not quite aloud, smoke sweeping upward in a thick black column tinged with rose. Russell exits the interstate and drives in the direction of Andrew's neighborhood, the whole southeastern sky rolling and fattening. Clouds expanding into clouds.

Emma

She crawls from beneath the table, minding the placement of her hands and knees, to find the dining room covered in glass. Glass on the carpet, the chairs. Glass on the tabletop, the hutch, the leaves of a potted gardenia. She felt the shower of it against her shoulders and back, she heard it spray the furniture, but she's astonished to see so much, all four windows gone.

Gingerly, Emma stands up and shrugs the flannel blanket from her shoulders, running her fingers over her arms and legs and face. Thanks to the blanket, there isn't a scratch on her, even though she wears nothing more than spandex cycling shorts and a cotton tank top. The chandelier, loosed from the ceiling, swings in a tired circle from two twisted wires, the bases of its eight tiny bulbs headless in their sockets. Fragments of glass stick to the wall and flicker like crystals in the orange morning light.

She steps with care to one of the empty window frames and peers outside. Smoke darkens the sky. A towering fire rages below— one of the plants in flames. Which one, though? *Which one?* It's impossible to tell. Near as they are, the distance is still too great, the smoke too dense, a reddish-black pall in the shape of a cauliflower.

Emma tiptoes through the house, searching in her white ankle socks for a phone and her tennis shoes, glass everywhere. On the kitchen countertops. On the armchairs and end tables. Arrayed in an abstract mosaic across the ceramic tile in the entryway. Knives of it, splinters, razor-edged sections the size of dinner plates. As far as she can tell, no window has been left unbroken, no vase or picture frame. Each room looks as it might in the wake of a powerful earthquake.

She can't catch her breath, though it's no exertion at all to walk so delicately from room to room. Emma feels as though she's in a semiconscious state. She is outside herself, she thinks—is that what people call it? There's a ringing in her ears, and she feels momentarily like she's lost—lost in this house she knows so well—everything a little murky all of a sudden, foreign-looking in some frightful way. Has she sustained an injury to the head? She touches her face again, smooths her palms slowly over her skull. No lumps, no blood. Her search for shoes and a phone seems a rational, self-orienting task, but she keeps having the strange sense that her thoughts are not her own, that they belong to someone else, and Emma moves aimlessly around the living room, hardly looking.

They are in the spare bedroom, her Nikes. She remembers now. She took them off, as she sometimes does, while riding the stationary bike, feeling lighter without them—before the explosions began, before she grabbed the blanket from a linen closet and hurried to the dining room for cover. Emma makes her way down the hall. Once or twice she missteps and a shard of glass crunches like a corn chip under the ball of her foot, though her socks remain untorn, her feet uncut.

In the spare bedroom she pulls on her shoes, leaving the laces untied. The ringing in her ears has abated, replaced by a sharp whisking sensation, a fretful feeling, at the back of her tongue. She finds the cordless phone on a nightstand in the master bedroom. She dials Andrew's cell phone and gets his voice mail. Emma bites her lip and tries the number again. This time a computerized voice tells her that all circuits are busy. She dials 911—it's the only other thing she can think to do—telling the dispatcher there's been an accident.

"Explosions," she says, absurdly. "A fire."

"The WEPCO plant?" the dispatcher asks, clearing his throat.

Emma feels a flush of heat in her neck.

"We're aware of the situation, ma'am. Are you hurt?" He speaks slowly, as if to a child or a drunk.

"I'm not hurt, no," she says. "You don't have to send anyone. I'm hanging up now," Emma says, and hangs up.

Back in the living room, she turns on the television. An aerial view of the plant: fire and smoke, so much smoke, a close-up of what she saw from the dining room. Abandoned automobiles, dented or windowless or overturned, obstruct the narrow roads that curve like tributaries through the flat sepia terrain. Studying the screen, Emma looks for Andrew among them, looks for his dark-blue Sonata, but can see no one, can spot no car that resembles his. There are no paramedics, no police officers, no firefighters. Nothing but flames and smoke—a holocaustal tableau that puts Emma in mind of before and after images she once saw of a mock town built for destruction and survivability evaluations by the Nevada Test Site, the first image depicting houses, commercial buildings, automobiles, even mannequins, the second only the charred, mangled husks of a few cars and trucks, desert earth smoldering around them.

The surrounding chemical plants are more or less okay, says the reporter, overwrought, while the Meyrowitz marshmallow factory, just down the road from WEPCO, has been leveled. The number of fatalities, if there are any, is not yet known. Because of the immensity of the flames, he explains, because of their extraordinary heat, firefighters cannot approach the WEPCO plant until the fire dies down.

Emma takes a breath. Where's Russell? On his way home from the tavern? Home already? He isn't at risk, she thinks, either way.

She closes her eyes, rubs the back of her neck. *This is happening*, she thinks. *This is real.*

•

Outside, neighbors stand open-mouthed in doorways, watching the sky. Others mill about in the street: women mostly, only a few men. High above them to the east, a massive ceiling of smoke. They observe it with tilted heads, with looks of hysteria and wonderment, as though it's a UFO about to touch down.

"Mother of God," one of them says, cradling a blood-glazed arm.

"Is everybody all right?" says another.

Emma watches dreamily as a snow of ash wafts through the air. Despite the condition of the windows, she turns and locks the front door.

She has to look for Andrew. She has to find out if Andrew is okay.

The ash powders his driveway and his sidewalk, and is all over the little patch of grass in front of his house, seeming to accumulate more heavily there, the green lengths of blades poking through. It carries a smell she can't quite place. Behind the wheel of her Civic, Emma lowers the windows, which are miraculously intact, and sniffs the air. The smell is sweet and familiar, and conjures a brief, hazy nostalgia. She knows what it is.

Marshmallow. The smell is roasted marshmallow.

Simon

The pickup ticks softly in the late-morning heat, perched atop a sandy bluff that overlooks a wide plain of rain-shadow desert. He considers the modest beauty of the Mojave, its clean and muted loveliness, distracting himself—keeping his mind from circling back to the plant and the explosions and poor Andrew Huntley. He sits studying the land, a marvel, as one might a work of art in the solitude of a gallery. He feels a deep-rooted connection to these flat, quiet expanses just outside the city.

What has he done? He can't allow himself to think about it.

Simon crosses his eyes and the landscape blurs. He is sorely thirsty. His pants are torn, stained with blood that leaks from the gash in his leg. His hands are tired from clutching the wheel as he sped eastward through the roadless desert. Deep within his ears, the sound of bubbles rising in a water-cooler bottle. In spite of these things, it is, in a sense, like meditating, staring this way into the openness before him: a dismissal of his self-reproach, an escape. He fights the temptation to remove himself from this state, to lift his eyes to the fire in the distance. It swells in the periphery of his vision but he won't look at it.

He turns his attention to the rearview mirror. It's cockeyed and dust-covered, and Simon straightens it, wipes it clean with the heel of his hand. His entire face stings as though razor-nicked, and he examines his reflection. The cuts, little blood-darkened slashes, are all over his cheeks and nose and forehead. He looks deeply into his own two eyes, whose color he's always liked but now seems deceptive and ugly, a silvery, fish-scale blue. Cowardly eyes, he thinks, marked in some uncertain way by weakness.

He is a coward. He has always known this—a secret he's kept since childhood—and now, as a consequence, a man's life has been lost. Simon fears so, at least. He can't stop his mind from returning to this unsettling place. He feels the need to weep yet no tears fall, held in reserve behind his eyes.

Broken glass blankets the dashboard, the side windows blown out, the rear window as well. Somehow the windshield is still in one piece, fractured in places though holding to the frame. Leaning forward, Simon can see that the right front fender is flattened. The passenger-side door hangs open, bent nearly in half. He unbuttons his shirt, slips out of it, and wraps it tightly around his thigh, wincing as he knots the sleeves over the gash. Simon isn't sure what caused it: something airborne during the first explosion, he thinks, a piece of shrapnel rocketing toward him as he climbed into the pickup. He felt nothing, anesthetized by adrenaline. Only now does the pain set in, an edgeless gnawing that works its way into his knee and down through his shin.

The fire spread too quickly to be extinguished. As the alarms rang out, people scrambled for automobiles, piling in and racing off through the desert. Simon stayed behind, longer than he should have, to make sure all of his men had evacuated. He was alone in the pickup, fifty yards or so from the plant, when he saw Andrew Huntley in the rearview mirror, running after him and waving an arm. Simon thought briefly about stopping. He knew that if he did he might never see his wife and children again—might never see his house again, or his big kidney-shaped pool, or his new Trek touring bike. He held his foot to the accelerator. The second explosion was twice as loud as the first, deafening. The pickup had been lifted into the air by the time he heard it, and when it landed glass was coming at him and he closed his eyes, and when he opened them the truck was out of control and the passenger-side door was dangling wedge-shaped from a hinge, and in the mirror Andrew Huntley was gone, replaced by a wheeling mass of dust and smoke. The world was dust and smoke and the rumbling clamor of destruction, and nothing more. Simon got control of the pickup. A couple of miles out he turned it around, fishtailing, and ascended the bluff. It was from here that he watched the third explosion, the largest, and as the shock wave rippled toward him through the dirt—as he braced for it—he was positive he'd had enough time to stop for Andrew Huntley.

Now, against his injured leg, Simon feels the vibration of his cell phone. He arches his back into the seat and digs the phone from his pocket. Rebecca.

"I'm okay," he answers. "I'm all right, hon."

She's crying. "Thank God," she says. "Thank you, God." She cries harder, sniffling into the phone.

"Hey," he says. "Honey. I'm alive." The noise is still there in his ears, thick and toneless—more of a gulping sound now. He can barely hear her.

"Where are you?" his wife asks him.

"In the desert—in the truck. I just drove."

"I kept calling but I couldn't get through. I thought…"

"Hello?"

"Can you hear me?" Rebecca says, her words clipped and staticky. Before Simon can respond, the line goes dead.

He doesn't call back. He sits still in the pickup, holding the phone to his chest, watching his shirt darken with blood around his thigh. Simon doesn't know Andrew Huntley very well. They work in different departments. Huntley is a technician, a subordinate, Simon a manager in charge of a sizable crew. But they've spoken, over the years, at holiday parties and company picnics. Huntley is younger than he is: early forties, long-faced and slender, with large, knuckly hands. He has an affable smile and keeps his dark hair combed flat against his head. A womanizer of sorts, Simon remembers thinking, though he can't recall anything he's heard, or anything Andrew Huntley has ever said or done, that might have given him this impression. Besides, Huntley's married, isn't he? Simon is sure he's met his wife at one of those parties, one of those picnics, a blondish woman with, he calls to mind somewhat ashamedly, larger-than-average breasts. She and Rebecca hit it off, he seems to think. He doesn't remember any children, and hopes they don't have any.

•

He looks at the fire now, at the black hive of smoke, tilted as if on an axis. He begins to question his perception, his memory. He *did* see a man in his rearview mirror, didn't he? He *did* see Andrew Huntley—right?

Maybe not. It's possible that his brain played a trick on him, fear and confusion commingling to produce a fleeting hallucination. It's possible that there was nobody there at all.

But the fragment keeps playing in Simon's head: Huntley in full stride, his arm sweeping back and forth, then gone.

It was automatic, the way Simon tore off through the desert, save for his brief thought about stopping. An animal effort of self-preservation. Rebecca would be horrified if she ever found out. So would his children, Daniel and Michaela—grown now, and critical of him. What he did will remain a secret, then, a guilt that will haunt him. Simon knows this. He feels the way he's imagined he would after an act of infidelity. He's never come close to committing one in the twenty-five years he and Rebecca have been married, but he's thought many times of how he might feel immediately following such a transgression, and it is this feeling exactly. The sourness below his tongue, the tightness in his throat, the kind of queasiness he gets after drinking coffee on an empty stomach.

At the same time—he can hardly admit it to himself—he has an overwhelming sense of good fortune. Here they still are: the plain, elemental beauty of the desert before him, the mounting pain in his leg. He knows how lucky he is to experience these things. To live and to breathe.

Maddie

They won't let her go.

They've summoned her here and told her the accident took place at the plant where her father works. They pulled her out of class, AP biology, and presented her with this information, only to hand her a cup of water and show her to a couch.

Maddie can hear them whispering around the corner, though she can't unravel the words. Mrs. Skinner—the office secretary—and Dean Langen. Maddie has called home several times by now. She's tried her mother and her father on their cell phones, tried her mother at her practice, but the lines are all tied up. Less than an hour ago, Maddie and two dozen of her fellow students watched the distant explosions through the old bowed windows of their sixth-floor lab. They rushed from their stools during the first lengthy boom, just in time to see the smoke topple upward.

Now she can't help feeling that she's being kept in the dark. Is her father injured? Dead? Maddie cries, drying her eyes with the sleeves of her shirt. She tries to picture him but the image won't sit still, spinning willfully into vibrant schemes of color that flash in the darkness of her mind's eye.

She listens to the whispers, hating them both: Mrs. Skinner, with her matted, fake-blond hair, her pear-shaped nose, her long and narrow teeth, and Dean Langen, with his bald, cylindrical head and dull-witted smile. Orchestral music plays faintly on an old portable CD player atop Mrs. Skinner's desk. Maddie hears what sounds like the local news coming from a television somewhere in the depths of the office—from a lunchroom, maybe—but like the whispering, the words are indecipherable.

There's a disinfected smell to the coffee table, an odor of cleanser or lemon oil that tickles Maddie's throat as she breathes. A water cooler stands in the corner, and she keeps getting up for more water, draining cup after cup. She's been here only four or five times before, in passing. Maddie prides herself on her general adherence to rules, and on her perfect record of attendance and near-perfect grade-point average (3.95). She's an academic-scholarship student, president of her class. She plays flute in the marching band. She runs for the varsity cross-country team. She secretly maintains a long list of words she's looked up in the dictionary, using them in conversation whenever she can. In her almost three years at Bishop Delaney High, she has never done anything that might have warranted a trip to the dean's office.

"Excuse me?" she says, scooting to the edge of the couch. "Mrs. Skinner? Hello? Can someone tell me what's going on?"

Dean Langen appears from around the corner. "Hi, Maddie," he says. He sits down beside her, rests his palms on his knees. "We still haven't gotten hold of your parents. Do you have any idea where your mother might be?"

"At her office is where she *should* be. How would I know?"

She's never spoken to the teachers or administrators of her school with anything but the highest respect, and it startles her to answer him in the bitchy tone she reserves for arguments with her mother. Maddie is still crying. She wipes her nose with the back of her hand.

Dean Langen stands up from the couch and plucks a yellow tissue from a box at the corner of Mrs. Skinner's desk. "Please," he says, extending his arm.

Maddie blows her nose.

"We're going to keep trying," Dean Langen says. "If you'd like to talk with one of the school counselors, you're welcome to do that."

"I'm fine," she says.

"Feel free to lie down as well, okay?" He nods at the couch, then goes back around the corner.

Through the window across the waiting room, Maddie can see a few dark leaves eddying in the breeze, vestiges of autumn. A chitalpa tree shaped like a tuning fork grows from a brick-edged plot in the concrete. Fat pink flowers droop from the branches, the petals like stockings hung to dry. As she tries a second time to picture her father, a memory comes to her from a far compartment of her mind, the two of them lying beneath the big woolly dogwood in her backyard, to whose gray-ridged trunk her father nailed three cherry-wood steps so that Maddie could climb with ease to the lowest branches. She is nestled in her Strawberry Shortcake sleeping bag on a warm April night in 2003. Her father—she can almost see his face now, *almost*—is stretched out beside her on the wrinkled blue tarp he's spread across the grass, his own sleeping bag in a roll beneath his head. Yard camping: something he did with his own father throughout his boyhood. ("*Yamping*," her father would say in a clownish voice, and Maddie would laugh.) They're looking up into a gnarl of branches illuminated by his flashlight. The dogwood is in full bloom. In a kind of reverential silence, her father moves the beam slowly across the inner canopy while Maddie watches the flowers appear and disappear, white and crosslike. They seem to go on forever.

"Don't ever forget how much I love you," he tells her, with reference to nothing, something foreboding in his tone.

"I won't," Maddie replies.

"No matter what happens," he says.

"No matter what."

Wherever the beam wanders, an ivory bouquet hangs striking and motionless in the little circle of light. She is eight years old, and she imagines the flower-covered branches reaching as far as the eye can see, traversing the globe until they converge somewhere on the other side.

Maddie wishes she could recall more of that night, one of many she's spent camping in back of the house with her father. As she stares at the chitalpa tree outside, she begins to wonder what her life would be like without him.

Dean Langen appears again from around the corner. "We're still trying your mom," he says softly.

Maddie doesn't look at him. A violent urge rises inside her, the urge to stand and strike him. Where in the world is her mother?

"I want to go home," she says, trying her best to withhold her tears. "I need to go."

"We can't just let you leave in a situation like this. I'm sorry, Maddie. The school's on lockdown. You'll have to wait here until we reach one of your parents, I'm afraid. Mrs. Skinner will be out in a minute." He pats her shoulder and walks away.

Maddie gets up from the couch and goes to the window. It's just barely open, air whistling through the dusty screen. She watches as the breeze continues to toss the left-behind leaves. After a moment, she opens the window all the way, pops the screen from the frame, and climbs out.

●

It was her only means of leaving, if she wanted to avoid the security guards at each of the school's two gilded gates. In the near distance, beyond the practice field, Maddie can see the section of fence she'll have to scale to complete her getaway. She hurries past the chitalpa tree, through the faculty parking lot, and across the empty field. The rails of the fence taper to pointed tips, and she places her feet on the soldered spirals and hoists herself up and over.

There's a meadow on the other side, emerald blades of grass as long as yardsticks. They sweep her bare knees as she runs, birdsong filling the air, dark smoke brooding over the mountains. The meadow dwindles to a spread of tussocks, and then the grass vanishes entirely at a stand of junipers, beyond which lies a short length of desert.

Maddie starts through the dirt. She's in exceptional shape. Since late November, when the cross-country season ended, she's logged thirty to forty miles each week on her own, rising early every morning. All the same, she's breathing heavily. She doesn't own a car—her mother shuttles her to and from school, or she bums rides off friends—and this is the quickest way home, a straight line to her neighborhood but a good distance nonetheless, three or four miles.

She can feel the big toe of her left foot butting against the leather of her black penny loafer, and she can already feel a dull cramp in her side. But she keeps running, her loafers turning the dirt, pebbles gathering in the hollows of her arches. As though competing in a steeplechase, she hurdles bursage and weaves through the dark volcanic rocks.

Again, Maddie cries. She is certain her father is dead. She can feel it, the weight of his absence—slowing her now as she runs, pushing her earthward. She can sense his sudden nonexistence in the world.

Russell

He's never cared about any other friend as much as he cared about Andrew. Andrew was almost a full year his senior. He had a waggish way about him that sometimes made Russell feel inferior, the way he imagines he might feel in the presence of an older sibling. But he never held this against Andrew. On the contrary, he admired his friend's wit and intelligence. He always liked that Andrew made him laugh, even when it was at Russell's own expense. He always liked that Andrew made women laugh, and when they were younger, Russell especially liked that girls seemed to find him more attractive with Andrew at his side.

He was with him the night he met Emma, six and a half years ago at the Bora Bora, where Emma deals roulette, blackjack, and pai gow poker. He and Andrew were there for a younger friend's bachelor party. They were playing a few hands of blackjack—the only two at her table—while the rest of their group ordered drinks at one of the bars. Andrew remarked on the many gin-and-tonics he'd had, pretending to hiccup, and Emma laughed as she dealt them their cards. Russell hailed a passing cocktail waitress for a pen and a napkin. Feeling woozy and brave, he asked Emma for her number. She angled her head and smiled, a tiny miracle. Then she gave it to him, just like that (against house rules, Russell later learned). He was mute with surprise.

"Jackpot," he said as they walked away from her table.

Andrew rolled his eyes.

Russell read the napkin, holding it up like a trophy: "Emma."

When they were married eighteen months later at the Clark County Office of Civil Marriages, Andrew was the best man.

•

Now he's gone.

How is it possible? His closest friend has been killed, a person Russell's known for most of his life.

Two hundred people are injured; eight, including Andrew, are dead. All of the deceased were employees of the plant, all of them men. Only three of the bodies have been found. Andrew's is among the five unaccounted for.

There's no official word as to what might have caused the explosions. Theories proliferate. A small brush fire in the surrounding desert. A lit cigarette carelessly discarded, even though smoking was strictly prohibited at the plant. The malfunction of some piece of equipment—the vaguest of all the speculation, save for the chatter of pundits and bloggers who hold, in the absence of any evidence, that al-Qaeda is to blame.

Day and night, the Western Engineering & Production Company is the lone target for criticism on Fox News, CNN, and MSNBC. It's come to light that WEPCO amassed a considerable surplus of ammonium perchlorate—nine million pounds of it, to be exact, equivalent to more than a thousand tons of TNT. The company was storing it in lime-green polyethylene drums that occupied an entire parking lot at the east end of the property. From time to time Andrew would stop by the All or Nothing after work, making the long drive from the plant, and Russell keeps thinking of him shaking his head one evening, eyes cast down at his drink, as he talked of the overcrowded lot. During the Cold War, WEPCO sold its ammonium perchlorate to the military for ballistic-missile engines. By the early nineties the company was selling it to NASA as well, for the boosters that powered the Space Shuttle. When *Atlantis* touched down on earth for the final time and NASA terminated the Shuttle program, WEPCO scaled down its production. But the fifty-gallon drums continued to accumulate.

The largest explosion registered 3.5 on the Richter scale, and residents have reported feeling shock waves—the slight remains of them, anyway—as far away as Spring Valley and North Las Vegas

Airport. The crater where the storage lot used to be is fifteen feet deep and two hundred feet wide. Homes and businesses within a four-mile radius suffered not only broken windows but caved-in roofs as well. Doors were ripped from their hinges, countertops dislodged. Property-damage claims are expected to exceed a hundred million dollars. One of the shock waves knocked a 737 off its course. Eventually, three different engine companies—about three hundred firefighters—were mobilized to battle the flames, which climbed almost four hundred feet. It took an estimated fifty thousand gallons of water to put them out. The cloud of smoke carried ammonia and hydrochloric acid, and both the Department of Energy and the Environmental Protection Agency dispatched emergency-response teams.

Russell watches the coverage whenever he can. The particulars have embedded themselves in his memory. The marshmallow factory was closer to WEPCO than he thought. Meyrowitz is its name. The only maker of kosher marshmallows in the world was located, of all places, in the desert outside Las Vegas. The workers managed to evacuate before the factory was wiped out along with the plant.

"It's a miracle there weren't more deaths," the governor said in a televised address. "We've got a miracle on our hands."

•

Russell feels a dart of nausea now, thinking of it all. His house—his neighborhood—was spared any harm. He's thankful for that at least.

Emma blots her eyes with a tissue as they walk through the parking lot of the Peppermill, a coffee shop and lounge at the north end of the Strip. It's almost five o'clock. She has to be at work by six, and they've decided to grab an early dinner, even though the notion of eating only intensifies his queasiness. They're returning from Andrew's funeral.

Inside, he takes Emma's hand. The lighting is neon—pink and purple and blue—and the restaurant smells of grease and butter. There are silk plants on high wooden shelves, and several potted trees: fan palms in need of pruning, each one hunched against a mirror-tiled ceiling. Video-poker consoles bleep and blip along the bar. "Here we are," Russell says, for no reason.

The hostess seats them at a table beside a window.

"He can't just be gone," Emma says, planting her elbows into the leather-bound menu. She sniffs and exhales, sniffs again. "How can a person go away forever? Here and then not here—it doesn't compute."

"I know," Russell says.

"None of it makes any sense."

"None of it does."

"I just wish…"

"What," he says.

"It's like he vanished. It defies…I don't know. *Logic*. No warning, no nothing. It's so crazy to me."

She's been quiet for the past couple of weeks, staring past him, empty-eyed and abstracted. The stricken look on Emma's face, the one she's been wearing since the day of the accident, is somewhat surprising. She knew Andrew for the better part of a decade, and it's natural for her to have feelings of grief. And to be sure, the whole city is in shock. There's been a local catastrophe. She has a right to a certain amount of gloom. But she knew him only through Russell. Emma only spent time with Andrew and Juliet on the rare occasions that the two couples went to dinner or to the movies or to some free concert in a park. She's been to their house no more than a handful of times. All in all, the four of them weren't that close, and it irritates him that she's acting as if it's her *own* best friend who's died.

He figures he just wants the attention that's due to him. Andrew was his, not hers. Emma should be the one consoling *him*. It makes Russell feel foolish, this pettiness. He should be flattered that she's so moved by Andrew's death—he meant more to her than Russell thought. But that look on her face. He's never seen it before, not even when her grandmother, who raised her, died of colorectal cancer last winter. Something about the way Emma's mouth keeps opening and closing, fishlike. Something about the slow blinking of her eyes. On occasion, in his most timorous moods, he used to wonder if there was something going on between them. He has no good reason to believe it, but he used to get this inkling sometimes. This soupy feeling in his limbs. Ropy currents in the mire of his gut. He sweeps the thought aside.

"I already miss him so much," Russell says, adjusting his glasses, running his fingertip back and forth along the wire bridge. "And poor Maddie. Poor Juliet."

"What those two must be going through right now," Emma says. "And not even a house to live in."

They're staying at a Best Western not far from their neighborhood, their room to be paid for by insurance money.

"How come FEMA hasn't gotten involved?" she says. "There should be a special fund or something, shouldn't there?"

"I keep getting stuck on this one idea," Russell says. "It's weird, but I keep wondering if maybe he didn't die. Maybe he survived the whole thing, crazy as it sounds. I mean, if they haven't found a body."

She gives him an impatient look.

"Remember after September Eleventh," he says, "when the news kept showing those posters all around New York? Those fliers, or whatever they were, advertising lost workers from the Trade Center? All those people refusing to accept that their loved ones were gone, hanging their pictures all around. I keep thinking of that." Before the service, Russell sneaked off to the parking lot of the church and smoked part of a joint, and he's still pretty high, and his voice sounds to him as if it's coming not from his larynx and his mouth but from someplace very far away. "That's me, I suppose. I can't accept that I'll never see him again. It's like you were saying: it makes no sense."

It was a closed-casket funeral, naturally. After a couple of weeks Juliet and Maddie had decided to go ahead with it, even though Andrew's body is still missing. During Juliet's tearful eulogy, Russell stared at the empty mahogany box—burnished to a gleam and overlaid with bright spring flowers—that they were all supposed to imagine contained his late friend. A symbolic gesture. Okay. But symbolic of what? A pretense, he thought finally, angrily. A waste of money. It's actually going to be lowered into the ground and buried; it's probably buried already, a casket with nothing in it. Throughout the service, Maddie sat beside him with dry, widened eyes. Nine or ten WEPCO executives sat looking bored in a rear pew of the church. Juliet had decided against any kind of post-funeral gathering, and as everyone filed out of the Guardian Angel Cathedral, its pitched metal roof glinting in sunlight, Russell saw in her face the distraught bewilderment of a refugee.

A waitress comes and they order a couple of burgers, Michael Jackson singing "Rock With You" from an invisible speaker close by.

"What if that's really the case, though? With Andrew," Russell says. "What if he's lost out there, in the desert somewhere?"

He doesn't believe this, and he hasn't, in point of fact, been wondering if Andrew survived. Andrew and seven of his coworkers are dead, undeniably. But it soothes Russell to talk this way, to make as if there's some faint hope that his best friend might return.

"You're not serious," Emma says.

"Of course I'm not. No. But still."

"He's in a better place now," she says mournfully.

That old line—that old platitude. It pisses him off.

"Heaven, huh? That's where he is?"

She closes her eyes, sips her water. "Why wouldn't he be?"

"I'm not saying that," he says.

"You're saying you don't believe in it."

"Maybe I am."

He *doesn't* believe. He's atheist, or agnostic. He can't remember if he's ever decided between those two defiant choices. He hates that latter word: *agnostic*. It makes people sound, ironically, as if they belong to some religious cult. Being atheist is more extreme, but the word has a much better ring to it.

"What are we talking about here?" Emma says, fidgeting with the collar of her black satin dress. Her wrist, her fingers, her neck—a wiggle of desire moves through him. Her dark hair, parted down the middle, hangs in two identical wings over bold blue eyes and a thin Greek nose, and she has the long, toned body of an athlete. Her beauty has always had a way of sustaining him.

When the waitress comes back with their burgers, Russell pushes his plate away. "Somebody's at fault, make no mistake. Somebody's going down for what happened," he says. "That deadly substance. So much of it just hanging around like that."

Once, around the Fourth of July, Andrew brought a vile of it home with him—ammonium perchlorate, granular and colorless, like fine white sand—and showed Russell how to make a firework out of a sheet of aluminum foil and a toilet-paper tube. Andrew had learned the technique from one of the engineers at the plant. They lit the firework on the sidewalk in front of Russell's house and watched, buzzed on beer, as it glowed in the mid-summer darkness, a knee-high fountain of flames that rained sparks onto the decorative rocks of his desert-landscaped yard.

"They'll get to the bottom of it," he says now. "The lawyers. They always do with things like this." He's talking nervously. He can't wait to get home and roll himself another joint from the new batch he picked up a few days ago. "The lawyers will make a killing. Or there'll be a cover-up. That wouldn't surprise me either."

The look is still there on Emma's face as she sips her Diet Coke. The fizz is like a throng of fleas, and she stares into it as if its presence is a mystery.

"I'm sorry he's gone, Russell," she says finally. "I'm so sorry."

"Thanks," Russell says. He feels friendless. Adrift. "Thank you."

She takes a bite of her burger, checks her watch. "Can you drop me at work? I won't have time to get my car."

"Don't you wonder what it was like? Not necessarily to *be* there, I don't mean. But close enough to really experience it. The shock waves and everything." He sighs. "Like the world coming at you, I bet. Or like some big hand shaking it. Shaking it like a snow globe." He nods his head. "Or maybe it was like getting hit by a giant gust of wind. To be nearby—I can't imagine. Juliet says it'll be another few weeks or so before they can move back into their house."

Emma glances at him.

"It must have been terrifying," Russell says.

"Yes," she says. "It must have been."

Emma

They head downtown on Las Vegas Boulevard, threading their way through traffic, passing the Bonanza gift shop and the Stratosphere, Dino's Lounge and the Talk of the Town gentlemen's club, tattoo parlors and wedding chapels and adult-video stores. Then the broken-hearted motels of a bygone Vegas, a profusion of washed-out neon: the Holiday, the Oasis, the Desert Star, the Monterey. Russell drives silently, his ponytail resting on his shoulder like a blond mink pelt. Clouds collected as they ate. The sky wavers in silvery light, and a heavy wind leans into Emma's window. The next thing she knows it's pouring, so suddenly it's as if the Corolla has veered into a waterfall, rain coming down like loose change on the roof and hood.

In front of the Golden Gate hotel, she leans across the console and kisses him. She was gruff with him during dinner; now's the time to apologize. His talk of Andrew's possible survival infuriated her, because Emma hopes against reason—single-mindedly, achingly—that Andrew will return.

"Thanks for the lift," she says, and kisses him again, then hurries from the car to the shelter of Fremont Street. Overhead is the massive barrel-vault screen that floats nine stories above the ground, stretching like a canopy from casino to casino, block to block, displaying magnified images of slot machines and showgirls that are synchronized to a jazzy instrumental of "Fly Me to the Moon." It's what everyone is looking at. Dubbed the "Fremont Street Experience," the screen was erected to poach sightseers from the Strip, to revitalize the downtown area, but the whole thing strikes her as tawdry and unnecessary, a disruption of the neighborhood's historic appeal. The Bora Bora is two blocks down. Along the crowded pedestrian mall, dark-skinned men sell peanuts and churros and foot long hot dogs, the aromas mingling in the humid air. Couples stroll toward her with upturned faces, eyes wide with reflected light. Beyond the Bora Bora is Vegas Vic, the famous neon cowboy that stands atop the old Pioneer Club, now a gift shop.

In the dressing room, Emma changes into her uniform: white button-down, black vest, black pants. She closes her locker and clocks in with one minute to spare. Ed Logan is filling out paperwork in the pit, leaning on his wood-paneled podium. He's often testy with the dealers, the only pit boss who makes Emma feel on edge, and she keeps glancing over her shoulder to see if he's eyeing her. He's assigned her to a roulette table for the first sixty minutes of her shift. Of the three games she deals, roulette is her least favorite. It bores her, watching a wheel spin around and around, a little ball skip about. Emma prefers the waxy stiffness of the cards. She likes tossing them to the players from a handheld deck, or fingertipping cards from a shoe. She likes to shuffle, likes fanning them across the tissue-soft felt. Blackjack and pai gow poker require a certain dexterity, and as dealer you're part of the game, which makes time fly. An hour of roulette is almost always a crawl.

Emma's table is unoccupied, and she spins the wheel lethargically, running through the payout chart in her mind. She stares out at the multitude of slot machines, column upon column; at the bronze chandeliers that hang from the low, tiered ceiling; at the stone waterfall fountain near the cashier's cage, pumping the white water that always looks to Emma like melted candle wax. Beyond the fountain, artificial coconut palms encircle a replica of a double-peaked volcano. Cocktail waitresses zigzag through the crowd, and bells ring out, and the casino burbles with conversation.

Russell wasn't toying with her during dinner. He has no idea that Emma was at Andrew's house, so close to the plant, when the accident took place. She's sure of this. She lied to him, as she so often has. As usual, Emma got away with it. She was having brunch with a friend: this is what she'd told him that morning, when he called her from the All or Nothing. How many times has she told

Russell she's going out for brunch, or going to do *whatever*, when in fact she's intended to meet up with Andrew? How many times has she deceived him, her husband who loves her unwaveringly? Lying to Russell has become second nature, and in the end it isn't just the relationship she had with Andrew and the fact that Andrew was Russell's dearest, boyhood friend that makes her feel she's a truly awful human being; it's her effortless dishonesty as well. Russell is so trusting of her, convinced of her everlasting integrity. It's torment to know she's made him into a fool.

It must have been terrifying, he said.

It was. So much so that Emma thought she was going to die. When she felt the first explosion, she was reading on the stationary bike, flipping through her father's copy of *Crossing the Water*, a collection of poems by Sylvia Plath—a gift her mother had given him in the final days of their lives, before Emma went to live with her grandmother. In addition to the bike, the spare bedroom contains a doorway pull-up bar and an elliptical trainer and a set of weights, equipment that, were it not for Emma, would have gone entirely unused. Andrew had given her a key, and she'd sometimes squeeze in a late-morning exercise session while she waited for him to come home for lunch. The recklessness, she thinks now. The audacity. Their routine was to eat their salads or sandwiches—whatever Emma had picked up for them—at the kitchen counter, then make love on the living-room floor (never in a bed or on a couch, for fear of leaving behind some odor, some hair, some stain). Andrew liked to play classical records on his mother's antique Victrola, and was always careful to collect the refuse of their meals in a plastic bag he'd later discard at work. The midday rendezvous were risky, but the cost of motel rooms would have quickly added up. Emma enjoyed making believe that the house was hers, that she could use its tidy white rooms as she pleased, that she and Andrew lived there together as a couple: she loved him, after all. She enjoyed too—secretly, guiltily—the rush of parking down the block and sneaking in through the side door, of worrying that a neighbor might question her or call the police, or that Juliet might return unexpectedly from her office, or Maddie from school. Without exception, though, Emma felt depraved afterward, and the knowledge that she'd worked out in the spare bedroom would somehow mitigate this feeling, a harmful act offset by a healthful one.

The explosion rattled the house, and she got off the bike and went to the window, thinking in the initial moments that a plane had crashed or a gas line had erupted. She looked out over the cinder-block wall in the backyard to the smoke-filled sky beyond and felt a stitch in her stomach. Minutes later, on tiptoes, forehead pressed to the glass, Emma watched the second explosion, recoiling as the pane shook and the flames rose spherically into the air. If it was WEPCO—*Let it be one of the other plants*, she prayed, the stitch in her stomach dilating—there might be more to come. She and Andrew had talked about the likeliest consequences of a fire at the plant. "God help us," he'd said, "if anyone ever strikes a match within a hundred feet of that place." She knew the next explosion, if there were one, could be even worse.

She crawled beneath the dining-room table, covered herself with the flannel blanket, and tucked her head between her knees, recalling civil-defense drills from elementary school—Bert the Turtle, the monkey with the dynamite—back in the seventies. If you saw the flash you were to "duck and cover," assume the fetal position and close your eyes, shielding yourself with a jacket or whatever was close at hand. She and her classmates had practiced the maneuver every couple of months from kindergarten to middle school, and for an instant Emma pictured her six-year-old self, horse-toothed and pigtailed, sitting cross-legged below the surface of her desk and staring at the pale-red wads of bubblegum stuck to its stainless-steel legs, her first-grade teacher, Mrs. Arnold, detailing the horrors of a nuclear detonation.

It was the third explosion, the loudest, that shattered the windows. With the glass came the hot, tremendous wind of the shock wave, the apocalyptic sound. Emma didn't scream, didn't move.

She thought: *I am dying. This is what it's like to die.* She wondered, almost tranquilly, why she felt no pain. In the ghostly silence that followed, before she removed the blanket, she was confused to discover herself alive.

Later, she drove as far as she could along Sunset Road, heading for the plant, before being stopped by a police blockade. She pulled to the shoulder. Standing on the hood of the Civic, she watched as WEPCO burned.

•

She hasn't seen her father's book since the day of the accident, and Emma has a sinking feeling that she left it in Andrew's spare bedroom. She's tired and wants to go home. She'll get a ride at the end of the night from Charlotte, one of the slot attendants—the friend Emma said she was having brunch with that day—but that's a full eight hours from now.

A few minutes later a man sits down. A regular, although he's never played at one of Emma's tables. He's trim and bespectacled, and wears a baggy white shirt, a sort of tunic. Around his neck is a string of small red beads. He always wears some draping outer garment, and he's a table hopper: she watched him one evening as he moved from blackjack to roulette to craps to Caribbean stud, looking for just the right game, just the right dealer. He gives a wink now as he draws a chrome money clip from a rear pocket of his pants, which are as white as the man's shirt.

"Marcus Bauerkemper," he says, and smiles. The man is nearly bald, with a gauzy semicircle of silver-gray hair. He looks for too long into Emma's eyes, as though he's forgotten what he was going to say. "I was over there for a while—in there." He motions with his head toward the poker room. "Now I'm here. With you."

"Okay," Emma says. She can't help but laugh. She feels bad about it, laughing on the day of Andrew's funeral.

The man smiles again, nostrils flaring—each one the size of a pumpkin seed, filled with untrimmed hair. He counts out a mound of old one-dollar bills and slides it across the layout. "Money," he says sourly, almost to himself. "Money, money, money. That's why we're both here in this place, is it not?" He sweeps an open hand over the table, then looks up at the ceiling and swivels his eyes, as if following a bird of prey that orbits overhead. "Cash-money," the man says. "The very root itself of all that is evil. You're here to earn it. I'm here to win it."

Emma nods, slipping the bills into the drop box. "Good luck to you, then."

Every once in a while, she ends up with a Marcus Bauerkemper at one of her tables: an oddball. It's best to nod politely, say as little as possible in return.

He names his denomination: five dollars, the minimum bet. Emma places a stack of four red chips on the felt.

"*Luck*," he says in a heavy voice. "'Success or failure apparently brought by chance rather than through one's own actions.' That's Merriam-Webster, if memory serves. Or is it the New Oxford American? Not sure now. In any case, you don't really believe in it, do you? Luck?"

"I guess I've never thought much about that," Emma says. But she has. She's considered herself unlucky for as long as she can remember.

"How could you *avoid* thinking about it, in your line of work?"

"Maybe you're right."

"No maybe about it," the man says. "The misguided belief in luck is what keeps this establishment here in business. Your employer, I'm talking about."

She laughs once more. Marcus Bauerkemper folds his arms.

"*Wonderful*," he says in the same heavy, stately voice. "'Exciting wonder. Marvelous, astonishing. Unusually good. Admirable.'" He speaks as though declaiming from a pulpit. "That one, I happen to know with absolute metaphysical certitude, is Merriam-Webster." He thumbs his black-rimmed glasses up the bridge of his nose. "The world's not wonderful, is it, Emma? It isn't trying hard enough, isn't doing its best. We feel this sometimes, don't we?"

"How do you know my name?"

He points to the small brass plate pinned to her vest.

"It's been a long day," Emma says.

"For that, I'm sincerely sorry."

He makes a series of basket bets, four in a row, each of which he loses. A basket bet is a five-number wager on one, two, three, zero, and double zero. Such a wager pays six-to-one but the house edge is nearly eight percent. It's a foolish bet, at a game that already carries the worst odds in the casino. Emma wonders what he meant—why the world isn't wonderful, how it isn't doing its best. She has her own answers to these questions but she wants to hear his, the perspectives of a man who evidently memorizes dictionary entries. She wants to know why someone she met only ten minutes ago would say such a thing to her.

The man draws his money clip from his pants again. He slides the clip from its wad of cash and peels off a fifty-dollar bill so crisp it looks as if it's been pressed and starched. He straightens the bill between his thumbs and index fingers and holds it out to her.

"Change fifty!" Emma hollers.

From the podium, Ed Logan answers, "Change fifty!"

When she gives Marcus Bauerkemper his chips, he places the entire stack on the layout: another basket bet. Emma spins the wheel, presses the ball to the rim and gives it a flick. The ball jumps from fret to fret, landing with its little patter on the number three. Marcus Bauerkemper grins.

She stacks his winnings on the felt, feeling the twinge of discontentment that often accompanies an ample payout. She and Russell, they are knee-deep in debt—credit cards, deferred student loans— their combined annual income barely enough to live on. On weekends, Emma cleans houses or walks dogs in their neighborhood for extra money, and just last month their bank threatened to foreclose on their mortgage. She isn't a gambler, but every once in a while she's tempted to take an entire paycheck to a nearby casino and see what she can turn it into.

"Back on top," she says. "And then some."

"It's official," he tells her. "You, Emma, are my rabbit's foot."

"Thought you didn't believe in luck."

"I don't recall ever saying that."

She hears Logan coming over, and then, from the corner of her eye, she sees him. He looks the part of a nineteen-seventies pit boss, as though he reports to Lefty Rosenthal himself, as though no one's told him that the Mafia was driven out of Las Vegas nearly twenty years ago. His dark, slicked-back hair is the thickest Emma has ever seen on a white person, and the dealers privately ridicule his bright solid-color ties, which hang inches shy of his waistline. Logan is tall and paunchy, and she can always hear him walking across the floor. He stops at Emma's back. Pit bosses don't like dealers getting too friendly with the players. Conversations are distractions, and distractions are opportunities for card sharps and other cheats. Emma can hear him breathing, hear his wing tips shifting on the carpet. A moment later he's back at the podium.

"I'm sorry it had to happen this way," Marcus Bauerkemper says. "Our meeting for the first time, that is. In a place like this. I have weaknesses, just like you. Just like everybody. We could have met anywhere, you and I—in a park, or an ice-cream parlor, let's say. But we met here, didn't we?" He shakes his head. "In this casino, which, I'm going to tell you, is the exact opposite of a park or an ice-cream parlor, Emma. The one-hundred-percent exact opposite."

"I'm not sure what it is you're talking about, sir."

"*Grace,*" he whispers. "That's what I'm talking about. 'Unmerited divine assistance given humans for their regeneration or sanctification.'" He studies her. "You won't find it in these parts. Not around here. I'm talking real, honest-to-goodness grace. The kind that isn't going to just fall in your lap."

Emma stares back at him.

"I'm not trying to alarm you," the man says. "We all need a *faith*-lift from time to time." He slaps the table. "That's funny, isn't it?"

She smiles dutifully, and he digs around in a front pocket of his pants, extracting a handful of items: a binder clip, a ring of keys, a tin of breath mints, a business card. He places the items on the table, pointing to the tin. "That's funny too," he says. The cover reads TESTAMINTS, each *T* a Latin cross. Below that it reads POWERFUL FRESH BREATH…POWERFUL MESSAGE. "Found those in a Christian bookstore. Couldn't help myself. This is what I want to give you, though."

He hands Emma the card. The backdrop is a pale blue sky that holds a single white cloud, tufty and cartoonish, shot through with a diagonal ray of sunlight. The card reads *Pastor Marcus Bauerkemper, Assembly of the Holy Redeemer*. Along the bottom are an address and a phone number.

"We meet every Sunday at five o'clock. Come," he tells her. "I would very much like you to." He pushes his heap of chips to the center of the layout. "I'll cash out now, please, if you don't mind."

A religious fanatic. She should have known. Emma thinks of her dinner conversation with Russell, when they touched uncomfortably on the subject of heaven. She believes in God, she always has—she's Catholic—but like a lot of believers she knows, she has no distinct conception of the afterworld, not when she really thinks about it. Wherever people go when they die, they aren't going to find themselves roasting on a spit below ground or winging their way around some paradise in the sky. Andrew was Catholic too, but it makes no difference where he is now; she knows he is no longer Andrew in any way she can fathom or comprehend. There will be no eventual reunion between them.

"Your church," Emma says, placing the man's new chips on the felt.

"Come," he says. "See for yourself."

Simon

Prior to the accident at WEPCO, Simon's morning routine, Monday through Friday, was to rise at a quarter after six, shower and dress, bolt down a low-calorie breakfast of yogurt and sliced fruit, and kiss his wife goodbye no later than seven o'clock.

Now he's been sleeping in. Some days he doesn't bother to shower. He's taken to eating Eggo waffles drenched in syrup. It surprises him that he doesn't miss the daily practice of waking up early and going to work—doesn't miss his job, not one bit. He is perfectly fine with the unpredictability and the time off.

Even if there were a plant for him to go to every day, he'd most likely be home on paid leave on account of his injury. When Simon finally drove himself down from the bluff and out of the desert, after half an hour or more of staring out the fractured windshield of his pickup, he went straight to the emergency room at Rose de Lima Hospital. He called Rebecca to meet him. Other victims were there too, bloodied and moaning. A portion of the hospital's multistory car park had buckled. Windows were webbed with cracks, or blown out. Simon waited for hours to be examined. He was X-rayed, given a tetanus shot in his shoulder. The shrapnel, or whatever had wounded him, hadn't ruptured any arteries, and a friendly female doctor stitched and bandaged his leg, wrote him a prescription for an antibiotic, and sent him on his way. The stitches ache every once in a while, but in general he can move the leg without pain or difficulty. The cuts on his face have healed. Even his hearing impediment, to Simon's relief, was mild and temporary.

He's done nothing about his Ram—it sits impaired, unsightly, nearly totaled, in the center of his driveway—and so he's borrowed Rebecca's Taurus for the day, telling her he's meeting over lunch with the other managers and the vice presidents to begin mapping out the future. He's been invited to no such meeting. The company, from what Simon can tell, is in a holding pattern—if you can even call it a company anymore. (What is left of it?) He's gotten numerous phone calls from the guys in his crew, but Simon has no idea what to say to them. The vibe community-wide seems to be that the residents of Las Vegas never want to hear the name WEPCO again, though there's been gossip, among the managers, of a relocation to Cedar City, Utah: a new, safer plant. Nevertheless, Simon is of the opinion that no one at WEPCO knows quite what to do. In a lengthy, excessively optimistic email, Bud Stone, the president and CEO, promised that all WEPCO employees will continue to receive a paycheck while the company makes plans to rebuild. As far as Simon is concerned, Stone's rambling, excessive optimism betrays his doubtfulness and fear.

•

Simon glances at the address he jotted onto an orange Post-it Note earlier in the week. The Post-it hangs from the edge of the dashboard, whiffling in the breeze of the air conditioner. The day is hot and cloudless, and as he drives, he passes office parks and apartment complexes and stretches of flat, littered desert. During a red light, he stares at a new-looking strip mall that's been abandoned: a treeless ghost town broiling in the sun, dispossessed of the signs that once hung above its nine or ten storefronts, its fenced-off parking lot smothered with weeds. When he locates the subdivision called Bighorn Heights, Simon follows the bend of a newly tarred road lined on each side with squatly tract homes in various states of ruin. Barring the damage they've endured, they're similar to the homes in his own neighborhood, Mojave Meadows, only smaller—pale-brown stucco jobs on miniscule plots of land. Simon is thankful that Mojave Meadows is just far enough from the WEPCO site to have remained undamaged. Here, plywood sheets cover windows and a few doorways. Rooflines sag. Garage doors hang aslant in their frames. Contractors' pickups are bumper-to-bumper along both curbs, and everywhere he looks men in work boots and tool belts are busy making repairs.

Simon reads the numbers until he comes to Andrew Huntley's house: 5850 Damselfly Drive. He parks the Taurus in an open space across the street, lowers his window. Like most of the block, Huntley's place is boarded up. No one's working on it, though, and the house looks spurned and lonely. Slate-green century plants, withering in orange clay pots, flank the concrete stoop. To the left of the driveway, an uprooted landscape light lies on its side in a border of mulch, a black cable trailing into the ground. The grass is yellow-tipped and overgrown. A hedge needs leveling.

Simon can't say why he's come. He googled Huntley a few days ago—he can't say why he did that either—and after skimming a slew of recent articles from the *Review-Journal* and the *Sun*, he came across Huntley's information on WhitePages.com. He wrote down the address and looked up a map of the city to see where the subdivision was situated. Even so, he had no intention of driving to Andrew Huntley's house. He stuck the Post-it Note to the driver's-license window of his wallet, thinking of it now and then, with no clear idea of what it meant to him or why it was on his person.

And now here he is.

Andrew Huntley was indeed married, with a daughter in high school. But there are no automobiles in the driveway; it doesn't appear that anybody is home. Simon sits for a while and stares at the place. Even if they *were* home, what would he do, ring the doorbell and introduce himself? *Hello. My name's Simon Addison. I, um…I watched Andrew die, you see, and I might have been able to save him but I was too afraid—too chickenshit—to try, and, well, I want the two of you to know that I feel just awful about the whole thing. Really awful.*

Three days ago, at the funeral, Simon sat in a pew with a group of coworkers, fellow survivors, and secretly pondered what might have been going through Huntley's head as he ran from the plant. *Live, live, live!* Simon decided. That alone. Not the actual words, though—just a blurry amalgam of instinct and panic and desire.

Simon didn't know any of the victims of the explosions—not really, not in any meaningful way—but he's attended each of the four funerals that have been held so far. For the past day or two he's managed to keep his guilt at bay, telling himself he did what almost anybody would have, but the guilt pants and snarls just out of sight, tracking him wherever he goes. The scene hasn't stopped returning to his mind: Huntley racing after the pickup, waving; the ear-splitting second blast; the dust and the smoke, and Huntley gone in the dark midst of it.

Simon closes his eyes, tries to snuff it out.

He starts the car and drives back home. He pulls into his driveway, stopping a few feet from the pickup, and goes around back, moving, it occurs to him, in an involuntary kind of way, as if directed by some remote-control device. Through the breakfast-nook window, Rebecca sits with her back to him at the table, writing checks for bills, her newly short hair tinted with the umbery gold her stylist talked her into, spreading out in the shape of a seashell at the bottom of her neck. As Simon walks to his shed, Lexie, his dachshund, rushes to greet him, scurrying around the pool. Simon takes a knee and strokes her haunches before the dog can bark. He carries his hedge trimmer, his push broom, and his leaf rake to the driveway, then returns for the lawn mower. Lexie lies down against the house and watches him. Simon walks the mower through the grass at a measured pace in order to curb a squeaky wheel, keeping an eye on his wife as he passes the break-fast nook. Her head is lowered—she's focused. He can hear NPR on the kitchen radio. He crams the four items into the trunk and secures the trunk in haste with a length of twine, then gets in the Taurus and closes the door very quietly. He's about to pull out when Rebecca appears in the doorway, waving to him. She comes outside in her blue summer dress, lithesome and groomed, moving down the driveway with a visible, springtime vigor. Simon lowers his window.

"What happened to the lunch?" she says, looking at her watch.

"Ended earlier than I thought it would. Just a preliminary thing, less than an hour. We'll start hammering out the major stuff next week."

"What's with the mower?"

"Oh," Simon says. "Needs a new starter rope, I think. Something. It's all jammed up. I thought I'd take it in while I have the time." He smiles. "TCB," he says.

"Good for you." She looks carefully at him. "You were talking in your sleep again last night."

"Anything incriminating?" He's been doing it ever since the accident.

"Rumbles and mumbles. Nothing coherent. You sounded so upset."

"Heartburn," Simon says, touching his chest. "I keep waking up with it."

She leans in and kisses him. "Milk of magnesia. I'll pick some up."

Simon watches her as she walks back up the driveway. Then he raises his window and drives back to Andrew Huntley's house.

•

He sets about mowing the lawn, what there is of it: a rectangle no larger than a king-size bed, hedged on one side with a thick green yew. He mows it both vertically and horizontally, leaving a crisscross pattern in the manner of a yard-care service. He'll have to sneak the lawn mower back into the shed now that Rebecca will expect it to be at the repair shop. If she catches him, Simon will come up with an excuse. One lie begets another, he thinks, resigning himself to the inevitable.

Before he started mowing, he peeked through a garage-door window to find the garage vacant like the driveway, but he keeps waiting, with a twitchiness approximating to fright, for someone to appear out of nowhere. He barbers the hedge and rakes out the trimmings. He plants the landscape light back in the ground, piling mulch around its neck, wondering if the light still functions. Simon leans against a fender of the Taurus, which is parked along the curb, and admires his work. This heat—it's a cramped room with no windows, no door. He notices a garden hose coiled against the side of the house, and drags it around front and screws it to the spigot. He turns on the spigot and drinks deeply, laving his face, then stands at the edge of the lawn with his thumb to the hose's coupling. A rainbow shimmers in the spray. He waters the potted plants too, sweeps the grass cuttings from the driveway and sidewalk.

Like he did on the morning of the accident, he finds himself appreciating the vast but simple fact of his existence. He thinks about what's truly important to him, what matters above all else, and the faces of his wife and children materialize predictably and happily in his mind. Then Simon pictures his house, a five-bedroom ranch with a three-car garage, and then the whole of Mojave Meadows, the sprawling gated community that makes him feel prosperous and safe. Before graduating high school and moving away, his children hated not only Mojave Meadows but the rest of Las Vegas as well. Daniel and Michaela: twenty-three and twenty-one, respectively. Simon thinks with sadness of their recent entry into adulthood, youth fluttering behind them like a shirt taken off on a windy beach. Daniel is completing his second semester of law school at Penn, Michaela her junior year at Columbia. Ivy League elitists, they are now, disapproving of the West—of its "shameless vapidity" (Daniel's words), its "lack of refinement" (Michaela's). Simon shakes his head at their sophomoric sentiments. All of a sudden, he misses them terribly. But hasn't he missed them, more or less, since they were infants, at all times anticipating their eventual departures, when they would leave home to live life in earnest? Hasn't he always felt this pain of fatherly yearning? A feminine quirk, he thinks, his attachment to his children. Further indication of his weakness.

Rebecca and Daniel and Michaela. Andrew Huntley, before he died, and the rest of the Homo sapiens who inhabit planet Earth.

Animals, all of them, highly adapted animals—nothing more—but with hearts and souls as vital and persistent as his own.

•

Simon loads the trunk and dries his forehead with his sleeve. Inside the Taurus, he spots a red Jeep in the rearview mirror, and as he puts the key in the ignition, the Jeep pulls into Huntley's driveway. Huntley's wife, Juliet, is behind the wheel. Beside her is their daughter, blondish like her mother, with her mother's thin, winsome face. Both of them with their hair pulled back, the way they wore it at the funeral. Simon considers getting out and telling them who he is, offering his condolences. But he doesn't want to explain what he's doing here, why he burdened himself with attending to their yard, and so he blinks and smiles, his hands two cinder blocks in his lap, while Juliet and Maddie Huntley emerge from the Jeep. He keeps on smiling as Juliet approaches, which seems to take an eternity. She is of medium height and uneven build: blocky legs, slender hips and waistline, the large breasts he called to mind as he sat in his pickup at the lip of the desert bluff. She wears a green T-shirt and too-short jeans and old white tennis shoes. Tilting her head to one side, she grimaces in a hangdog sort of way, moving so slowly and cautiously down the driveway it appears as if trepidation is chronic to her demeanor. Simon doesn't know what to do.

Just as she reaches his window, he nods and drives off.

Maddie

"Weird," Maddie says. "Totally weird."

"We're getting an alarm system installed." Her mother leans against the tiled counter, picking absently at a trench of grout, looking around the kitchen as though she's misplaced something. "Russell's right. It couldn't hurt, now that it's just the two of us."

"Who do you think he was?"

"I feel like I've seen him before. His face was so familiar."

Maddie roots through a drawer beside the range until she finds a pen and a small spiral pad.

"What are you writing?" her mother asks.

"White car. Four doors. Ford, I think—right? Or was it a Buick?"

"Ford. Pretty new-looking, with a bumper sticker on the back: 'Proud Parent of a Dachshund.'"

"Caucasian. Short hair, brown." Maddie taps the shaft of the pen against her lips. "Child molester's smile." She tears the sheet of paper from the pad and folds it in half. "Just in case we need a description."

"He did clean up our yard for us," says her mother. "I mean, I *assume* it was him. He had a lawn mower sticking out of his trunk."

They've let the yard go. Maddie was planning on tending to it—something her father always used to do—today or tomorrow.

"The guy was a weirdo, Mom. Who just drives away like that without saying anything?"

"I know him from somewhere. I'm sure I do."

Even as she leans against the counter, her mother has an upright, soldierly posture. When she drops her arms to her sides, puzzling over where she might have met the strange man they found sitting in a car in front of their house, she looks as if she's standing at attention.

"The way he was smiling," Maddie says. "*Sickola.*"

Her mother looks around the kitchen again, sighing. Four tow-colored planks, nailed to the exterior of the house, cover the window above the sink. The glass inserts of two cabinet doors are gone, so that Maddie and her mother can reach through the wooden frames for a bowl or plate. Shards from the windowpanes flew clear across the room, and little scratches scar the glossy black cladding of the refrigerator. Overhead, a recessed bulb drones like a cicada. With no natural light, the small galley kitchen has the aspect of a cave or a mine shaft.

"Oh, kid. What are we gonna do?"

"Call the cops," Maddie says, "for starters."

"I mean about everything." Her mother runs a hand over the sheeny surface of her hair. "Where do we go from here?"

•

Maddie has asked herself the same question a hundred times in the two weeks since her father's death, or some variation of it: *What now? What next?* They'll swallow the loss and continue to exist, she guesses, feeling mature, knowing how levelheaded it is of her to come to this decision. Such a sharpness to that line of thought, though. It surprises her, her own no-nonsense reply to the situation they've discovered themselves in. She's heartbroken, of course—devastated, just as her mother is—and it's the first time Maddie has dealt with the passing of a loved one. And it's her father who's died, for God's sake. And she's so young, so young to lose him. And his very *body* is gone as well—blown to nothing, probably, or cremated in the fire—and Maddie longs for the closure that might come from at least getting to lay eyes on him one more time. Yet she's accepted that their only real option is to proceed with their lives.

Something else surprises her too. Her heartbrokenness, her devastation, Maddie has realized in the small amount of time she's been mourning her father, has a dirigible quality. She loves that word. It's on the list she maintains, and describes her grief's readiness to be steered to the rear of her mind whenever it suits her. Is she foolish to believe she has such control of her emotions? Maybe she won't later on, when their lives quiet down, when they aren't so preoccupied with the house.

Her mother has met with a man from their insurance company, and with another man, a salesman, about the windows, nearly every one of which shattered during the explosions. A few days ago the salesman's crew replaced the windows in the bedrooms and said they'd be back soon to finish the job. They're inundated with work, and the rest of the order hasn't arrived yet. Thanks to Russell, who went to a hardware store on the day of the accident, the remainder of the house is tightly boarded up. The worry around the neighborhood is that looters will pry off the planks and the sheets of plywood, but some of the neighbors have banded together and are taking turns standing watch for hour-long shifts during the night, pacing up and down the block with a flashlight and a thermos of coffee.

Russell has offered to put Maddie and her mother up at his place. Emma would love it, he said. But Maddie's happy to be staying in a spacious room at a Best Western, instead of in the tiny guest bedroom off Russell's den—where he keeps his synthesizer and, displayed along both windowsills, his collection of vintage G.I. Joe action figures—or with her aunt and uncle on her father's side, who have four tabbies and live all the way out in Summerlin. Her mother's been taking time away from her practice to deal with the funeral and the house, using all of the vacation leave she allows herself each year. And indeed, despite the circumstances, every night seems a sort of vacation, as the two of them nestle into the king-size bed and fall asleep to the enormous television that sits atop the dresser. Along about dawn, though, Maddie awakens to her mother's quiet weeping.

Her mother's voice has acquired a tragic tone that becomes even more tragic at times, when her eyes turn watery and she blinks in rapid succession, like a camera in continuous-shooting mode. Maddie first noticed the tone the day of the accident. After the explosions, her mother searched for Maddie's father at all the nearby hospitals, then came home to find Russell on the stoop. She sent him to get Maddie from school, and Russell spotted her on his way to Bishop Delaney, at the corner of Nellis Boulevard and Desert Inn Road. Her mother was on the phone when they walked in, talking to her sister, Maddie's Aunt Hailie in Tonawanda, New York. Crunching glass as she circled the living room in her heels, her mother raved about the explosions in a manner that seemed to belong to an actress from one of the old movies they always show on AMC and Showtime: Meryl Streep or Glenn Close. When she looked up and saw Maddie and Russell in the doorway, she uttered a deep, woeful cry, slumping in tears against the wall.

Dean Langen has done nothing about Maddie's disappearance that morning. She ran into him at school the other day and he only apologized for her loss and gave her an ungainly, wooden-armed hug. She still hasn't told her mother about leaving his office the way she did. Her mother's an emotional wreck right now, and Maddie finds herself speaking to her with great care—choosing each word with prudence—her voice calm and cordial and reassuring. Being in the house only makes her mother feel worse. With her written permission, Maddie's been skipping school on and off since the accident, and they've come here almost every day, cleaning up a little more of the glass each time, clearing corners and baseboards with a toothbrush. Russell has helped. But there's so much of it, scattered from room to room in aqua-edged geometric shapes: rectangles and trapezoids, crescents and parallelograms. They're beautiful, actually, and if you bend down and look at one from the proper angle, you can see a kind of movement, this quiver of imprisoned light. She's kept the observation to herself, lest her mother think that Maddie's mind isn't completely on her father, that she isn't grieving to the same degree her mother is.

•

Her mother relaxes her posture now, her forehead puckered as if she's just remembered something important. She gets a bag of frozen peas from the freezer. The open end of the bag has been twisted and secured with a blue rubber band, and she removes the rubber band and sticks her hand inside the bag and pulls out a pack of Pall Mall cigarettes. A few peas spill like gravel onto the counter. "Pretend this never happened," she says.

Maddie's mouth drops open. "Are you kidding me?"

"Don't get excited. It's not a habit. I quit years ago, before you were born. These are for special situations only."

"I can't believe what I'm witnessing. After all the lectures? *Don't drink and drive. Don't do drugs. Don't smoke if you don't want to die.*" In her entire life Maddie has never seen her mother smoke a cigarette. "How long has this been going on?"

"I told you—I'm not a smoker. I do this maybe once a month." Her mother pinches two cigarettes from the pack and holds one out to her. "You can have it if you want. Our secret. A few puffs aren't going to land you in the ER."

Maddie's never smoked before. Most of her friends do every once in a while—at parties, or in the parking lot after school—and suddenly it amazes her that she's never even wanted to try it. "Right here in the house?" she says.

"I can't see how a little smoke could make this place any worse."

Maddie takes the cigarette.

"Just don't make a practice of it," her mother says. "This one time only. If it makes you feel better, I'll chuck the pack and then neither one of us ever does this again. Deal?"

"All these years I've been so clueless. It turns out you're a really bad mother."

Maddie sticks the cigarette between her lips, and her mother digs a matchbook from the drawer beside the range.

"When I light it, inhale, but not too fast," she says. "Hold it for a second and then blow it out."

"Do I look like a person with special needs?"

Her mother strikes a match and lights their cigarettes. When the smoke fills Maddie's lungs—two hot fists in her chest—she feels immediately lightheaded, a little sick too, like the time she inhaled nitrous oxide at the dentist's office for a root canal. She coughs it out, holding the cigarette between her index and middle fingers the way real smokers do.

"Well?" her mother laughs. "What do you think?"

No wonder people say smoking can kill you. It tastes like death. "I think I might throw up," Maddie says.

"Pace yourself. You'll be all right." Her mother opens the pantry and removes a box of red wine. "It goes much better with something to sip," she says. She goes into the dining room and gets two glasses from the hutch. The feet chime as she sets the glasses on the kitchen counter. "Again, our secret."

"Who *are* you right now?"

The boxed wine is kept on hand for her grandmother on her mother's side, who visits once a year from Tonawanda—on Easter or Thanksgiving—and drinks copious amounts of it. She drinks only wine, and only boxed, insisting that bottled wine gives her gas. "Drunk in the Box," Maddie's father used to call her when she wasn't around. Several relatives from Tonawanda came to Las Vegas for the funeral (all of them at the Best Western, down the hall from Maddie and her mother, all of them gone now, mercifully). Her grandmother was among them, and when the funeral ended she grumbled that the sacramental wine had tasted like the priest's halitosis.

Her mother fills the glasses. "We both need to decompress a bit, wouldn't you say?"

Maddie inhales on the cigarette again, less deeply this time. Again she coughs. "Are we actually going to drink all that?"

Her mother hands her a glass, then crumples the pack of cigarettes in her fist and tosses it onto the counter. "Let's see where this takes us."

•

When a friend drops her off at the Best Western after school the next day, Maddie uses a house phone to call up to the room, to make certain her mother isn't there. She needs a break from that tragic tone of hers, from her mother's escalating strangeness. The reception area reminds Maddie of a Skittles commercial, all sunlight and pastels: a two-story bay window, two pink armchairs angled in front of a teal-blue couch, a painted coffee table with broad diagonal stripes of peach and citrus green. Adjacent to the desk is a small convenience store that's never open, and opposite the store is a Starbucks. She presses her lips to the window, leaving an O-shaped smudge, as the phone rings and rings.

Maddie goes up to the room, with its tacky carpet, wallpaper, drapery, and bedspread, primary colors and abstract patterns everywhere you look. She calls Russell on his cell phone.

"What's another name for maggots?"

He laughs. "You working on a crossword puzzle?"

"'Disco rice.' Isn't that great? Garbage men came up with it. It's not a joke. I read it somewhere."

She lies on the bed, the hotel-room phone pinned between her shoulder and her ear. Russell laughs again. He gave her his number when she turned sixteen, telling her to call him if she's ever been drinking and needs a ride home and doesn't want to involve her parents. Mostly she calls him when she needs advice.

"Is this the reason we're talking?" he says.

She gets up from the bed and goes to the window. "They have an especially charming sobriquet for used condoms." She's put on a French accent. "Care to hear it?"

"Quite a conversation we're having here, kid."

"'Urban whitefish,'" Maddie says in her regular voice, then thinks with a shock: *All of a sudden there's this person who isn't in your life anymore, this person you loved, who belongs to a part of your life that no longer exists.* Her father is gone and she doesn't know if she can really do it, swallow the loss and carry on without him.

Jet planes stripe the distant sky. Maddie wouldn't have noticed them but for their finger-long vapor trails, white on blazing blue.

"Shakespeare's got nothing on garbage men when it comes to metaphors," she says.

Russell

The All or Nothing is faintly lit and smells of patchouli and cigarette smoke, the walls concealed by hundreds of vintage record sleeves affixed this way and that. Neon beer signs flicker in the windows. Glass ashtrays brim on the small square tables. The tavern exudes grunge and procrastination and a kind of connate disinterest in whatever the world might have to offer, and Russell feels immediately at home whenever he arrives at work.

A crowd of regulars, bedraggled thirty somethings with piercings and tattoos, sit in pairs around the ring-shaped bar. Most of them are here three or four nights a week. They challenge one another to darts and foosball and gorge themselves on the complimentary Buffalo wings. They play cloying glam-metal songs on the jukebox—music enjoyed almost exclusively, Russell imagines, by car mechanics and ski-lift operators, the guitar-laden ballads of Winger, Def Leppard, and Skid Row—laughing and singing along, pretending to bang their heads. Once a shift one of them will order a bacon martini, the house specialty, which consists of Smirnoff, dry vermouth, Tabasco sauce, and olive juice, garnished, of course, with a greasy slice of bacon. For now, though, the All or Nothing is quiet, everyone slouched and smoking and nodding, speaking with a funereal air. Big Paco sips coffee as he fills a plastic pitcher with Miller Lite. He's a stout Spaniard who always wears the same faded black Galaxian T-shirt. Russell is here to relieve him.

An hour and a half into Russell's shift the door edges open and in steps Maddie. She's dressed in a yellow polo shirt, tight-fitting jeans, and white Jack Purcells. She moves between the straggle of tables, sliding onto a barstool, heaving a sigh.

Behind the bar, Russell folds his arms and says, "What are you doing here?"

"Do you have some time?"

"How did you *get* here?" he asks.

"I wouldn't guess you could serve me a beer."

"You know what the manager will do if he comes out of the kitchen and finds a teenager sitting at the bar?"

"I thought *you* were the manager."

"How'd you get here, Maddie? Did something happen?"

"Nothing happened. Can't we just chat?"

"Not until you tell me why you're all the way out at Desert Inn and Industrial at eleven thirty on a school night. Did you take your mother's Jeep?"

"You should consider hosting a quiz show. *Ten Thousand Questions*, starring Russell Martin!"

She wears a little straw purse as if it's a messenger bag, the chain strap crosswise between her breasts, accentuating them to a degree that makes him uncomfortable. She's a delightful girl. In less than a year she'll be eighteen, an adult—on her own soon after that, in college. She's been calling him all the time since her father's death. Russell doesn't mind. Emma's never wanted children, and Maddie is the nearest he's going to get to having a daughter of his own. He feels a protective fear for her.

He lifts an eyebrow. "What's going on here?" he says.

She took the keys from Juliet's purse and sneaked out of the hotel room, where her mother is asleep in bed. Maddie pulls the keys from a pocket of her jeans and drops them onto the bar.

"It's not like I don't have a license," she says.

"You need to leave right now," he tells her. "You need to drive straight back to the hotel, and you need to call me when you get there. Understand?"

"Are you going to tell my mom?"

He looks at her. "You better pray to the sweet baby Jesus she doesn't wake up."

"I was missing him," Maddie says shakily, kneading her temples with her fingertips. "I've been missing him all day long. I thought you'd understand."

Russell hesitates. "Okay," he says. "Fair enough."

He goes into the kitchen and asks Tim Woods, the manager on duty, if he can take a break. Woods comes out to cover for him, eyeing Maddie doubtfully. He's a short, doubtful-looking man regardless.

"Ten minutes," Russell says, placing a hand on her shoulder. "Then you're on your way."

•

The Jeep is parked in a space near the door, and they sit on the hood, heels against the high tubular bumper. Beyond the lot is Industrial, a three-lane thoroughfare parallel to the Strip. This is the Vegas tourists rarely see. Railroad tracks and power lines and faded billboards. Low, windowless buildings trimmed with dreary neon: head shops and dives, strip clubs gone to seed. A few streets away, the resort casinos give off a collective radiance that's tremulous and bright. A swamp cooler gurgles nearby.

Maddie tells him that missing her father makes her feel the way you do when you put your wallet or sunglasses in the wrong place: as though he's close at hand and she has simply to find him. She's accepted his death, she says; nevertheless, she can't help thinking that she'll stumble upon him somehow, somewhere.

"I know the feeling," Russell says, demonstrating for Maddie the way he often whispers to her father. He catches himself doing it, this whispering, throughout the day, as if Andrew can hear him. *Hey there, buddy*, Russell will say. *How's things?* He'll imagine Andrew beside him, responding. *Do you miss me? Do you miss the world?* This will happen while Russell showers in the morning. It'll happen during his commute. It'll happen as he stands at the kitchen sink loading the dishwasher. *Come home*, he'll plead. *Come back.* "Did you say something?" Emma might ask, and Russell will answer, "Hmm?"

He hates that his best friend is dead, but the whispering, Russell feels, is an emblem not of grief but of self-absorption. As though he so craves the attention Andrew can no longer provide that Russell has to envision Andrew listening to him, answering his constant, senseless questions. When the pretending ceases, when Russell sets foot back in the real world, he feels as if he's been shoved from behind into an ice-cold swimming pool. That sense of falling, of shock.

"I don't know," Maddie says, looking sidelong at him, something gentle in her voice. "It sounds really nice. You talking to my dad like that."

Wind soughs through the alleyway between the All or Nothing and the twenty-four-hour tattoo parlor next door, sending an empty can rattling over the ground. A few stars struggle in the sky.

"Maybe someday he'll answer you," she says, smiling at him. It's the same smile she's always had. Russell remembers her at age six, age ten, age fourteen—that sweet, sassy beam of self-assurance.

Her purse sits between them on the hood of the Jeep, the strap lying loosely around it, like a drizzle of sauce on a plate. An old paperback peeks from the purse: *Crossing the Water*, by Sylvia Plath. Russell does a double take. He bends to study the cover. A furrowed strip of painter's tape covers the book's spine. Only the title—in thin white letters at the upper left-hand corner—is visible, but he knows without seeing the rest of the cover that it features what appears to be a black-and-white aerial shot of water lapping a shore.

He takes the book from Maddie's purse, turns it over in his hands. He flicks through it, back to front. The inscription reads simply, cryptically:

I lean to you, numb as a fossil. Tell me I'm here.

It's a line from "Two Campers in Cloud Country," a poem from the collection.

"How'd you get this?" he says.

"I found it in the spare bedroom a few days after my dad died. My mom and I were cleaning up. He must've given it to her at some point. There's a message in there from him, a quote from one of the poems. I'm pretty sure it's my dad's handwriting." Maddie kicks the bumper with her heel. "My mom doesn't know I've got it. I should give it back to her, but I like having it with me. It reminds me of him, and the poetry's really beautiful."

"I see," Russell says.

The book belongs to Emma. Her grandmother entrusted it to her on Emma's thirteenth birthday. It's the last thing Emma's mother gave her father, or so her grandmother claimed: an anniversary gift, one week prior to the accident that took their lives, their Oldsmobile T-boned by a drunk college student who ran a red light. Emma treasures the book, and occasionally carries it around like a talisman in her own purse. She's read it, or read selections from it, so many times the binding has weakened.

"You found it where?"

"On the floor of our spare bedroom, under a bunch of glass."

Russell's mind is in disarray. He went in there the day of the explosions, measuring the damage the house had suffered, walking on fragments of broken window that sounded like thin ice cracking beneath his soles. He didn't notice the book. He flicks through the pages again now, thumbs the royal-blue tape. He can't see how Emma's mother's handwriting looks a thing like Andrew's. More important, Russell can't see how the collection of poems found its way to the floor of Andrew's spare bedroom.

"Would you care if I borrowed this?"

Maddie shrugs. "Sure," she says. "Enjoy."

She lies back on the windshield, gazing upward. Russell feels the approach of a panic attack, and then it's upon him. He's sweating and his mouth goes desert-dry. His hands shudder, his heart rate ramping up. He needs a toke. His left eye begins to water, and he pulls off his glasses and sets them on his thigh, taking a long, deep breath.

Scant as it might seem to anyone else as proof of an affair, the book is enough to convince him that there was indeed something going on between Emma and Andrew. Is he crazy to draw such a conclusion? Russell doesn't think so. When was the last time she went to Andrew's house? It's been a number of months, as far as he knows, maybe a year. Possibly longer. She didn't even go there with Russell after the accident. But he saw her father's book in the days leading up to the explosions, on Emma's nightstand, and on the kitchen counter once, and in the outer pocket of her purse—he knows he did.

His long-standing suspicion about them has always come and gone. Russell tried to suppress it for years, telling himself he was being unreasonable, he was insecure, he was imagining things. It was difficult, though, to ignore their behavior toward each other. Whenever he and Emma went to dinner with Andrew and Juliet, there was this flirty awkwardness between Emma and Andrew that somehow seemed less than innocent. She'd talk more quickly in front of him, dashing headlong through a story and leaving out a pivotal event, tripping over her words, slugging her cocktail or her wine. Andrew, in turn, would tease her for it, making Emma laugh, touching her back or her arm or her hand. He might have imitated her, for example—her rushed and muddled syntax—and then, taking hold of himself, he'd have glanced uncomfortably around the restaurant or left the table for a visit to the men's room. Russell wonders if Juliet ever noticed any of this. It was all so obvious to him.

Then there's the curious fact that until just recently—until Andrew's death—Emma would often shower when she returned home from the Bora Bora ("scrubbing off all the vice," she'd joke). Not to mention the three or four times, over the past year, he thought he heard her whispering on a phone call in another room of the house. And there's also the pink Victoria's Secret slip Russell once came across while looking in her closet for a spare hanger— he's never seen her wear it. She's rarely in the mood for sex anyway, and when she is, or pretends to be, she puts forth a bored, lazy effort that fills him with shame and makes the whole thing reek of an obligation.

He's never mentioned his suspicion to Juliet, nor to anyone else. He'd sound like a jealous fool, with his half-baked ideas—with no proof at all. But since Andrew's been gone, Emma's been out of sorts. As often as not she goes around with that same stricken look she wore in the days immediately following the accident. Russell has talked himself into thinking he's reading too much into it. He loves her beyond everything. He loved Andrew as well. In his heart of hearts, though, Russell knows he's right about them, the way you always know when you've caught a cold, with no more confirmation than a pinhead tickle at the rear of your throat.

"Imagine creatures so advanced they can build a machine to propel themselves off their own planet," Maddie says. "That's us. Think about that for a second."

He twists around, pats her on the arm. The wind flattens her hair against her forehead. "Off you go now. Your father would kill me for letting you stay as long as you have."

"My father's not around anymore."

"Don't joke about that."

"Who's joking?"

Russell clutches the book with both his hands. "Time's up, Maddie."

"In a moment," she says, still focused on the sky. "I like the view from down here."

Emma

In the thirty-four days since Andrew's death, Emma has consulted two fortune-tellers and a medium. Each was a heavyset woman of late middle age who wore some kind of peasant blouse and several eyeball-size rings. Each had a downtown storefront with a neon sign. Emma doesn't put much stock in the occult. Supernatural, mystical claptrap, it all seems to her. But she's never felt so out of alignment, so close to toppling over, and she's willing to try anything to recover her equilibrium.

The first fortune-teller, a palmist, traced Emma's fate line with a ballpoint pen and told her to expect a life-altering event in the next few weeks. The second, a tarot reader, fingered her summary card—the Ten of Swords—and said Emma's circumstances were about to change. The medium closed her eyes and held Emma's wrists and whispered that a loved one from the hereafter was deeply concerned about her. None of them offered any specificity, any idea of what the time ahead might actually hold—any indication of her future contentment.

Emma hopes she can find that contentment with Russell. She hopes she can come to adore him the way she still adores Andrew, and she hopes the secret years she passed with Andrew will remain just that: secret. She hopes Russell will never suffer for the weakness and selfishness that guided her away from him. Emma hopes, in the deepest and truest part of her, that her guilt and her grief can be replaced somehow by an abiding love for life, for *her* life, the one she opted for when she married Russell Martin.

There are people, she knows, who possess such love—a great, unbroken enthusiasm for everything around them. She sees these people all over the city. They stride the sidewalks downtown with their wide, expectant eyes. They can be found at supermarkets and department stores, heads tilted thoughtfully, not so much shopping, it appears to Emma, as simply marveling at the items on display. Every once in a while, as she looks into the crowd from behind her green felt table, Emma spots one of them at the Bora Bora. They seem to smile for no particular purpose, emanating neighborliness and joy, a little caper in their step. She wants desperately to be one of these blessed few. She wonders how they've come by their unmistakable sense of appreciation and curiosity and (she has to assume) belonging.

Sometimes Emma feels that she's never really belonged any-where. She was orphaned at nine years old, raised by her mother's mother, and all that time—despite her *yiayia*'s best efforts to make Emma feel at home, converting into a bedroom the fusty little loft Emma's dead *papou* had used for his model-ship building, giving her free rein to play as she pleased in any part of the house—she was aware of her status as visitor. She was a burden, most likely. A charity case for sure. Someone to feel sorry for. Certainly not a little girl with any kind of place in the world.

Well. Poor Emma. Poor thing. Enough of the pity party, she tells herself. There's no shortage of people who are worse off.

It was Russell, at last, who gave her the emotional security she was short of in her youth. In bed, he'll prop himself on an elbow, leaning over her, and skim her body slowly with his fingertips—a blind man reading Braille—his thin blond hair draped over his nose so that he has to keep sweeping it aside with his index finger. He'll explore her breasts and her arms and her stomach and her legs with an expression that borders on wonder, the same way the life-lovers she sees at supermarkets and department stores consider the items on display. It's as though he's a child reaching into a petting tank to touch the fin of some exotic marine animal, and when they make love, Emma's stomach turns at her own duplicity and gall. Through his intense and unconcealed attraction to her, Russell has given

Emma a gift: a constant reminder that she is loved. She's thanked him with betrayal.

•

She wasn't able to help it. She felt something for Andrew the moment he sat down at her blackjack table, drunk and silly, all those years ago: with his solicitous green eyes, his dark and angular face. She gave Russell her phone number when he asked for it only because she thought she'd have a chance of seeing Andrew again, unaware that Andrew was married.

And then Russell called her.

"We met the other night. At your table. The Bora Bora."

"Andrew," Emma said buoyantly, though she knew it wasn't him.

"His friend," Russell said. "The other guy. Russell."

Before long they were seeing each other. He was a nice enough guy, and it seemed that Emma was always meeting guys who weren't nice enough—who were proud or domineering or opinionated or sarcastic. It had been three years since her last boyfriend, and she lived alone, and she was…well, lonely. That was the sad, solitary word for it. Emma savored Russell's attention, and could maybe see herself with him long-term—she guessed, she supposed. All the while, though, she thought about Andrew, getting to see him only occasionally, when he and Juliet hired a sitter and the four of them went out on a double date.

She'd grown so weary of her loneliness. Emma waited a reasonable twelve months before hinting that Russell ought to propose. She can say in all honesty—can't she?—that she didn't marry him to gain greater, permanent access to Andrew. She isn't crazy. She simply settled, and a byproduct of having done so was that she could hang out with Andrew from time to time, as difficult as that could be. Emma may not have been in love with Russell, she may not even have been that attracted to him, but she cared about him immensely—he was her best friend now—and he was in love with her, and these things were more than enough.

•

Then one evening she ran into Andrew at the All or Nothing. Emma had stopped by after work for a beer, and to chat with Russell. So had Andrew. But it was Thirsty Thursday and in no time customers were clamoring for drinks around the bar, swarmed along the padded arm rail, ants at the mouth of a hill. The customers waved impatiently at Russell and Big Paco, both of whom hustled back and forth among the bottles and taps. Emma and Andrew made small talk and ate pretzels from a wooden bowl. Russell shouted, "Sorry!" and shrugged. At some point Emma got the feeling that she and Andrew were connecting in a way they never had before. He seemed to look at her with a new intensity, a potent curiosity, resting his forearm on the bar and sipping from his pint of Guinness. "I like this," he said. "Talking to you this way. Just the two of us. It's nice."

Emma was afraid—the memory of this fear will never leave her—because she knew from the way Andrew nodded when she spoke, from the way he kept allowing his knee to fall lightly against hers, that something was happening, and that something more was going to happen, something she might be powerless to stop if she even wanted to stop it. Big Paco kept watching them suspiciously, knowing, or so it seemed to Emma. As exciting as their flirting was, it was also like swallowing a wad of gum that ends up lodged in your esophagus—pulsing there, a little threat.

She kept glancing helplessly at Andrew's skin, the skin of his face and neck and hands. Emma had to remind herself not to. But it was beautiful, suntanned and smooth, and she imagined other skin, skin she couldn't see. His stomach. His inner thighs. The small of his back. The skin behind his ears, weirdly, and then the skin inside them, even that: the shadowy depths of each canal. Skin she wanted to kiss and lick. Skin that belonged to her husband's best friend, his best man, and the entire time Russell was only a few feet away, oblivious. Emma could almost taste the briny sweetness of Andrew's body. She willed herself to stop seeing the two of them entangled in the sheets of a bed, Andrew slipping inside her and simply resting there on top of her, his nose to hers. He called home and told Juliet he'd be late, and by eight thirty or so he and Emma were drunk. Russell was too busy to notice, even though he'd been the one serving them their beers. They said goodbye to him. Emma had parked in a garage a few blocks away, and as Andrew walked her to her car she got this splintering feeling within. Something was breaking free, like an iceberg calving from a glacier, and the summer sky darkened and the streetlights winked in their own coppery glow, and at her Civic he kissed her, pressing her against the door, and Emma plucked her keys from her purse and they clambered inside and made love for the first time, right there in the backseat.

Afterward, they sat sweating among their clothes. All the familiar words came to her. *Cheater. Adulterer. Tramp. Slut. Whore—dirty rotten whore.* Nevertheless, how thrilling and wonderful it had been! She felt vile, of course—utterly vile—but she was also overcome with a kind of vertigo, as if beholding the earth from the basket of a hot air balloon, that was not at all unpleasant. She couldn't let go of Andrew's hair. Emma had grabbed a clump of it at the back of his head and still held it tightly in her fist. Finally, he whispered, "Uh, that sort of hurts," and they both laughed, and he leaned over and kissed her, and they laughed again. She felt completely sober then, as though she hadn't consumed a single drop of alcohol. Beside her, Andrew pulled on his pants and said, "Okay. What do we do now?"

•

Emma still can't believe she did it, cheated on Russell. And with Andrew, of all people. It was something she'd fantasized about, sure—she'd fantasized about Andrew all the time—but to go through with such an act is to transform oneself. She is, she thinks, a completely different person now. The kind of person who would have an affair. With Andrew's death, though, has come the possibility of renewal. Now that he's gone, as much as she misses him, as greatly as she continues to love him, she can become herself again, can she not? If nothing else, she's been given the chance to right her marriage. She will do her best to put Andrew behind her and devote herself to the man she's chosen as her husband. She hates to admit it, but her grief is balanced by a profound sense of freedom. She's been released from the imprisonment of infidelity. Also, she can't help feeling that Andrew's death has saved their lives: Juliet's and Maddie's and Russell's, her own. His dying, in the end, was a sacrifice. If she and Andrew had been found out, each of them would have been devastated, even more than they are now. And it's up to Emma, the lone custodian of the secret she and Andrew carried, to keep their lives intact. To protect them all from the truth.

Which is no small feat. Hiding her sorrow, tucking it in like a shirttail, is proving as difficult as hiding the affair itself. To make matters worse, she still hasn't found her father's book. She thinks of it as a link between her and her parents, and likes to imagine, reading one of the poems aloud, that her mother and father are listening from some nonmaterial realm, that they hear their grown daughter's voice and are lifted by it. She left Andrew and Juliet's in such a stupor after the explosions. She had the presence of mind to grab her tote bag, but she's almost positive she forgot the book—on the floor, or on the seat of the stationary bike, or on the windowsill. She can't remember fully, so much of that day remains out of focus, but Emma has no idea where else it might be. There are no names written in it, not her father's or her mother's or her own; there's no reason for Maddie or Juliet to connect the book to Emma. Still, it's evidence. She was negligent, even if she *was* in a state of near-unconsciousness.

Additionally, she's had a feeling for the past couple of weeks that Russell is angry with her. He's been moody and rude, keeping to himself. Does he know something? On the day of the accident, after she left Sunset Road and started for home, Emma stopped at a gas station to wash up and change out of her exercise gear, but it didn't matter. Russell had gone straight to Andrew's from the All or Nothing. Thank God Emma left the house when she did. Maybe, though, instead of finding *her* there, he found the collection of poems. Maybe—helping Juliet and Maddie dispose of the broken glass or board up the place—he came across it in the spare bedroom. When Russell returned from Andrew's that night, his thumb swollen and blood-encrusted because he'd hammered it into a plank, Emma didn't let herself cry. She narrowed her eyes, firmed her lips, pretending she wasn't sick with panic, affecting, she believed, a self-possessed concern.

•

How will she find the contentment she hopes for, the love for life? What will devotion to Russell be worth after so many years of disloyalty? How will Emma become herself again? And what does that even mean? *Did she know who she was in the first place?*

Where will she begin?

After work—at the wheel of her Civic, in the Bora Bora's ill-lit parking garage—she takes Marcus Bauerkemper's card from her purse. It was three weeks ago that he gave it to her. She thinks of the conversation they had that evening, his presumptuous and eccentric manner. There was an innocence to it, though—to his whole farcical performance at her table—and Emma found herself drawn to him. Not romantically, of course, but the way one might be drawn to a grandfather or an elderly uncle. He's played at her tables four or five times since then, reciting the dictionary, cajoling her to visit his church. Emma can't see any harm in it. Perhaps he can help her, tell her what it is she needs to hear, whatever in the world that might be. Anything's better than feeling sorry for herself, living in dread of an unknown future.

The engine idles noisily, echoing through her open window. She contemplates the card, taps it with her fingernail. Sky. Cloud. Sunlight. She reads the embossed, calligraphic print: *Assembly of the Holy Redeemer.*

Simon

He follows the Jeep as it swings idly out of the subdivision, past the stone-slab sign that reads Bighorn Heights in shining white letters. He keeps his distance, low in his seat, elderly-driver low, such that he finds himself peering over the wheel at the Jeep's receding taillights. The bill of his gray Runnin' Rebels cap obscures his eyes, and for a broader margin of security Simon pulls it down even more. Juliet respects the speed limit, though a few times she exceeds it suddenly and then hugs the corner in a right turn, as if aware of Simon's presence. She tacks southwestward, sailing the generous thoroughfares of suburban Las Vegas. Simon watches from a strip mall across the street as she fills the Jeep's tank at a Texaco station. He puts the pickup in park and lowers his window. It's June, an endless month of arid heat, but now and then an evening like this will come along, the temperature having lowered at nightfall, the air having dampened in some secretive way, and the city's residential areas will give forth the cool, wet-turf scent of a golf course after dark. Desire bores through him, augering down through his center, hollowing him out. Even from far away Andrew Huntley's wife is so eye-catching, so unassumingly pretty.

He follows Juliet to the Crapshoot, a boxy, signless dive some of the guys in his crew go to after work—"the Crapper," they call it. The Crapshoot has no kitchen but is known for its hamburgers, the only food you can order, which the bartender broils in a heat-stained toaster oven beside the register. Simon parks in a far corner of the lot and waits for nearly an hour, wondering what Juliet is doing inside. Drinking alone? Having a drink with a friend? Eating a late burger for dinner? (It's well past nine o'clock.) Finally, she emerges, climbs unsteadily into the Jeep, and pulls away.

He still hasn't returned to work, so he has the time and energy for this. Now that the pickup has been restored to working order—now that he's finished dealing with the claims adjuster and the body shop—a range of open hours lies before him each day. He's stopped reading Bud Stone's emails. Oh the joy and release of hitting "delete" when they appear in his inbox! Simon has stopped opening company correspondence altogether. What he knows about the condition of WEPCO he's gotten from the news. Lawsuits have been filed, dozens of them. Three more bodies have been found at the site; Andrew Huntley's is still missing. Not much else has been reported. The investigation into the cause of the explosions continues. Simon can't get himself to care. He hasn't quit, not officially. He's merely gone silent—off-grid. (Can he call it that?) He and Rebecca have enough socked away for when he's inevitably let go. For now, Simon still receives his bimonthly paycheck. Maybe when it ceases to arrive he'll look for a new, low-tension job, a job of another sort entirely. Driving a school bus. Shelving books at a library. Some line of work that provides just enough income, if they're frugal, to offset the dwindling of their savings. Work that carries little risk, little danger of something blowing up.

Juliet travels farther into the city, ending up on Las Vegas Boulevard, passing the Monte Carlo, Bellagio, Bally's, the Flamingo and Caesars Palace and Harrah's. He stays several car-lengths behind, the Strip glowing like a Lite-Brite. It always reminds him of that old toy from the sixties, the casinos and their multistory signs showering a hazy incandescence onto everything below, calling out to the endless passersby, *Look at me! Look at me!* Through his open window, the ruckus of automobiles—revving engines, honking horns, the low-frequency output of high-priced sound systems. He changes lanes whenever Juliet does. As far back as he is, he feels connected to her by some invisible string stretched tight, as though the Jeep and his pickup are opposite ends of a tin-can telephone, as though he might say something, sending his eager vibrations her way, and Juliet will hear him and respond.

"You are not the kind of person who does a thing like this," he says under his breath. "You, Simon Addison, are not this person."

•

He's been to the Huntleys' house many times since the day he mowed the lawn and trimmed the hedge. Making sure Maddie and Juliet aren't home requires a measure of reconnaissance that makes him feel not a little creepy, not a little unhinged. For a few weeks they stayed at a Best Western, but once the windows were replaced, they moved back in. At first Simon simply continued to mow, trim, and water. But then, with additional equipment from his shed, with an exalted sense of purpose, he dug out a dead copper-tone and planted a new one he'd picked up at a nursery close by. He pruned the bushy white dogwood in the backyard. Before long he was weeding and edging, replenishing mulch, checking the landscape lights for spent bulbs. The place looks like a botanical garden, and thinking of it puts a proud if discomfited smile on Simon's face.

He brought even more equipment, turning his attention to the alga-afflicted pool, brushing the steps, walls, and floor, then treating the water—which was the sloughy color of pea soup—with algaecide and shock. He emptied the skimmer basket and skimmed leaves and dead insects into a peatlike clump on the deck. He hosed out the filter cartridges, refilled the tablets in the floating chlorine dispenser. With his test kit, Simon checked the chlorine level and the pH, making sure the water was halfway up the mouth of the skimmer.

He keeps waking to a mental to-do list, a day's work to occupy the hours of his new, jobless life. He pressure-washed the house's beige stucco exterior, which was grimed with blown dirt, the desert being just beyond the Huntleys' backyard. The front door was scratched in places, its paint chipped off in others, and so Simon smoothed its surfaces with a putty knife and sandpaper, spackling a nail hole above the textured-glass window in the center. Though he had no way of opening the door, he gave it a fresh coat of nut-brown, coaxing the bristles as close as he could to the frame. He shoveled debris from the gutter and swept a row of doughnut-size anthills from a joint in the sidewalk. The driveway was a line chart of three prominent cracks, and he filled each of them with a bead of polyurethane sealant.

He hopes Juliet has noticed everything he's done.

•

Now, in lieu of maintaining her yard and pool and house, Simon is following her. He doesn't know why, exactly, just as he doesn't know what's compelled him to care for Juliet's property. It has to be about more than his attraction to her, which has crept up on him only in the past few days. He goes to Bighorn Heights at various times throughout the week, parks two or three corners from Juliet's block, and waits like a cop on a stakeout until her Jeep appears. He follows her to the bank and the supermarket, to Au Bon Pain and Barnes & Noble and Walgreens, to the tan adobe-style office park where, he's come to learn, she practices as an art therapist. On one occasion, feeling bold though creepier than ever, he sat only rows behind her as she took in a matinee by herself on a Friday afternoon. Another time Simon glided behind her in the pickup through a car wash.

Sometimes Juliet will be out already and Simon, from his nearby vantage point, will see her arriving home and he'll call it quits and go home himself. And sometimes he'll sit parked in Bighorn Heights for an hour or two to no avail—he won't see her at all. When he spots her leaving the subdivision, though—the Jeep slowing to a stop at the end of Damselfly Drive—his heart floats up in his chest, and as he pulls out behind her he imagines Juliet next to him, in the passenger seat of the pickup. He imagines they're together, a couple. In love.

He doesn't peep in her windows at night—nothing like that. He doesn't own any binoculars, and he's never taken a photo of her. Simon gets no sexual pleasure from spying on Juliet. He isn't a criminal or a pervert.

•

He's right behind her now and can see the top of her head above the headrest, her eyes in the rearview mirror. They pass the outdoor pirate show at Treasure Island: loud music, a dazzling strobe, cannon fire from a listing ship. Simon reduces his speed, allowing distance between the Jeep and his pickup. He turns after she does onto a short side street, stopping across from the Guardian Angel Cathedral, the venue for her husband's funeral.

Juliet parks in the lot and walks around to the front of the church. There's a row of six wooden doors, and she pulls at each of the handles. She takes a step back and looks up at the gabled mosaic that rises enormously over the doors, wedged between the edges of the roof: the Guardian Angel amid three smaller angels, labeled PRAYER, PEACE, and PENANCE. Juliet wears dark jeans and a striped blouse, her hair down around her neck, the way Simon likes it. She takes a cigarette from her shoulder bag and stares off to the east, hip cocked, as she smokes. Far away, above Frenchman Mountain, silvery stars speckle the black night sky. She stamps on the butt, and Simon coughs. A single, unaccountable cough: he isn't sick. He's parked a good thirty yards away, but Juliet wheels around and looks directly at him. His window, he realizes, is still open.

As she walks to the pickup, Simon feels his bowels loosen. Then comes the sensation that he's lost his balance, and he jolts upright in his seat. Like he did a few weeks ago in front of her house, he nods when Juliet reaches him. This time he doesn't drive off.

"Can I help you with something?" she demands.

"What do you mean?" Simon does his best to look puzzled, racked now with an insistent flatulence. He lifts his Rebels cap but it falls back down. The fitted cap is too large, containing his forehead and the tops of his ears, its bill as stiff and flat as a vinyl record. He feels like one of those preteen wannabe-gangsters he always sees loitering in front of convenience stores.

"What do I *mean*? I mean who are you and why are you stalking me, or whatever the hell it is you're doing?"

"I'm not—"

"Don't lie to me!" She talks as if with a wired jaw. "You know I've seen you. What business do you have taking care of my house? Why are you here right now?"

"Listen, I—"

"What's the story, goddammit? Before I call the police."

"Please," Simon says, emitting a silent stream of gas. He removes his cap. "I'm a friend. Of Andrew's."

"What's your name?"

"Simon Addison."

"How did you know my husband?"

"From work. I work for WEPCO." He takes out his wallet and shows her his ID card.

"I *thought* you looked familiar."

"I was at the funeral," Simon says, tipping his head toward the church.

"How do you think it feels to see some man I've never met hanging around outside my home?"

"I'm so sorry. Really, I am. Can we talk about this? Would that be acceptable? I feel like I need to explain myself. I can clarify everything, I promise."

She glares at him, a hank of hair falling over her nose.

"A cup of coffee, maybe," he says. "If you have a few minutes."

Juliet folds her arms, swaying a little.

"Coffee," she says. She tightens her lips. "All right, whoever you are. Let's have some coffee. Somewhere close. With lots of people."

"How about Tiffany's? Down the street." Simon has a sudden appreciation of his own nerve, even as he fears that Juliet will indeed call the police. "You know it?"

"Of course I know it," she says. "Tiffany's. Fine. I'll meet you there."

•

Tiffany's Café is inside the old White Cross Drugs, a few blocks north of the Stratosphere. He parks in the lot, snugging the pickup between a conversion van and a flatbed truck. The drugstore is lit with a dim, gray fluorescence, and the lone cashier nibbles her thumb in a posture of weary submission. Simon makes his way through the aisles to the rear. It's all sleek tan surfaces in the café—the tile floor and the tabletops and the long counter. Two letter-board menus hang above an archaic register. The place itself is ancient, an institution. The booth benches and the pedestal stools are of a rich red vinyl, and in the center of each table a glass vase holds a long-stemmed daisy. A minute later, Juliet walks in, meeting his eyes with a nettled brow. They take a booth by a window.

"So it's Simon," she says. She folds her hands and leans her elbows on the table, her breath soured with liquor. "Tell me, Simon, do you think it's okay to do what you've been doing?"

"No," he says. "I definitely do not. I do *not* think it's okay. Just so we're clear on that."

"Good. Because it isn't. It's against the fucking law."

Simon isn't sure if, strictly speaking, this is true. But then he doesn't know exactly what she's referring to. "Your place, you mean. All the stuff I've been doing there."

"I mean *following* me. I've seen you more than once, you know." Her voice has turned loud and coarse. "Who do you think you are, James Bond?"

"I don't think that. No," he says. "I just figured I could help in some way."

"By harassing me?"

"Now wait a second. I've never harassed you. Please don't say that. Let me back up, okay? I started doing some things to lend a hand with your house. I don't know why. I thought it would give you time to focus on other matters, I suppose. You lost your husband, and—well, once I started I couldn't stop. And then I wanted— I don't know *what* I wanted." He lowers his face, feeling stupid. He knows nothing about this woman. "I know I'm in the wrong here. I'll understand completely if you want to go to the authorities."

A young waiter comes and takes their orders for coffee.

"Pie as well," Simon says, then worries that he's just diminished the gravity of the conversation. What's more, his flatulence has escalated; it's all he can do to hold the gas at bay. Pie will only make things worse. "Slice of cherry, no ice cream."

Juliet glances at him. "For me too," she says. "The same."

"I can't express how sorry I am," Simon tells her.

"Did you think I wouldn't recognize you if you showed up in a pickup truck?"

"What? No, I wasn't trying to—"

"And why didn't you just ask, like a normal person, if you felt the need to help me?"

"I wanted to remain anonymous, I guess."

"Don't misunderstand me," Juliet says. "My front lawn's a putting green. The house looks better than ever. It's like the Palace of Versailles over there. That doesn't mean it's reasonable for you to become my gardener without permission. That doesn't mean I want a chaperone wherever I go."

"I agree," Simon says. "You're absolutely right."

"Most women would have a restraining order against you. I can't believe I'm sitting here talking to you like this." She points at his wedding ring. "How would your wife feel if she knew where you are right now?"

He told Rebecca he was going to see a new action flick at the multiplex near their neighborhood. On the whole, Rebecca thinks going to the movies is a waste of time, and she dislikes action movies anyway. Like Juliet, Simon is a solo moviegoer, but he's used this same story three times in the past two weeks and he wonders if Rebecca's growing suspicious. Many mornings Simon tells her he's off to another meeting: the company is renting office space downtown, he's said. Sometimes he says he's going to the driving range, or to the Trek store to check out accessories for his bike. Until lately, Simon was never deceitful with her, not really. After all their years together, he loves Rebecca with the fervor of a newlywed, with a day-to-day awareness of how lucky he is. The frequency of his lying shocks him. He has only to open his mouth and the falsehoods come tumbling out.

He flicks the vase in the center of the table. The daisy, white as a cloud, bobs in the gentle wind of an air-conditioning vent. "I'd rather not think about my wife at the moment," he says.

"And what about my husband? Speaking of spouses. How come I never heard Andrew mention your name?"

"Hmm," he says. "We were *work* buddies. That's different sometimes." He feels immobilized by his guilty conscience. "I've taken it pretty hard, his passing. Like I told you, I only wanted to help."

"Well—" She breaks off. "Thanks, I think." Her voice is softer now, tinctured with a will to trust him. "But I want it to stop, what's been going on. All of it. I'm giving you permission. I'm *telling* you."

"You have my word." He places his hand flat on the table. "Listen, I hope you're all right, all things considered."

Juliet shrugs. The waiter returns with their cups of coffee and plates of cherry pie, and they sip and eat in an uneasy silence.

"There aren't enough people in here," she says at last, setting down her fork, her plate empty. "I told you there needed to be a lot of people."

"You're right. Sure. I take responsibility for that. If you're worried, we can go."

"I'll go when I want to go."

"Are you always so confrontational? Sorry, I don't mean right now. In front of the church, walking up to a stranger's car in the dark. That was a brave thing to do, don't you think?"

"You aren't very threatening, even from a distance. Besides, do I have a reason not to feel safe around you, Simon?"

"No," Simon says, another pocket of gas building painfully inside him. "Of course not. Still, though."

"I no longer have a husband, in case you haven't noticed. I'm learning to take matters into my own hands."

He nods, searching his mind for something else to talk about. "That church," he says. "The Guardian Angel? On most Sundays it's standing-room only. The place fills up with out-of-towners praying for luck. Have you heard this?" He wants to ask her why she went there tonight. "There's even a special tourist mass where people drop casino chips into the collection baskets. Then once a month a priest they call the 'chip monk' drives around to all the casinos and cashes them in."

Juliet looks away, letting out a small, cheerless burp. When the waiter brings the check, Simon lays down a twenty-dollar bill. "On me," he says. "The least I can do."

Juliet says, "There's no pain when I talk about him. Not the way I expected there to be. I can say his name and it just hangs in the open for a while. But it doesn't hurt—not yet, anyway. I should feel bad about that, shouldn't I?"

"We all grieve in different ways. It's nothing to feel bad about."

"I'm a therapist. What am I asking *you* for."

"Are you able to drive home, do you think? No offense. I just want to be sure. You won't be surprised to know I was outside the bar earlier." He offers an apologetic smile.

Juliet rubs her eyes. "Don't leave," she says. "I don't mean to be so sharp. Stay with me. Have another cup of coffee."

She reaches across the table and touches his arm, and Simon's shoulders grow warm inside his shirt.

"Stay," Juliet says, looking at him now. "Please."

Maddie

On a Monday in the middle of June, Maddie and Russell visit the WEPCO site together. Maddie's been wanting to view the wreckage, but not by herself. For her mother it's still too soon. Russell too has had misgivings, though he finally agreed to join her. There are concrete barriers obstructing Sunset Road, but they're able to drive far enough along it to see what's left of the plant. They stand looking out at the piles of twisted steel, which rise uniformly in single file, like humps on a camel's back. The heavy-duty vehicles trundle back and forth—dump trucks and flatbeds and bulldozers and forklifts—hard-hatted men in the small rectangular cabs. Blackened girders slant out of the ruins like giant insect legs. Large objects—you can't tell what they once were—look like crumpled-up paper or burned pieces of coal. The automobiles, peeking through the piles, are indistinguishable: paintless and mangled, the tires melted away. All around, hooks and wrecking balls swing from the wire ropes of cranes.

To the east, a sweep of desert stippled with the gray-brown growth of summer: sagebrush, creosote, yucca. In the opposite direction, spilled flatly across the low-lying land, are houses and strip malls and casinos, backdropped by the far Spring Mountains. There were wild grasses on this land, Maddie once learned in her fifth-grade Nevada-history class, warm-water springs that flowed so rapidly, so plentifully, a man couldn't sink if he wanted to. In the 1800s, Spanish-speaking traders, en route from New Mexico to California, bathed and quenched their thirst here. Before that, the Anasazi people diverted the water and grew corn, beans, and squash. And before that—thousands of years before—the terrain was dense with foliage, roamed by antelope and deer, ground sloths and buffalo, mammoths and saber-toothed cats. Now, only twenty minutes east of the Strip, there is this: churned-up dirt and the taste of dust, the dry, earthy smell of it. The groan of diesel engines. The scattered fragments of a disaster.

Maddie takes pictures with her cell phone. She searches for her father's Sonata but can't tell one mutilated car from another. She lowers the phone and stares silently, blinking.

"I just don't know what I want anymore," she says as they get back in Russell's Corolla. "It's like I've always been so focused, so motivated, and now everything seems so laughably unimportant to me. Like, disposable or something, if that makes any sense. I thought I was dealing with it at first—missing my dad, losing him. Now I keep thinking that I want to run away from it all. My whole stupid life."

She waits for Russell to console her. Driving to the site, he was quiet, almost irritable, his eyes restless and distant, and Maddie felt that something wasn't quite right with him, sensing it was about more than just her father. Now she slides her cell phone into her purse. In the near, heat-hazy distance, a backhoe moves slowly among the remains of the plant. Russell closes his eyes for a long moment, then puts the key in the ignition and says, "Okay, then."

Instead of taking Maddie home, he makes his way to Interstate 15, then to US 93. He says nothing at all, and something dense, something warm, shifts inside her, tipping.

•

They're heading due north, through Coyote Springs and the Pahranagat Valley, filling the time with irrelevant topics of conversation, neither of them willing to acknowledge what's happening. Is this some exaggerated game of chicken, or is it for real? Russell's mood seems to have improved, brightened, Maddie thinks, by the glow of their sudden departure. She hasn't packed a suitcase. She hasn't asked her mother's permission. They've simply taken off, with no destination, no tangible purpose.

Where are they going? She doesn't care. The whole thing is outrageous and thrilling. And *right*. It feels perfectly right, as though, since her father's death, the total effort of her existence, without her knowledge, has been concentrated on this single end.

Sun-dulled pavement tapers to the horizon like the nib of a fountain pen. In an hour or so they reach the town of Alamo. At a Sinclair station they fill up and buy bottles of water and a bag of roasted pistachios. Then back onto 93, the old Great Basin Highway, the desert earth blond in the noonday light, the mountains striated and majestic, so freakishly stunning that for an instant it seems they're a figment of her imagination. A legion of transmission towers—inverted isosceles triangles with what look like arms and antennae, retrofuturistic—link east with west in an endless line. Every so often a hawk or an eagle planes down in the distance.

On either side of the highway, globemallow and bear poppies. Y-shaped Joshua trees whose fury branches end in a cluster of bristlelike leaves. Motor homes and eighteen-wheelers flash by in the opposite direction, ribbons of dust sidewinding across the land. Everything domed by a big Nevada sky, blue as an iris.

•

They decide to camp out in Cathedral Gorge, a state park just south of Pioche. "I've got all the equipment we'll need," Russell says, pointing over his shoulder. "In the trunk."

He has a tent and a sleeping bag and an air mattress, a ground tarp and a cook set and a kerosene lantern. Maddie can use the mattress and the sleeping bag, he says. There are a couple of Mexican falsa blankets back there. He'll be perfectly fine.

"Have you been secretly planning this or something?" She digs her hand into the bag of pistachios, cracking open her window. "What's all that stuff doing in your car?"

"I don't know. I mean, I don't know if I can tell you that," he says. "I don't think I'm ready to talk about it." He wrinkles his forehead. "Maybe later, though. Maybe that's a campfire conversation."

Maddie rolls her eyes at him, tossing two shell-halves into the scorching wind. "Whatever, fruit loop. Why don't you stop being so mysterious and just tell me."

Russell gives a chuckle. "Follow your nose," he says dryly. "It always knows."

By now they've been through Ash Springs and Crystal Springs and Caliente—cruising below the speed limit, taking their time—passing cattle-crowded ranches that bear names like Whipple, Buckhorn, and Sharp. Each town consists of a diner, a saloon, a gas station/convenience store, a post office, a make-do cemetery, a motel or two. Maybe a crumbling train station, deserted. Maybe, in the middle of some backyard, a cinder-block outbuilding converted into a laundromat or a taqueria, the name spray-painted in black along a street-facing wall.

Maddie has never been this far north of Las Vegas by car. The drive seems like a fantasy, a waking dream. She watches the landscape slip past as if it isn't even real: pre-filmed background footage in an old-time movie. She contemplates Russell's response to her question about the equipment in his trunk, then feels a tightness around her eyes, something akin to an ice-cream headache. School is out for summer, so Maddie isn't worried about missing any classes. What about Russell's job, though? When is his next shift at the All or Nothing? How long will they be gone? She wonders what her mother and Emma will say when she and Russell get around to calling them. There's been no discussion about this, just as they still haven't discussed the reality of what they're doing. Namely, that it's illegal—is it not?—for Maddie and Russell to leave town without her mother's permission. According to fact, she supposes, Russell is a kidnapper now, even though Maddie has given her consent.

She isn't that hungry, but shelling the pistachios is a way of passing the time. Maddie remembers the day she used her thumb to pry off her middle toe's dead, purplish nail, a few weeks after dropping a can of tomato sauce on her foot. She felt a flicker of achievement as the nail dislodged and fell to the floor, and she feels the same pleasant flicker each time she frees one of the nuts from its muzzlelike shell. She stuffs the half-empty bag into the console. Cell-phone reception is spotty, and on the dashboard lies a foldout map from the gas station in Alamo. Maddie spreads it open, holding it up like a newspaper. "We're close," she says, and Russell nods.

A minute later she says, "I kind of did something. Something not so good."

His wrist sits limply atop the wheel and he stares out at the highway through the wire rims of his glasses, a man in a vegetative state. He's grown quiet again. He wears a white, threadbare T-shirt that reads LIVE LONG AND FESTER. Maddie can usually tell when he's high. She wonders if he is right now.

"Hello?" she says, snapping her fingers. "Earth to Russell."

"What's that? Sorry," he says. "Just thinking. Okay—something not so good, you said. You in trouble?"

"Not that I'm aware of. I feel really terrible, though. I need to get it off my chest."

"All right, fine. How bad are we talking?"

"Not very. Bad enough. I don't know."

She closes one eye, squinting with the other until the highway grows streaky and blurred. Maddie tells him what she did. A few weeks ago, she went for a long training run and ended up at a Smith's Food King near the hotel. She walked a slow lap around the row of checkout counters, passing the in-store bank, the dry cleaner, a line of slot machines. Behind the counter at the end, three long shelves held an assortment of cigarettes and snuff and chewing tobacco. The cashier was busy ringing up a grapefruit, and when Maddie went by she reached behind him and took a pack of Camels from the middle shelf. She palmed it at her side, made her way past the produce to the condiments aisle, where she tore away the cellophane and opened it. There were security pillars at both pairs of the supermarket's sliding glass doors, so Maddie removed three of the cigarettes and ditched the pack between a couple of ketchup bottles. Then she left, simple as that. Walked right out and ran back to the Best Western.

She's only seventeen, and looks her age, if not younger. She would have been carded if she'd tried to buy cigarettes, and unlike the majority of her friends, she doesn't own a fake ID. Maddie had never stolen anything before, and in her chest she felt not the heaviness of remorse but a high, fluttery delight. What shocked her was not so much that she'd committed a crime as that she'd committed one with such composure and expertise. She'd gotten away with it. Or had she? Sitting on the bed in the hotel room, Maddie thought of those tinted half-globes you always see suspended from the ceiling of a supermarket, lifeless eyeballs that record your every move. She hadn't considered them. She deadbolted the door, stashing the Camels in a nightstand drawer. For half an hour or more she waited for a knock, but nothing happened. No one was coming. She took one of the Camels from the drawer, rode the elevator downstairs, and bought a mocha Frappucino at the Starbucks. Outside, she asked a college-age girl smoking a clove for a light, and went around to the back of the hotel and smoked her cigarette. She coughed only once this time, sipping the Frappucino between drags, dizzy from the hulking double rush.

"Is this the truth?" Russell says now.

"I'm going to hell, I guess." Hearing herself admit to what she did, Maddie sees the distance of years that stretch between them. "I know—you're disappointed in me. *I'm* disappointed in me. That's why I'm telling you this."

He shakes his head at her. "Maddie."

"My mom let me try one of her cigarettes and I liked it. I wanted another one."

The cigarette Maddie smoked with her mother made her lungs burn, made her nauseous, and it tasted awful at first, yes. But she can see what people like about smoking. She feels more mature with a cigarette between her fingers—almost worldly, in some indeterminate way. And holding one gives you something to do with at least one of your hands during a conversation. And once she got used to the taste, she enjoyed the buzz she's heard her friends describe, as good as the buzz from a can of beer—though different—and it takes effect more or less instantly. The day she stole the Camels, Maddie had awoken with a strange desire to smoke, the way a child awakes the day after Christmas with a desire to resume playing with a new toy. She couldn't call it a craving. Rather, it had been a kind of novelty-induced eagerness to put another cigarette to her lips and inhale.

"Your mother gave you a cigarette?"

"It was so easy," Maddie says. "I walked into the store and I took what I wanted."

"So you're a smoker now. And a thief." Russell reaches back and adjusts the green rubber band around his ponytail. "A general miscreant, really. Let's not forget the fact that you climbed out the window of your dean's office the day the plant blew up."

"I didn't steal a whole pack. Just a few cigs from one that I opened."

"*Cigs?*"

"That's better, isn't it? Just taking a few?"

"No, it's not better," he says. "It's the same. You shoplifted. Quantity doesn't matter. Or maybe it does—I don't know. That's not the point. Be thankful you didn't get caught."

"I'm thankful we're doing this," she tells him. "I'm thankful to be gone."

He looks at her.

"Aren't you?" Maddie says.

"Since when does your mother smoke?"

•

At the Cathedral Gorge visitor center—a small, single-room cabin with several racks of glossy brochures—they buy parking passes and a bundle of firewood. Then they have to drive along a narrow road that winds for a mile through the vacant desert park. They pull into a gravel lot and get out, stretching. A small brick building labeled RESTROOM stands a few yards away. "Time to lift the leg," Russell says, making a beeline for it.

Maddie leans against the hood. The campground contains eight or nine sites, each with a wooden picnic table, a grill, a stone fire ring, and a green aluminum ramada. The gorge is walled by low, buff mountains that indeed put her in mind of cathedrals. The place looks as if it were designed by Antoni Gaudí, the dead architect she studied in AP Spanish—she calls to mind the Sagrada Família, the Colònia Güell—towers, spires, columns, and arches defined against the cloudless sky, lit up by the high yellow sun. Steep outcroppings thrust themselves from the valley floor among primrose and ricegrass and long, ripply sand dunes. A jackrabbit darts from one jumble of rocks to another. There isn't a person in sight.

Juniper trees grow in a huddle near a trailhead. Maddie walks down the trail a bit, watching for snakes. She picks up a fallen branch, slender and spiny, jade green. She spins it between her palms, letting it prick her, thinking of her father—his love for camping, in the backyard or elsewhere. How he would have enjoyed this place.

A thought unfolds: *What if he's still alive?* The notion grips her, crazy as it is. Russell put it in her head the week of the accident, as they were cleaning up the glass in her house. He told her about this weird urge he had to search for her father in the desert around the WEPCO site. "I keep seeing him out there," he said, "roaming around like some kind of ghost. I keep picturing him running away from the explosions, running and running, and then, I don't know, getting disoriented—maybe because he's injured or something. Getting lost. But lost *where? How?* It makes no sense. I just miss him, I guess." Russell apologized and hugged her, saying he ought to keep his big trap shut.

But what if her father really is lost somewhere? *What if?* The question is there in her head—a fly she can't swat. It's madness, she knows, but she lets herself consider it, lets the prospect buzz. His body still hasn't been found. What if he *did* manage to get away? What if he ran, as Russell suggested, and was knocked senseless by one of the explosions, knocked off his feet, but not killed? What if he got himself up at some later point, wounded and confused, and wandered unknowingly into the Mojave? What if he's out there somewhere, astray in those low desert mountains on the way to Lake Mead, surviving miraculously on the prickly pears, which people say you can do—sucking their moisture, eating their fruit?

What if he can't find his way to a road, his cell phone dead, his sense of direction impeded by delirium? What if her father's heart is still beating, if his lungs are still drawing air? Is it so far-fetched?

Back at the car, she says, "Sixty-one for every human on the planet." Maddie twirls the juniper branch as though it's a lasso.

The passenger-side door is open and Russell's bent over, rooting around in the glove compartment. He sticks his head up. "What?"

"Trees. There are sixty-one of them for every living person." During the drive—three hours in all—Maddie displayed her fondness for obscure trivia. She wonders if Russell is sick of hearing her talk. "That's about four hundred billion worldwide."

"Lotta raking come fall."

"They don't all lose their leaves," she says. "Consider the evergreen." She plucks a needle from the branch, blows it like an eyelash from her fingertip, feeling rebellious and free and…doomed. Maddie can't deny it. There's a leaden feeling of doom in her stomach that's making her nauseous, as though she's eaten something rancid.

Russell takes a Ziploc bag from the glove compartment. He unseals the bag, holds it to his nose. She gives him a reproachful look.

"Not for you, little lady," he tells her. "Don't even think about it. *Pour moi.*"

"I'm gonna go ahead and say it's bad enough that you and I are here at all. Now we're adding narcotics to the brew."

"The voice of reason. An unwelcome visitor if ever there was one." Russell smiles. "Not to worry," he says. "It's medicinal."

Russell

It's been a week since he confronted Emma with the book. He walked in after his shift at the All or Nothing, ten thirty on a Monday night, and pitched it onto the coffee table. Emma sat cross-legged in the middle of the couch with a bowl of ice cream, watching *The Brady Bunch* on TV Land. The lamps were off and the wooden blinds were closed, and the television filled the living room with a flat, ashen light. Russell went to the kitchen and got himself a beer. He dropped down into the La-Z-Boy opposite the couch, flicking the bottle cap into the air and then catching it with a swipe of his hand.

"I figured you might be looking for that," he said.

Emma leaned forward, peering at the book, its tattered black-and-white cover, the lower right corner frayed, cottony—curled like the crest of a wave. "Oh." She set the bowl of ice cream on the coffee table. "I haven't, actually. Why? Where was it?"

Russell picked at the label on his bottle. "Where was it, she says." He hadn't let himself light up that day, and he felt lucid, authoritative. "Where was it." He tilted his head. "I guess you've decided I'm an idiot," he said. "A big old dumb-shit. A big dumb dipshit."

"What are you talking about?"

"You're right, too. Big stupid dumb-fuck me." He sipped his beer. "Probably because of all the weed I've smoked over the years. I'm sure that's the explanation—gotta be. You know what they say: 'They don't call it dope 'cause it makes you smart.'" Russell felt a whirling in his chest, the emergence of some inner vortex. "If I were smart, if I had a brain in this thick head of mine, I would have trusted my intuition. We would have had this conversation a long time ago."

Just then his resolve wavered and he thought about easing up a bit. What, after all, was his intuition worth? He felt silly, however convinced he was of Emma's unfaithfulness, presenting her with nothing more than the book of poems. (Russell had hemmed and hawed for a full two weeks before finally getting up the nerve to broach the matter.) He didn't know for sure that she'd done anything wrong; it wasn't as though she'd confessed. Perhaps there was a perfectly valid reason the book had ended up at Andrew's house.

Emma picked it up from the coffee table and put it beside her on the couch. "I'm not following you," she said, tightening the belt of her white fleece robe. She placed her hand on the book as if to protect it from him. It angered Russell more every time he looked at it. On the television, Christopher Knight was doing a bad impression of Humphrey Bogart. When Emma started to say something, Russell cut her off.

"Were you at his house recently?" he said.

"Whose house?"

"Don't do that to me, babe. Don't pretend." He finished his beer in three loud gulps. "You know whose house. And I'm pretty sure you've been there without me, haven't you."

She looked frightened now, blinking her eyes at him. "You're talking about Andrew?"

There was a rippling in Russell's stomach—like butterflies, only heavier. The sensation spread to his chest, into his shoulders, and up around his throat, dispersing along the line of his jaw. "Were you over there or something, the morning he died?"

"Russell—"

"I feel like you were. Call it a hunch. Or maybe it was the day before that, or a *few* days before. But you were there at some point." With his palm, he pressed the cap back onto the bottle. "That much I know. I may be a dumb-fuck, but I'm pretty sure your father's book didn't get up and walk itself over to my best friend's house."

Emma began to cry, her left hand twitching in her lap.

"Oh, God," Russell said. "Oh, my God."

"Russell."

"Did you see him that day?"

"I was waiting for him," she said, wiping her nose with her robe.

"Oh, Christ."

"He thought the world of you. He adored you."

"Don't tell me that!" He sat forward, pointing the bottle at her. "Don't ever tell me that again!"

Emma nodded.

"What a dipshit I am," Russell said.

"Stop saying that."

"I knew all along and I let it go on right in front of me. I just kept on being his friend."

"I wanted it to be over," Emma said. "We both did."

"Well fuck you! You got your wish. Did he wear a rubber, at least? He didn't, did he."

"Please, Russell."

He got up from the La-Z-Boy and stood at the edge of the coffee table, his toes clenched so tightly inside his shoes he could hardly feel them. "Did he pull out? Tell me."

She hid her face in her hands, then dragged herself from the couch and went to their bedroom, closing the door. Russell locked himself in the hall bathroom. Quickly—violently—he jerked off, punching a hole in the wall when he came.

•

Now he crouches inside the stone fire ring and assembles a little tepee of kindling: sticks and twigs Maddie has gathered from the surrounding wilderness. The sun is setting behind the mountains; clouds are dying embers in a low purple sky. His kerosene lantern burns brightly on a nearby rock, and the desert air is cool on his skin. Far away, some coyotes yelp and howl.

Maddie sits hugging her knees in an old aluminum lawn chair from the trunk of Russell's car. She wears a pink button-down, white shorts, and her Jack Purcells, the toes of her tennis shoes poking downward through the chair's faded orange webbing. "What's the craziest thing you'd do for a million dollars?" she says.

"It's a bit late for an icebreaker, don't you think?"

"Come on. Just tell me."

He steps outside the fire ring, strikes a wooden match and holds it to the tinder in the center of the kindling. With a small whoosh of air, the pile of ricegrass and dry conifer needles ignites. "I don't know," he says. "You're kind of putting me on the spot here."

"Would you drink a glass of cat barf? The white, frothy variety."

"No," he says, kneeling down and blowing.

"Suck the blistered toes of a dead homeless man?"

"Nope."

"Walk up Fremont Street with your pants around your ankles?"

A flame rises and gutters, and he stacks slender pieces of wood in a loosely fitted square around the fire: a log cabin to encompass his tepee. "Pants only, or underwear too?"

"Underwear too—what do you *think*?"

"I don't know. *Of course* I would."

"Would you shave 'Engelbert Humperdinck Rocks My Universe' into the side of your head?"

Russell stands up, laughing in the velvety twilight. He stares at her, her sun-kissed cheeks and nose. "Perhaps," he says.

Maddie blows a raspberry.

"Could all those words even fit?" Smoke drifts over him, and he takes off his glasses and rubs his eyes. "'Humperdinck' alone would take up most of the space. I've got a pretty small noggin. Plus, I'd have to cut my hair."

She lifts her eyebrows, sizing up his head. "Hmm. Never really noticed before. Sort of a little pygmy skull you've got there, isn't it?" Then she asks him, "What would you do to see my father again? Only for a minute. One single minute. And it'd really be him, too—in the flesh. Not some spirit or something. You could say a few things to him, put your arms around him. You could say goodbye. Then at the end of the minute he'd be gone, forever this time."

He looks to see if she's crying. She isn't.

"What would you do?" Maddie says.

He doesn't know what to tell her. The only thing he feels toward her father now is abhorrence. Yes, Russell abhors him with an inner darkness he finds startling and inhuman. A *way-down* darkness that, were Andrew still alive, might pour forth and inhabit the outermost corners of Russell's being, might take full possession of his faculties and impel him to some unthinkable violence against his purported best friend. He feels so witless, so put-upon, for caring as much as he did about someone who was only stabbing him in the back. Russell wants to punish Andrew, physically. It is almost all he can think about. He wishes there were a way.

"The cat barf," he says, putting his glasses back on. "I'd drink the barf. I'd drink a whole wheelbarrow of it."

He imagines Emma and Andrew having sex in Andrew's bed. Then Russell imagines them meeting at some park somewhere, one of those sterile rectangles of grass in the center of a newly erected subdivision, far from where any of their friends or relatives would ever go, to walk hand-in-hand among the saplings and gazebos on a summery afternoon—lovers in love. The darkness inside him darkens.

It's ironic, he supposes, that he's always enjoyed picturing Emma with other guys—several at a time, as he watches. In one of his fantasies they're guests at a hotel in some remote and nameless city, and Russell goes out to a bar and brings back three strangers for Emma, then stands in a corner of the room while the men strip off their clothes and go down on her, one after another, Emma spread-legged on the bed. Once, Russell went so far as to peel a banana and proceed to suck on it as he thought of her giving a blow job, of what it might be like for her to do that to another man. It turned him on immensely. He still can't believe she gave herself to someone else—*to Andrew*—in real life.

"So what's with all the gear?" Maddie asks him. She pulls her tennis shoes from the lawn chair, leans forward and licks her knee, smells the wet skin. "Why couldn't you talk about it? Were you supposed to go on some kind of clandestine camping trip or something?"

"Isn't that what this is?" he says.

The campfire pops and wheezes. Sparks squiggle in the air like lightning bugs. Russell drags the picnic table from beneath the ramada to the edge of the fire ring. He sits down on one of the benches and, with his Swiss army knife, begins whittling a long stick coated with tiny wartlike nodes.

"Mr. Mystery again, huh? That's all right. You don't have to tell me."

"Look," Russell says, "I don't mean to be mysterious. It's complicated. It's a difficult thing to discuss." He works at two of the larger nodes, shaving them from all angles. "You're too young to hear about it anyway."

"Dick."

"I'm sorry," he says. "I shouldn't have said that." He looks eastward at the mountainous horizon, a shadowy line that resembles the waves of an EKG. "Emma cheated on me, okay? She had an affair." It's jarring to say it, as though an invisible arm has taken forceful hold of him. "I packed up my car. I was going to take off. I didn't even know where—I didn't even pack all my things. My plan was to hit the road and set up camp wherever I landed, but I couldn't do it. I couldn't get myself to leave."

"Whoa," Maddie says.

"You put it best: I wanted to run away from my whole life. I still do."

"Looks like you're doing it. For the time being, anyway."

The severity of the circumstances makes his heart flitter. He's a forty-three-year-old man on an unauthorized camping trip with a teenage girl. That he's known her all her life is of little consequence.

Earlier in the day, Russell put up the tent—a two-person dome—and they drove to the nearby town of Panaca, where they bought bottled water and instant coffee, hot dogs and buns, marshmallows and bars of chocolate, bacon and eggs, paper plates and hot cups, toothbrushes and a styrofoam cooler and a bag of Reddy Ice. He called the All or Nothing from the parking lot of the convenience store and told Tim Woods he was under the weather and wouldn't make it in today. Maddie called her mother but got no answer. She left a voice mail, short and sweet: she and Russell had decided on a whim to go camping in Cathedral Gorge. No big deal. Then Russell got on, trying to sound reassuring. "I know we should have asked you first," he said. "There's nothing to worry about. I love her like a daughter, Juliet. You know that."

Ever since they left the WEPCO site today—when he drove them, in a kind of delirium, to US 93—a thought has been knocking around in his mind: *Your life is falling apart.* He smoked a bowl an hour ago, in the shade behind the brick restroom, but he needs more, much more.

"So that's why you didn't call home today," Maddie says now.

"She doesn't need to know where I am. She's lost that privilege."

A viridescent darkness has come to rest around the gorge, shaggy clouds covering the sky like a mohair rug. Insects chorus, and when the woodsmoke pulls back for a second or two, the air smells of clean, uncorrupted earth.

"That information's strictly confidential," Russell tells her. "It stays between us. Not even your mother can find out, you hear?"

"Do you know who he is?"

"Who *who* is?" He's playing for time.

"The guy. The dude Emma cheated with."

"It doesn't matter. I'm done talking about it. I shouldn't have mentioned it in the first place." Russell has stripped the stick of its bark—has blunted each of the nodes—and sharpened one end of it to a fine, whitish point. He tests the tip against his palm. His green backpack is behind him on the picnic table, and he twists around and unzips it. "Here," he says. "Before I forget." He gives her back the copy of *Crossing the Water.* He took it from the coffee table, unsure what to do with it, the night he confronted Emma, after she retreated to their bedroom—the same night he secretly packed to leave, tiptoeing into the room as she slept. It's the possession she cherishes most, and Russell thought about burning it, or simply throwing it away. He's never had such cruel and vindictive thoughts before. Suddenly, painfully, he misses his wife's body, her skin against his own.

"Oh. Right," Maddie says. She presses the book to her chest. "Thanks."

He won't tell Maddie or Juliet about Emma and Andrew. Why defile their memory of him? What good would it do? What the eye doesn't see, the heart doesn't grieve over. What would happen, though, if Maddie gave the book of poems to her mother—assuming, as she does, that it was a gift from her father?

Russell sets the stick and the knife on the bench. He reaches behind him and pulls the backpack into his lap, digging out his flashlight and passing it to Maddie. "Read something," he says.

She turns on the flashlight and opens the book. A moment later she says, "Check this out. There's a poem in here called 'Sleep in the Mojave Desert.'"

"We're in the Great Basin now. But close enough."

Maddie considers the page, then reads:

"*The desert is white as a blind man's eye,*
Comfortless as salt. Snake and bird
Doze behind the old masks of fury.
We swelter like firedogs in the wind."

She closes the book. "Spectacular," she says. She shines the flashlight on the styrofoam cooler, which sits in the dirt beneath the ramada. "I'm hungry, though. Let's have ourselves some dogs."

"Let's," Russell says, but he doesn't move. At the bottom of his backpack, beneath his socks and his underwear, is the handgun he bought a few years ago, a Ruger LC380, swaddled in his paisley-print bandanna. The gun was supposed to quell his anxiety about a home invasion, but it only makes Russell fearful of an accidental shooting. Emma hates guns, and he had to talk her into letting him get one. It's as heavy as a mallet; he feels the Ruger's ominous weight in his lap. He packed it for protection against grizzlies or wolves or mountain lions, depending on where he might be.

And who can say what sort of individuals one might encounter on the road? Who knew, Russell thought as he was filling his backpack, where he would end up, how far he would go? (He was only kidding himself: apart from a firearms course and a single visit to a range in North Las Vegas, he has yet to put it to use.) Now it crosses his mind, horrifyingly, that he can use the gun on himself. The option is there. He knows the famous story of Sylvia Plath, and he thinks of her in her London apartment, four o'clock in the morning, cramming wet towels beneath the doors, her children asleep in their beds. He thinks of her turning on the gas, placing her head, like a bread loaf, into the oven. Andrew's death was traumatic enough; the knowledge that Emma and Andrew were carrying on behind his back—and that Emma, too, will soon be gone from his life, for he is unable to imagine how he can remain married to her—is about all Russell can handle. They were, in effect, the only family he had, his father having died of a pulmonary embolism a couple of months after 9/11, his mother, senile at seventy-three, residing in an assisted-living facility in Summerlin. What is he left with?

Deep down, he knows he'd never really do it. Still, the gun is right here, right here in his backpack, and he chills at the thought of his forefinger against the trigger, and then: nothing. His life's terminus.

"What happens in the morning?" Maddie says. "What happens if my mom decides to have you arrested?"

There's no reception this far from the highway, so he doesn't know if Juliet has called them back. He doesn't know what'll happen in the morning, or what he was thinking when he drove them here.

He zips the backpack and places it back on the picnic table, then goes to the cooler and gets the hot dogs and the buns and the paper plates. With the sharpened stick, he spears two dogs tip-to-tip and looks at Maddie and says, "It'll be a long time before we're back to normal. You and me, your mother. That's all I can tell you for now."

"Sometimes there's no such thing as back to normal," Maddie says. "Sometimes all you can hope for is a slightly better version of what you've got."

Emma

The Assembly of the Holy Redeemer church is a converted bowling alley that dates from the early nineteen-fifties. Nuclear Strikes Lanes & Lounge, it was called, back when mushroom clouds from the Nevada Test Site could be seen from the upper-floor windows of Fremont Street hotels. The north-side address on Marcus Bauerkemper's card didn't register at first, but Emma remembers Nuclear Strikes from when her grandmother threw her a bowling party for her tenth birthday. The neon sign has been removed from the roof (she calls to mind three electron orbits around a flashing bowling-ball nucleus), replaced by a vinyl banner that bears the church's name in big capital letters. The building's exterior, its campy, doo-wop aesthetic, is otherwise unchanged: the fieldstone walls, the plastic paneling around the double glass doors, the tail-fin roofline with the boomerang pillar.

The interior has been gutted and remodeled. Emma stands in a vestibule beyond the doors, where framed watercolors of farms and forests and rolling fields hang against a dark floral wallpaper. A card table holds a coffee urn and plates of frosted cookies. Past the vestibule is the nave of the church—where the lanes and ball returns used to be—low-ceilinged and windowless and unadorned, with rows of padded folding chairs. Emma takes a seat in the back. At the pulpit, Marcus Bauerkemper regards the congregation with his nostril-flaring smile.

"The great Baptist preacher Charles Spurgeon was once criticized by a member of his church for using humor in his sermons," he says. "The sermons came across as trivial, a woman told him. They lacked weight. 'My good lady,' Spurgeon replied, 'if you only knew how much I restrain myself.'"

The congregation laughs uncertainly. Marcus Bauerkemper wears a black cassocklike robe, his string of red beads loose around the collar.

"Psalm 126 shows us the importance of humor, people. The importance of laughter," he says. "Psalm 126 shows us that God and laughter go arm in arm. Because—tell me now—what is laughter equivalent to?" He cups his hand around his ear. "I'm sorry, but I don't think I can hear you." The congregation is silent. "That's right: *joy!* *Joy*, my brothers and sisters, is what Psalm 126 is all about."

A couple of women wave patterned folding fans, despite the frigid, air-conditioned atmosphere. From up front comes a lonely and mechanical "Amen."

"And I'll tell you what, ladies and gentleman. I've got a secret for you. Lean in now, listen to me. *Joy*," Marcus Bauerkemper whispers into one of those headworn microphones, "is the direct result of being restored by God." He claps his hands. "Make no mistake about it! *Joy* comes only from legitimate God-given restoration!"

Emma catches a whiff of Southern dialect in his speech, which she hasn't noticed during their conversations at the Bora Bora. He dances around the pulpit now, kicking his legs and tapping his knuckles against the inner part of his forearm, as though his fist is a tambourine. Someone in a middle row chuckles. Marcus Bauerkemper makes his way down an aisle between the folding chairs, stopping beside an obese, wispy-haired woman with door-knocker earrings. He rests a hand on the woman's shoulder.

"Verse four reads, 'Restore our fortunes, Lord.' Now, I don't need to tell you that fortune in this context does not mean chance. It does not mean luck. It has nothing at all to do with the slot machines or table games of our fair city." He smiles. "Here's what Psalm 126 is saying to you, my good brothers and sisters: when the Lord restores your fortune, he transforms you into the person you once were, the person you were designed to be."

A man gets up from the front row and faces the congregation, an acoustic guitar hanging from a strap over his shoulder. He's boxy

and wears a flattop, and is standing directly beneath a large recessed
bulb, so that he appears lit by some preternatural radiance. What
looks like a burn scar spreads taffylike from his earlobe to his chin.
He ambles around the perimeter of the folding chairs, strumming
the guitar while Marcus Bauerkemper delivers his sermon.

What is Emma doing here? Has it really come to this, looking
to some evangelical crackpot—a pathological gambler to boot—for
answers? Weren't the fortune-tellers and the medium enough?
With the exception of Andrew's funeral, she can't recall the last
time she attended a *Catholic* service, let alone whatever this is. Las
Vegas has more churches per capita than any other city in the country, and Emma's chosen one with a name that evokes prophesying,
faith healing, and speaking in tongues. Well, she's driven all the way
out here, she may as well stay for the remainder. At the very least,
it's mildly amusing. She feels herself in slightly better spirits than
when she arrived.

If Marcus Bauerkemper has anything at all to offer in the way of
a psychic remedy, Emma needs it more than ever. She hasn't seen
Russell for several days, hasn't heard from him. She's beside herself
with worry, so much so that she took two days off from the Bora
Bora, lying in bed with the phone on her chest, going out only for
short, unaccompanied meals. For a week after she admitted to her
affair with Andrew, Russell slept in the spare bedroom. He wouldn't
speak to her, walking out of whichever part of the house she walked
into. Then he took off six days ago, on Monday morning, and didn't
come home. She couldn't reach him. That night, around ten thirty,
she called some of his buddies. A guy he knows from college. Big
Paco from the All or Nothing. Two guys Russell plays disc golf
with a couple of times a month, one of whom was sleeping. None
of them knew where he was.

When Juliet called, Emma was just about to dial her number.
(She'd hesitated, wondering if Russell had told Juliet about the
affair.) Russell and Maddie were camping together at some state
park out in the desert, Juliet said in her stiff, disdainful way. They'd

left a voice mail but weren't answering their phones. She said nothing about the affair. *What*, she wanted to know, was Russell doing taking Maddie on a camping trip without telling anybody? *Was he out of his goddamn mind?* Russell and Maddie have left no additional voice mail. The only other communication Juliet has received are some emails from Maddie, which Juliet has forwarded to Emma, adding terse little messages of her own, the forwards as stiff and disdainful as her tone of voice. The emails are nearly identical: Maddie telling her mother that she's perfectly safe, defending Russell and his character. The most recent one read:

Mom—

Please don't worry about me. I'm perfectly OK, although I can't say I'm of entirely sound mind, not at this difficult moment in my life. Russell is a good guy, a GREAT guy. I don't have to tell you that. Don't be angry with him. He would never do anything to hurt me. We both just needed to get away for a while, our souls being the big fat messes that they are. The freedom of the highway and the SO BEAUTIFUL (!!!) desert have been endless blessings. We'll be home soon. Please find it in your heart to understand.

Maddie

P.S. This mizzle fits me like a sad jacket.

The postscript is a line from *Crossing the Water*, from the poem "Leaving Early," one of Emma's favorites. Her father's book is missing again. Obviously Russell took it with him. He probably *is* out of his mind, after what he's gone through over the past seven weeks. Who wouldn't be? Emma herself can no longer prepare a meal, such is the magnitude of her anguish. She loves to cook yet she can't get herself to do it. She has an appetite, she can eat something that's been prepared for her at a restaurant, but sautéing an onion in a skillet will strike her as an impossible undertaking. Other things, too, seem unreasonably demanding. Flossing her teeth, tying her shoes, reading words on a page. She's like a child who has yet to possess the most basic human abilities.

She has lost not just Andrew, but now Russell as well.

•

The man with the guitar passes her a second time, grinning as he strums. He wears an orange polo shirt that's loose and untucked, widening like a bell around his waist. His scar is pink and red, fleshy yet almost translucent, and reminds her of the skin of a newly hatched bird.

Marcus Bauerkemper is back at the pulpit. "Bear with me now," he's saying. "I have a little mnemonic that explains precisely what God is asking of you. Because I've got some news, ladies and gentlemen. You don't get to sit back and let Him do all the work. No, you've got to contribute. You've got to bring something to the table if you want to be restored, and these five letters will explain just what to do: *H-A-P-P-Y*." He counts them out with his fingers. "H-A-P-P-Y, folks! That's all you've got to remember."

He pauses, shuffling through some papers as though he's lost his train of thought. Adjacent to the pulpit is a spindle-legged stool, and the man with the guitar sits himself down on it and begins a leisurely rendition of "Jesus Loves Me."

"The *H*, my good people, is for 'humility,'" Marcus Bauerkemper says. "Restoration requires the humility to ask for it." He shuffles the papers again, in a kind of agitation this time. "The *A* stands for 'advice.' Yes. If you're feeling sad, ladies and gentlemen, if you're down in the dumps, in a blue funk, heartbroken or glum or despondent or depressed, then you have an obligation to talk to someone. It's imperative that you seek the professional healing you're in need of. Like I said, folks, you've got to contribute. You've got to *prepare* yourself for God's joy."

Emma can't get over how easily her resolve fell apart in the face of Russell's questioning. He seemed so sure of himself, so convinced. She wasn't able to lie to him any longer. Leaving behind her father's book was a disastrous accident. On the positive side, she has the same sense of freedom she had just after Andrew's death: she carries no secret anymore. Regardless, she should have denied the affair, concocted some explanation. (In the end, what kind of evidence is the book of poems, anyway?) What has her confession accomplished? Now Russell is so shattered he's run off with Maddie. Now their marriage, in all probability, is over, and Emma doesn't want it to be. *She does not want it to be.*

She thinks back to that party for her tenth birthday, Emma and five or six of her fifth-grade classmates eating pizza and sheet cake in this same drab space, lugging their bowling balls around and dropping them onto the polished wood lanes, her grandmother wiping up icing with a paper napkin. Her *yiayia*: a woman who believed so fundamentally in life—that strong-willed optimism she had—enduring the worst of her disease with good cheer, rarely letting on that she was in a great deal of pain, certain until the end that she would pull through. She had a deep affection for Russell, and Emma puts her hands together and silently implores her to bring him back.

"The first *P*," Marcus Bauerkemper says, "represents 'perspective.' The story of the gospel is that God has sent Christ to rescue us. My friends, the only way to experience true joy, to be rescued and restored, is to adopt a gospel perspective." He adjusts his glasses, then his microphone, with a steady, theatrical hand. "The second *P* is for 'prayer.' God wants to *hear* from you, people. God wants you to pray for the restoration that He alone can bestow upon you. This takes us back to the *H* now, doesn't it? Having the humility to ask for God's intervention."

Russell, Emma thinks, *Russell*, his name announcing itself over and over in her mind. She has always disliked his bowl-packing, his joint-rolling, his daily (costly!) reliance on marijuana. Ordinarily Emma doesn't allow it in the house, and she dislikes that he's always stealing out to the garage or the backyard to smoke. She dislikes the *reason* he smokes, or what he claims is the reason: his panic attacks, whose omnipresence in their lives tends somehow to make *her* anxious as well. She dislikes that he's slightly overweight and takes little interest in his appearance, rarely dressing in anything other than a T-shirt and cargo shorts and his old suede Pumas. She dislikes his constant laments for his 1961 Chevy flatbed, the truck he drove when they met. "Old as the hills," he'll say, "but that baby purred like a kitten." The Chevy was a grayish beige, the color of phlegm, and one of the bed's steel edges read POOR MAN'S PORCH, spray-painted in yellow by the previous owner. Emma begged Russell to sell it, and finally he did, for six hundred dollars, putting the money toward his used Toyota—but he'll never let her forget how much he loved that truck. She dislikes that he makes this low guttural sound when he chews, and that he'll strike up a conversation with any stranger in the aisle of a supermarket, and that he leaves his fingernail clippings sprinkled like grains of white rice around the drain in the bathroom sink. Emma dislikes each of these things about him, but she wants him home. She wants him home so very much.

Marcus Bauerkemper tidies his papers and raises a finger above his head. "And now, people, we come to the *Y*. I guess I lied when I said the five letters explain what God's asking of you, because the Y lets you off easy. It isn't advising you to do anything. The Y stands for—you've maybe guessed it by now—'you.' *You*, ladies and gentlemen. Like I said, Psalm 126 tells us that joy comes from being restored by God. We're full-circle now, aren't we? God, and only God, will restore you. Only God can make you joyful. Only God has the power to turn you back into the person you were meant to be, that glorious and beautiful and original *you*!"

The man with the guitar concludes his strumming and returns to his seat in the front row. Marcus Bauerkemper's mnemonic seems redundant and amateurish—oratorical snake oil—the whole service, the church itself, cartoony and unreal. (What did she expect?) For all this, Emma still finds herself oddly drawn to him. She has an overwhelming desire to confide in him. She's no sucker, nobody's fool; she isn't one to fall victim to empty rhetoric. And Emma's

Catholic, not Protestant. But his goofiness makes him seem accessible, and she senses a bona fide wisdom beneath his stagy, preacher-man persona. Her thoughts turn to his gambling. As far as Emma can tell, he makes no effort to conceal what is surely a compulsion—she knows one when she sees it. He wore all white to the Bora Bora the day they met, with no concern at all about being spotted by a member of his church. He's nothing like the sanctimonious, fat-necked priests she remembers from Sunday Mass with her grandmother, their noisy strictures during the homily, that straight, superior way they always carried themselves. As Marcus Bauerkemper told her, he has weaknesses, just like everybody, and he isn't too proud to admit it.

He scans the congregation now, passing a hand over the waxy dome of his head. For the first time since Emma sat down, their eyes meet across the rows of folding chairs.

"Only God can pardon you for your sins," he says, giving her a slow, hospitable wink. "And for those who put their trust in Him, the world is filled with joy."

Simon

Each Monday, first thing, Simon visits Andrew Huntley's gravesite at the Palm Mortuary and Cemetery on Eastern Avenue. He brings a thick bundle of lavender phlox and a box of Keebler Sandies—the Sandies because he overheard a coworker mention at the funeral that Huntley had a known weakness for them. The phlox Simon picks from the garden in his backyard, and the cookies he purchases at a Circle K on his way to the cemetery. He sits down cross-legged in the closely mowed grass, the skin of his mended leg stretching with moderate soreness where the stitches used to be. He opens the box and removes one of the cookies and raises it in honor of Andrew Huntley. Eating it, Simon looks around and thanks God for having delivered him from death on the morning of the explosions. The grounds are treeless and flat, the headstones level with the grass. The place looks to him like the surface of some strange green moon. "Yes," he might say aloud, a great sinkhole of regret opening inside him. "Yes, well. Damn." There's never anyone there to hear him, the cemetery as empty as Huntley's casket. When Simon arrives the next week, the box and the flowers are always gone, and he takes a particular delight in imagining a hungry groundskeeper parking his riding mower to swipe the cookies. He hopes they're eaten and not thrown away. He hopes Andrew Huntley has found himself in close, blissful proximity to a celestial ocean of Keebler Sandies.

Simon has been meeting up with Juliet ever since their coffee and cherry pie at Tiffany's Café. It's a nonromantic, nonsexual sort of thing, in spite of his attraction to her. A friendship, he supposes. Purely platonic—they haven't even hugged each other. Harmless, Simon assures himself. He hasn't told her he's been visiting her late husband's grave. Nor has he told her how much he loves his wife, Rebecca, how very *in love* with her he is. Or that he lied about having been Huntley's buddy at work. Or that he left Huntley behind to die as the plant erupted all around them.

Over the past two weeks, Simon and Juliet have had lunch together a handful of times. They've gone to an afternoon movie, and the other day Juliet gave him a therapy session for the fun of it, during which Simon sat at their table at Marie Callender's and doodled on his napkin while she leaned across and interpreted his clumsy drawings. She's a completely different woman than the one from that night at the café. She's nice to him—she's sweet. And Juliet's funny. She makes him laugh. At least when she isn't worrying about her daughter, who's run off on some road trip with Andrew Huntley's best friend, a forty-something bartender, some guy named Russell. Simon tries his best to spirit her up. He regards her the way he might an insect in a spiderweb: with compassion and curiosity. He feels so pleasantly off course when they're together. It's what the French call *dèpaysement*. A change of scenery. Disorientation. The word sprang into his mind during that impromptu therapy session over lunch. Where has he heard it? On NPR, no doubt. Rebecca always has it on, in the kitchen, in the car.

Rebecca. Yes, he loves her. Of course he's said nothing to her about any of this.

•

Simon still follows Juliet, still studies her with his private admiration. He likes the way she moves, the daily rhythms of her body, which make her far prettier than she already is. The way, for instance, she tips her head—as if pouring something carefully from her ear—to rummage in her shoulder bag. The way her chin juts out when she answers her cell phone. The way she steps into and out of the Jeep with a scarcely discernable hesitancy. The way she walks, this especially: her tight-ankled hustle. He observes her with fervid attention, a bird watcher entranced by some rare avian behavior.

The next Monday he spots her at the cemetery, from a length of about two football fields. He sees the red Jeep make its way into the parking lot and out the other side, onto one of the gravel roads that twines through the flat, green grounds—the one that leads to Huntley's plot, to where Simon sits cross-legged next to his bundle of flowers. He hurries to his pickup and drives to the end of the road. Alongside the mortuary—a white, hip-roofed building with huge tinted windows—he gets out and peers around an overgrown lilac, watching as Juliet kneels before her husband's headstone. He watches her pick up the box of Sandies and turn it over and set it back down. She remains there beside it, unmoving, for five minutes or more, and then he watches her stand up quickly and leave.

Simon gets back in the pickup and catches up with her, or almost. He keeps a wary distance. He has to be careful. He can't let her catch him in the act a second time. Like she did that night two weeks ago, Juliet drives to the Guardian Angel Cathedral. Simon pulls into the parking lot of a gift shop next door, where a sign reads T-SHIRTS SOUVENIRS INDIAN JEWELRY ELVIS. Again she tugs at the handles of the six wooded doors, and again the doors are locked. Simon is struck this time by the church's name. There is, by his reckoning, something protective about his spying on her. If Juliet falls into trouble, if she's accosted or harmed, if her Jeep breaks down, he can go to her aid. He's a guardian angel of sorts, is he not? He once saw a television program on famous Christian mystics—Maria Valtorta, Saint Gemma Galgani—and their claimed relationships with the messengers of God who looked after them. What if, unbeknownst to him, he's been divinely commissioned to keep an eye on Juliet? Maybe what Simon is doing at this very moment, watching her from the open window of his pickup, has been designed by a higher power.

An absurd, self-aggrandizing thought. He laughs inwardly. What he's doing, *everything*—his entire demeanor over the past seven weeks—is just plain peculiar, and Simon has no illusions about it.

Exactly as she did the last time, Juliet takes a cigarette from her shoulder bag and cocks her hip and then stares in the direction of Frenchman Mountain while she smokes, the hem of her yellow sundress blowing like a curtain in the dry June wind. Above the mountain's summit, thin white clouds fan out across the sky. A few minutes later she steps into the Jeep with that charming little hesitancy of hers and drives away.

•

"One kiloton," says Rebecca in the living room that afternoon, the *Review-Journal* spread out beside her on the couch. "The size of a small nuclear weapon, it says here. That's what those blasts equated to, according to a report by"—she leans closer to the paper—"Sandia National Laboratories. Whatever that is." She looks up at Simon, who stands in the archway to the kitchen, hands in his pockets. "That's what you lived through. That's what you survived."

"Hmm."

"Two hundred million dollars in total damage. Can you believe that number? It also says that several small earthquakes were triggered around the city. As if the explosions weren't enough."

"Huh," he says. "I hadn't heard that."

She turns a page. "'The US Fire Administration, working with the Clark County Fire Department, has traced the accident to welders repairing the steel frame of a fiberglass structure on the property.'" She looks up at him again. "You didn't tell me this."

"I didn't know."

"'Sparks from a blowtorch set the fiberglass ablaze, accelerated by ammonium-perchlorate residue,'" Rebecca reads. "None of this came up at any of the meetings you've been going to?"

He's ignoring the news these days as much as he can, particularly reports on the investigation. Andrew Huntley is dead and Simon is to blame: nothing else is important. But WEPCO, to Simon's annoyance, is all Rebecca can talk about. Of late she's been most concerned about the state of their drinking water. An aquifer beneath the site has been found to be contaminated, due to improper waste disposal by company employees back in the seventies. The aquifer feeds a small spring that flows directly into Las Vegas Wash. The Nevada Department of Conservation and Natural Resources has sampled the groundwater numerous times. Local agencies are debating just how much ammonium perchlorate—which is thought to hinder the production of thyroid hormones—can be safely consumed. Simon isn't worried. The amount in the aquifer is estimated at one part per billion, half a thimble in a backyard swimming pool. Rebecca, on the other hand, wants to harvest the rain—in the middle of a desert. For now, an entire corner of the garage is stacked with twenty-ounce bottles of Poland Spring drinking water.

"There haven't been any meetings," Simon says. He sits down next to her. "At least not that *I've* been asked to attend. Look," he says. "There's something I have to…well, disclose."

She closes the paper. Simon takes her hand.

"I quit," he tells her.

"What?"

"At first I only stopped answering my email. I couldn't bear to think about that place, or what happened to it. I still can't. Then about a week ago—like I said, I quit my job. I don't work there anymore."

In the days of confusion that followed the accident, Simon's superiors let his unresponsiveness pass. He was home when the VPO, Bruce Westerfield, finally called. Simon went into the den and closed the French doors and officially resigned, half-whispering into the receiver.

Rebecca stands up from the couch. "What are we supposed to do?" she says. "The house, the Taurus. Tuition for Michaela. Simon."

"My last paycheck should arrive sometime soon."

"Well, that's just wonderful. Honey, I love you, and I want to support you, but how do you expect us to live? The mortgage alone…"

Their mortgage, a long-running subject of contention between them, another thing for which Simon is to blame. He looks out the window at the tilted mimosa tree in the front yard, which he and Rebecca planted the month they moved in, fifteen years ago this fall. They'd come west from Livonia, Michigan, the place of both their births. Simon was laid off by BASF after a decrease in profits, but in no time he landed the job at WEPCO. The move was difficult, bidding farewell to family and friends, to their old tree-shadowed neighborhood, from which the four of them had walked on summer evenings to the nearby main drag, with its bar-and-grill and diner and ice-cream parlor, their haunts. When they'd flown to Las Vegas to shop for a house, a couple of months before leaving Livonia, Rebecca pushed for a place in the city—an afford-able place—close to established restaurants, to malls, to the Strip. But Simon had been set on buying in Mojave Meadows, an expen-sive, gated development on the southern fringe of the valley, only fifteen minutes from the plant. "A nothing commute," he'd told her.

Feeling guilty for the cost and location of their home—for its unwarranted size, and for the fact that Mojave Meadows was vir-tually treeless—he showed up from work one day with the mimosa tree hanging out the window of his car, a worn-out Mazda he owned before the pickup. Rebecca stood in the doorway with a hand on her hip. Simon kissed her and smiled, and they planted the sap-ling that evening, Daniel and Michaela somersaulting in the grass. They all laughed at its angle: the tree insisted on leaning, first this way, then that, no matter how many times they held it square and tamped down the soil and repositioned the wooden stakes. They laughed, too, at their new surroundings. Low, earth-toned houses with red tile roofs—with decorative rocks in place of lawns! Highs of a hundred-plus five months out of twelve, and, in three directions, miles and miles of desert.

"I've done the math," Simon says now. He puts his tennis shoes up on the coffee table. Lexie comes in from the kitchen and stutter-steps into his lap. "We have enough to coast for a while, until I work out what to do next."

"And what might that be?"

"I just told you—I've got to work it out. I'm in the process."

Rebecca crosses the room, sliding a hand through her hair. "How could you keep this from me? How could you not discuss it with me first?"

"I'm sorry," he says. "I'm sorry I lied."

"Where have you been going all these days you've been gone? What have you been up to?"

"Pounding the pavement," he says. "Looking for work." Which is true, to an extent. When he hasn't been hanging out with Juliet—when he hasn't been following her—Simon has applied for positions at Tommy's Hamburgers, Fabulous Freddy's Car Wash, and the Circle K he goes to on his way to the cemetery every Monday. "I'll know the right opportunity when it presents itself. For now, I'm just putting myself out there."

"Out *where?*" Rebecca presses him. "What *kind* of work?"

"Not the kind I had at the plant, that's for sure. Something different. Something mindless is what I'd like. I'm trying to reinvent myself a bit. I'm almost fifty," Simon says. He scratches at one of Lexie's hind legs. "I know what you're thinking: midlife crisis. That's not it, though. It's deeper than that, more fundamental."

"'Mindless.' What exactly does that mean?"

Simon feels an acidy dribble of annoyance—a burning in his chest like indigestion. "Maybe this is why I haven't said anything to you. Here I am apologizing and all you can do is make critical comments."

"I'm concerned," Rebecca says.

"If you're so concerned, why don't *you* go out and get a job?" He's being intractable now—a prick. She was a stay-at-home mom (a "house spouse," they'd joked) throughout the children's childhoods. Only in the past three years has Rebecca considered herself unskilled, unneeded. It's a delicate issue.

"Because that's not our arrangement, Simon. Our arrangement is that we depend on your salary. That's a decision you were a part of. Your livelihood is our survival." She shakes her head at him. "You asshole. To say that to me." She kicks a leg of the coffee table, and Lexie flinches in his lap. "It was the plant that brought us to this city in the first place. *Las Vegas, Nevada.* You know what my mother said when I told her? She didn't believe me at first. I left my family to come here, and now you up and quit without even running it by me?"

"You *wanted* to move here. You said so, at least. Was that a lie?"

"You're the liar, my friend. You've made that abundantly clear." She turns toward the kitchen, then spins back around. "I changed my mind. I'm glad you quit. It's because of WEPCO, because of whatever mistakes you were all making out there, that I can't even drink a glass of water out of my own faucet."

"None of that happened while I was at the plant," Simon says. "You know that."

"The only thing I know is that you need to find a new job, ASAP."

Quietly, he sets Lexie down on the carpet and goes out to the garage. He searches a plastic storage bin until he finds Daniel's old Little League bat—an Easton, black and lightweight, aluminum. The yellow grip is discolored and coming off, dangling from the handle like a banana peel. Simon opens the automatic door, then gets one of the water bottles from the stack in the corner and carries it out to the driveway. Rebecca comes out behind him. "What are you doing?" she asks.

Facing the street, Simon points a finger toward the horizon, Babe Ruth calling his last postseason home run. He tosses the bottle into the air and strikes it with the bat as hard as he can, surprised he's gotten hold of it on his first try. He expected the bottle to split right open, but it flies head over heels down the block, landing intact on the sidewalk.

"Wow. This is so mature of you," Rebecca says. "This is stupendous, Simon."

She goes back inside, slamming the door. Simon gets another bottle. This one he misses three times before the bat connects. Mrs. von Keppel, his eighty-year-old neighbor, watches him from her cactus garden. Simon waves. He hits four or five more, two of them bursting on impact, spraying his T-shirt and his shorts. The final bottle careers through the purple-green canopy of the mimosa tree and explodes in the middle of the street.

Simon takes one into the kitchen and pours the water straight down the drain, crushing the plastic in his fist, feeling a sense of pleasure that is plump and succulent. In the archway, Rebecca claps her hands.

"Way to go, honey. Way to lash out at *me* when you're the one in the wrong. Bravo."

He pitches the mangled bottle onto the counter, snatches his keys from the row of hooks near the door, and walks out.

•

On his bike, he attacks the wide, traffic-heavy streets, sweating through the dry patches of his T-shirt. He rides without stopping, up and down the sinuous hills, as if the Trek is not a sturdy touring bike but one built for speed. His quadriceps tighten, burning, and he leans into the corners, head forward like an arrow, a high, clear sun cooking his helmet and his back. In twenty minutes or so he reaches the office park where Juliet works.

He pulls into the parking lot as she's walking to her Jeep. Simon can see the tension all over her face, the continued grief combined with the unease about her daughter. It's half past four and she's just seen her last client. Does she want to join Simon for a ride? Fresh air? A little exercise? "Take your mind off things," he says. She looks him up and down, rubbing the side of her neck. Simon wishes he were wearing better clothes. She closes her eyes and nods. Yes, a bike ride might be just the right thing. "Sure," Juliet says, exhaling decisively. "Why not."

She lowers the soft top of the Jeep and he lifts the Trek into the backseat. At her house, Simon sits on the stoop while she changes. She comes out in running shorts and a sleeveless shirt and they set off for Wetlands Park, a couple of miles away, her old Raleigh mountain bike squeaking as she pedals. They ride along the bank of Las Vegas Wash, cruising the dusty loop trail. In some places the water flows clean and white over rocks and fallen branches, through tamarisk and phragmites and bulrushes. In others it's nearly stagnant, a flat, chalkboard green. Maybe Rebecca's right to be cautious. It doesn't look good.

They park their bikes and skip stones and talk about Maddie, who still has not returned. Juliet has gone to the police, but Maddie is seventeen, a gray area in the eyes of the law. She's a missing juvenile, not a kidnapped child, particularly since the one voice mail she's left implied consent. Huntley's friend, Russell, has been entered into the National Crime Information Center's database, and there's a statewide BOLO out on him ("Be On the Lookout," Juliet explains). If he's pulled over for a traffic violation, he and Maddie will be detained. There's nothing more the police can do.

The sun seems to expand with the intensity of its own bright heat: a blue-gold pupil dilating in the sky. By the time Simon and Juliet get back to Bighorn Heights, she, too, has sweated through her shirt. She invites him in for a glass of water. The walls of the house are bare—not a single photograph or print—the living room as generically furnished as a model home but lacking all the coziness and allure. You can't even tell that less than two months ago the windows were blown out by a shock wave. On her way to the kitchen, Juliet stops and tugs her shirt over her head, standing in front of him in a shiny black sports bra.

"Does this bother you?" she says.

Her breasts are low and hefty—Simon can't keep from glancing—her shoulders smooth as plums. Stretch marks gather around her navel, an outie, the knotted seal of a balloon.

"Not at all," he answers, trying to sound indifferent. "Why would it?"

"Because you're married. Because you used to work with my husband. Because you barely know me." She blinks three or four times. "Because you're married," she says.

"Hey, all we're doing here is—"

"Is what?"

"We haven't done anyth—"

"Is what?"

"I don't know," Simon says. "I don't have an answer for you."

Juliet's arms are down at her sides, the sweat-soaked shirt bunched in her fist. She stares into Simon's eyes.

"I had a difficult afternoon," he says, "and things aren't easy for you at the moment, with the whole Maddie situation and everything else, so how about we just—"

"Do you want to take it off?"

"Excuse me?"

"You heard what I said."

Simon laughs. "Do I want to take *what* off?" He can hear her breath now, her expression grave. He feels a hot weight at the base of his skull. "Do I want to take off your bra? Is that what you're asking me?"

"Yes, that's what I'm asking you." Juliet blinks again. "What would happen if you did that? How would it feel to see me standing here without it on?"

"Is this some sort of therapy game or something?"

"Would you touch them?"

He laughs a second time, scratching his forehead, looking away. Behind her on an end table, a row of books between two bookends casts a dark shadow on the wall, the silhouette of a city skyline.

"Would you hold them in your hands?" Juliet says. "Would you kiss them?"

"I never got that glass of water."

"What would you do to me, Simon?"

The sound of his name sends a jolt of dishonor up his spine. He thinks of Rebecca. Of Daniel and Michaela. The mimosa tree in his front yard.

"Would you kiss my shoulders?"

"Yes," he tells her.

"My neck?"

"Yes."

"And then what?"

"I'd—"

"Tell me."

The firm set of her jaw. The dense stillness of her eyes. She's a pocket watch swinging from a chain. "I'd take off your shorts," Simon says.

"How would you take them off?"

"Slowly," he says. "I'd push them down to your knees and... you'd step out of them, and—"

"And then?"

"I'd..."

"You'd what?"

"I'd pull down your underwear," Simon says, feeling faint. He doesn't know the person he's become, or the new, bewildering reality that has constructed itself around him.

"Uh-huh." Juliet lifts her chin. "Keep going."

"I—"

"Would you put your hand between my legs? Is that what you'd do?"

"Yes," he says.

"Uh-huh. And after that?"

"I'd put my...I'd..."

"Would you put your fingers inside me?"

"My God."

"That's what you'd do next, isn't it?"

"Yes," Simon says.

"Would you kiss me while you did that? On the mouth?"

"Yes." She's turning him inside out. Turning his inner surfaces outward. "I'd kiss you."

Neither of them moves.

"You're right," Simon says. "I'm married. And you...your husband—Andrew. It's been less than two months. This isn't—"

"We didn't love each other. We pretended to, but we never did." She folds her arms over her chest and gives a little shudder, as though she might begin to cry. "You should go now, I think."

He starts to say something. He doesn't even know what it is.

"Goodbye, Simon," Juliet says.

And Simon leaves.

Maddie

She can't stop stealing. They'll be in some small desert town—Majors Place, Ely, Eureka—getting gas or ice or firewood, or eating lunch at another ramshackle diner, and Maddie will take something. An empty coffee cup. A fork or a spoon. A pepper shaker. She's stolen candy bars and packets of chewing gum. Dental floss and batteries. A ballpoint pen, a hairbrush, a tire gauge—anything she can slip into her pocket or her purse. Stealing has become nothing less than a compulsion, and Maddie has a talent for it. It's no harder than it was the first time, when she swiped the cigarettes from the Smith's Food King back home. Afterward, alone in her room at the Best Western, her chest fluttered with that high, unexpected delight. Whenever she leaves a convenience store, another of her petty thefts complete, the sensation returns.

Maddie regrets the thefts she's committed, and a lot of what she's taken sits unused in her purse anyway. She feels like a bad person, a *despicable* person. But the urge will not relent. Sometimes it's as though her hands are moving of their own free will, picking things up and tucking them away. Despite the quantity of her spoils, Russell doesn't have a clue. Maybe he's too preoccupied to notice; he talks under his breath all the time about Emma and her affair. Most of the items Maddie has simply disposed of when he hasn't been paying attention.

She hasn't stolen any more cigarettes, though she really wants one right now. What Maddie wants, in actual fact, is something to *do*. They've been driving for the past hour or so, since they left the old mining town of Austin, and she is bored, bored, bored. She's read all the poems in *Crossing the Water*, some of them twice, three times, thinking about her father—missing him—and she's solved half a book of sudoku puzzles she found in the Corolla's cluttered glove compartment. Over the past nine days, she and Russell have run through every possible topic of conversation. Now Maddie has to occupy herself staring at the long, lonely highway in front of them, Highway 50, which is in fact called "The Loneliest Road in America." It runs from one end of the state to the other, from the Utah border all the way to Lake Tahoe, past ghost towns and old Pony Express stations and ridiculous roadside attractions such as a house in the shape of a cowboy hat. In between are unending miles of Great Basin Desert, whose beauty, as far as Maddie is concerned, has petered out.

Back in Austin she shoved an orange Harley-Davidson bandanna into the waistband of her shorts. She takes it out now, folds it diagonally, and ties it around her head.

"Where'd you get that?" Russell asks, stretching an arm out over the wheel.

"I bought it," Maddie says. "At the last gas station."

"I didn't see you buy it."

"That doesn't mean it didn't happen."

She stares out the windshield. The sky is blueprint-blue, the flat terrain on either side of the highway a frail, chalky brown, all but empty of vegetation. In the distance, a ragged mountain range slowly reveals itself.

"Let's talk," Russell says. "Tell me something of no importance, one of those factoids you're always pulling out of nowhere." He winks.

"Where are we going?"

"I don't know, Miss Daisy. Your call."

She has only herself to blame for her restlessness. The morning after their first night camping, in Cathedral Gorge, he made them bacon and eggs over the campfire and said they needed to head back. Her mother was going to kill them. "Here we are having ourselves a genuine adventure," Maddie said, "and you want turn around and go home? No way, Jose. Sorry, Charlie. I'll hitchhike if I have to." After a while Russell sighed, acquiescing in her resolve. They finished breakfast and packed up the tent and got back on US 93, continuing north, turning west onto Highway 50.

•

They still have no destination. Carson City? Sacramento? Maybe they'll head south instead, end up on the Baja California peninsula. Ensenada, San Felipe, Cabo San Lucas. Mexican vacation towns where, Maddie imagines, people lounge around all day and forget about who they are. Silvery sands and clean green waters—the tail of the continent, five hundred miles from Las Vegas.

They camped for three nights at a place called the Hickison Petroglyph Recreation Area, hiking and taking pictures, tracing the prehistoric rock carvings with their fingertips. They made a detour to Berlin-Ichthyosaur State Park, camped for another three nights there. Maddie felt like a tourist as she snapped away at the ancient, fifty-foot fossils with a single-use camera she'd swiped from the visitor center. She felt, too, like a runaway, which is what she is.

They've decided, for better or worse, not to call her mother again; they've made a pact. A phone call, they both know, will only mean they will have to return home. They've ignored the voice mails and text messages her mother and Emma have left, their cell phones dead now anyway. In place of calling, Maddie's been emailing her mother from public libraries in the towns they visit. "This is crazy," Russell says at least once a day. "This, hands down, is the dumbest thing I have ever done."

Boredom isn't the only thing getting to her. She's been wearing the same underwear for over a week. The nights are chilly, and at a travel center in Ely she bought a fleece jacket and sweatpants to sleep in, as well as the only long-sleeved T-shirt the place had, one that reads I'M HERE TO *HAUL* ASS, NOT KISS IT. But travel centers don't sell women's underwear, and so she's had to make do. Which also means showering each day in some filthy, curtainless stall and drying off with a wad of paper towels. And even though they sleep separately—Maddie on the air mattress, zipped up in the goose-down bag, Russell swaddled in the falsa blankets—they have to share the extremely small tent, an awkward, confined arrangement, both of them clothed from head to foot with a self-consciousness verging on the neurotic. Russell snores throughout the night, and Maddie rises crabby and exhausted to a triplet of torments: blinding sunlight and cold desert air and the deathly reek of his gas.

He glances at the orange bandanna, drumming the wheel with his thumb. "Emma's always wanted a motorcycle," he says. "A Harley." He blows air through his teeth. "She's too afraid to actually buy one, scared she'll crash. Well. Who cares what she wants now."

"People make mistakes," Maddie tells him. "Right?"

Is this what she's supposed to say, what he wants—or needs—to hear? She doesn't know the first thing about long-term relationships, or about being cheated on. She's had only one boyfriend, the second half of her sophomore year: Darin Swordoski, a soccer player who goes by the name Swords and sings in an emo band called Sweatshop Photo Lab. The whole relationship was a colossal mistake.

Maddie looks at Russell now, at his dismal expression, and feels inadequate. Should she say something more? He's always so good at comforting *her*. The banalities display themselves in her mind like selections on a jukebox, each one hokier than the last. *You'll get over this. It just takes time.* Or: *She never meant to hurt you.* Or: *You take the good, you take the bad*, which Maddie's pretty sure is the theme song from an old sitcom.

"This too," she says, "will pass."

Russell lifts his glasses and says, "Take a look at that."

A few hundred yards ahead of them is a miragelike figure on the shoulder: ripply, shimmering at its edges. A woman, Maddie sees as they get closer—waving at them. Russell slows the Corolla and pulls it over, the rumble strip making it feel like they're driving along a railroad track. They come to a stop ten or so feet from her.

"You sure this is smart?" Maddie says. The urgency of the woman's waving seems to reveal an awareness of some hazard down the highway, as if she means to holler, *Stop! No, no, no!*

"What are we gonna do, speed on by? She obviously needs our help."

She is all alone, without an automobile. She wears ratty tennis shoes and stonewashed jeans and a white roll-neck sweater, despite the fact that it's got to be ninety degrees outside, her face secreted beneath the brim of one of those khaki sun hats worn by British soldiers in the eighteen-hundreds—a pith helmet, Maddie thinks it's called—its chinstrap tightened against her cheeks. In the gravelly dirt in front of her sits a paisley duffel bag. She holds a black umbrella like a parasol, the fabric torn and frayed, one of the spokes bent like an elbow, another dangling at her ear like a snapped twig.

Russell turns off the car, and the woman stops waving. Her hair is rain-cloud gray, corkscrewing from beneath the helmet and resting heavily upon her shoulders. Instead of walking toward them, she rocks back and forth on the balls of her feet, unsmiling. And then she does smile, only for a second, and Maddie can see that her teeth are straight and white. Her skin is clean, so are her clothes. She doesn't appear to be homeless, not that a homeless person could survive out here. It's fifty miles to the nearest town.

"This," Maddie says, "is way north of strange."

Russell reaches into the backseat, tugs his backpack onto the console. He feels around inside and draws out a small black gun.

"What the hell is that?"

"Protection," he says. "What if someone's hiding somewhere, waiting to ambush us?"

"Hiding where? In a snake hole?"

"How do I know that lady doesn't have a weapon of her own?"

"I thought we were here to help. And where'd you get that thing, anyway? Suddenly you're a gun owner? You're the Lone Ranger or something?"

He holds the gun tenuously, queerly, in his hands, as if he hasn't the faintest idea what to do with it—as if it's a newborn chick that has fallen from its nest.

"Do you even know how to use that thing?"

"Relax, Tonto," he says. "The safety's on. Sit tight. I'll be right back." He tries to stuff the gun into a front pocket of his jeans but it's too big. "Fine," Russell says, and replaces it in the backpack, then gets out and walks around to the trunk and locks the backpack inside.

Maddie's never seen a real gun before, and a good part of her is angry—frightened—that he hasn't disclosed its presence until now. Is it actually loaded? Could the gun go off, even with the safety on? She knows he has issues, panic attacks, but is he really so alarmed by this stranger and her safari hat that he felt the need to take out a deadly weapon?

Maddie watches from the Corolla as they talk, a spotted lizard skittering across the pavement. The woman's mouth twitches in a rabbitlike fashion, a reddish-haired doll peeking from her unzipped bag. She follows Russell to the car and gets in the back.

Maddie twists around in her seat. The woman sets the duffel bag on the floor, fastening her seat belt with a jerky urgency.

"Maddie," Russell says, "this is Latifah. Latifah, Maddie." He starts the Corolla and pulls out onto the highway. "Latifah here is going to join us for a while. We're taking her to the next town."

"Nice to meet you," Maddie says.

"Right," says the woman, giving a military salute. She has eager blue eyes, a dainty, V-shaped face. "Not as in the rapper, by the way."

"What?" Maddie says.

"I wasn't named after her—the Queen. Everybody asks." The woman laughs loudly. "I'm a lot older than she is, for one, and my name's Arabic, if you really want to know the truth. It means that I'm tender. I'm pleasant."

"It's a pretty name," Maddie says.

"My parents aren't Arabs, though. They're Midwesterners. They're white as angel food cake. Go figure!"

Russell grins.

"So what happened?" Maddie asks her. "You broke down somewhere?"

"The answer to that question is no. The answer is that this gentleman who picked me up in Eureka tried to put his hands on me while he was driving us down the highway, and when I screamed at him, he pulled over and kicked me out of his rusty old car. I was hitchhiking, which my great-grandfather said you should never do. This man was what my great-grandfather would have called a *prevert*. 'Boys are *preverts*,' he'd say. 'Don't let 'em get their hands on you, Latifah.'"

Her speech is inflective and melodic, each sentence its own little song. Russell tells her he likes her accent. Where is she from?

Moose Lake, Minnesota.

How long has she been hitchhiking?

Two weeks, three days.

Where is she headed?

Santa Barbara, to visit her sister.

"Haven't seen her in years," the woman says. "I was working at the Piggly Wiggly in Duluth—I was a bagger there—but every once in a while they let me bring the shopping carts in from the parking lot, and I'd usually mess that up pretty good, and sometimes a girl just needs a change of pace, I say. Sometimes a girl needs to do something different with her life, and right now that girl is me, and I'm on my way to see Sweet Baby Jane, which is what we called her when she was a baby." They pass a green traffic sign and the woman shouts, "Forty miles to Fallon!"

Maddie examines her in the wing mirror: her twitching mouth, her cockeyed hat, still strapped tightly to her head. "Does she know you're coming? Your sister?"

"I dig the pig!" the woman says with a snort. "That's what my T-shirt had on it that I used to wear to work every day. Before I quit, that is." She pats the headrest. "Is this thing a luxury vehicle? It drives like a luxury vehicle. My great-grandfather used to call his nineteen fifty-eight Edsel Citation a big fat bucket of bolts."

"I used to drive an old Chevy truck," Russell tells her. "A sixty-one. A real pearl."

"I bet you did, Mr. Long Blond Ponytail." She snaps her fingers, hums a bubbly tune. "The good times are right in front of us now," the woman says. "Believe you me. They're right up there on the horizon."

•

In Fallon it's raining. Traffic is at a standstill on the short main street. Flat-roofed buildings stand shoulder to shoulder along the sidewalk, made of dark brick and rotting wood, two and three stories. Maddie stares out her window at a rusted iron bench. Beside it is a four-armed streetlamp with a shattered globe, shivers of wet white glass sticking up like the teeth of a shark.

Behind her the woman is quiet, though she talked most of the way—interjections and non sequiturs delivered in her loud, lilting voice. The rain touches down in wind-blown pellets, marbling the steamed-up windshield, lifting oil from the asphalt in blurry streaks of color, little drunken rainbows. In the gutter, some brown sludge resembles a mound of soggy bran flakes. Maddie cracks the window to a breath of warm, damp air. Then they're moving again, driving wordlessly down the rain-glossed street, until the woman whistles and says, "Pitchforks and hammer handles out there! Good thing I've got this umbrella."

It's half past five. Maddie and Russell decide they'll stay the night here, treat themselves to a hotel. The woman joins them for dinner at a western-themed café with glass-laid wagon wheels for tabletops. She reads out the entrées one by one, descriptions and all, her triangular face enfolded in the menu, the umbrella resting on her lap. She bounces the doll on her knee and combs its reddish hair with her fork, paying her portion of the bill with fistfuls of loose change from the bottom of her duffel bag. Maddie wonders how old the woman is. Is it safe for such a person to be traveling by herself? She's come this far, but can she make it all the way to Santa Barbara on her own?

On their way out, Maddie pockets a roll of Certs from a box next to the register. The weather has cleared, everything hushed and dripping. They stop in a bakery with a striped awning, glass-domed cake plates squatting in the window, and Russell buys Parisian macarons and chocolate-hazelnut biscotti and apple turnovers and cranberry scones—the macarons and biscotti for later that evening, the turnovers and scones for breakfast, all of it piled in a big pink box tied with yellow twine. The wind blows agreeably as they walk back to the Corolla, beads of rainwater trembling on its windows. Just as she opens her door, Maddie sees him, her father, stepping from a car that isn't his—some sporty hatchback thing at the far end of the block—wearing a denim jacket and shouldering a leather satchel.

Her stomach hitches itself up. He's alive—wonderfully, astonishingly!

And then: no, he isn't. It's only a man who resembles him, a man with her father's build. And mouth. And nose. And hair. A man who could be his twin. She wants to walk down there and tear the satchel from his shoulder and hurl it into the street. She wants to cry.

This isn't the first time Maddie has seen a man she thought was her father. It's been happening for the past few weeks, and during each sighting she's convinced—convinced to the core, if for the briefest moment—that he is really there. Ironically, she still has difficulty picturing him. There are photographs, of course—she slipped a three-by-five of him into her wallet—but her memory of her father's face, when she tests it, is insubstantial, thin as tracing paper. Her memory likes to tease her. His face will appear smokily, like a genie wisping from an oil lamp. It will float for an instant or two in the empty black field of her head, then it'll be gone. Most often Maddie can conjure only a single feature. His chin. A cheekbone. The tip of his nose, which used to move up and down when he spoke. The whole of her father's character, as well, is difficult to remember. With ease Maddie can call to mind the thoughtful things he used to do. That he made blueberry blintzes on Sunday mornings, for instance, served with the maple syrup he'd order from the Vegas Food Co-op. That whenever he came across an automobile whose parking meter was expired, he'd deposit any coins he had on him. That when Maddie was five years old and collected pebbles and other kinds of stones, her father bought her a children's book on the subject of geology and wrote in the inside cover *A book about rocks for a girl who totally rocks.* But it's effort to remind herself of his unpredictable fits of temper, or that, if truth be told, he used to drink too much, downing beer after beer as he watched college football on Saturday afternoons, or that sometimes he was a poor listener, distracted by some nagging thought or another, staring into a corner of the dining room during dinner, only partially there.

Maddie's shoulders heave and she's seized by a painful hiccup. Standing at her side, the woman says, "Anyways," and plunges the folded umbrella into her duffel bag. "I very greatly appreciate you—both of you. And not just for the ride, I'll have you know. I like to be nice and clear and straight about these things."

Russell flattens his hands on the roof of the car, pressing his stomach against the driver-side window. "You okay, kid?"

"I have no idea how to answer a question like that," Maddie says.

"Maybe you should stick with us," Russell says to the woman, who is already getting in the back.

Russell

They find a room at a historic brick hotel a couple of blocks away. The Overland, it's called. The brick is painted a deep, tomato red, and a long balcony with a white balustrade runs below the second-story windows. The side of the building reads BASQUE DINING, SALOON, and EST. 1908 in blocky white letters. A bronze commemorative plaque hangs beside the entrance.

Russell checks in at the front desk while Maddie brings in the air mattress and the falsa blankets. Their room is old-timey and spartan, reminiscent of the American frontier. Festooned curtains. A dark wooden dresser with tarnished brass pulls. A cast-iron radiator. Patchwork quilts on the double queen-size beds. No television, no radio. There's no shower either, so they take turns bathing in the claw-footed tub, and then the woman, Latifah—back in her jeans and her white sweater, sitting cross-legged on the hardwood floor—tells a series of coiling, dragged-out stories that each seem to start in the middle, stories without a beginning or an end, all of them connected, an infinite spiral staircase. Stories about her great-grandfather and her sister, Jane, that at times turn the woman's voice tinny and blue as she clutches her doll fondly to her chest, her helmet tipped back on her head. Russell and Maddie lie flat on the beds. The woman is barefoot, her big toes nail-less—squarish pads that are pink and shriveled. The nails she does have are the color of Manila paper, thick as corn kernels. Bathwater drips from her tangled gray hair. She sways from side to side while she speaks, so rhythmically Russell feels as if he's watching the pendulum of a metronome.

Who *is* this woman? Why is she so far north if she's on her way to California?

What is Russell even doing here? How is this whole situation going to end?

After nine long days of sleeping in a tent, he's happy to be staying the night in a hotel room, with a bed, clean towels, running water. But he has lost control of himself. This entire trip is nothing more than an act of folly, a fool's errand. They've taken flight, they've set themselves free, but for what? Campsites and desert roads and the brown barrenness of Nevada. Their pain, of course, would not be left behind; it is right here with them. Regardless, Russell has no desire to go home, and he can't get himself to care—really care, the way he should—that he is dragging Maddie down with him, to wherever it is he's headed. He feels even farther adrift than he did before they left.

He's tired, and his eyelids keep lowering, and he sits up against the wall. For a couple of weeks after the explosions, he wandered back to that bright Tuesday morning once or twice a day, sometimes remembering with shame how he wanted to see the fire up close. He caught sight of it amid the smoke as he exited the interstate, on his way to Andrew's—the fire blazing with an angry, skyward determination. Now he's there yet again, in his Corolla on the morning of the accident, like a soldier returning in his mind to a field of battle, the recurring vision almost tangible. A single, towering flame wriggles free from the trundling clouds of black, and Russell thinks for several moments about driving toward it, for no other reason than to get a better look, anxious though he is. He's so worried about Andrew, and about Maddie and Juliet too. But he doesn't know for certain that any of them is in danger, and he's pretty high—he just finished off that pinner of a joint—and some fraction of him wants, out of basic interest, to see the fire in all its immensity. There is something almost seductive about the whole dire scene, even about the smoke, with its encompassing proportions, looming on the horizon. Russell feels like an outsider, viewing it all from where he is, as if it's some grand festivity to which he hasn't been invited. He knows, coasting down the long, bowed exit ramp, that the weed is playing with him. It gives and it takes, never to be trusted. But he can't help it: he wishes he were there, at ground zero, or as close as he could get without risking injury or death. *Fire*, he thinks, watching it from the ramp. (His stoner's brain.) *Fire*. It's at once so deadly and so beautiful. What *is* fire, anyway? What are its properties? Did he ever learn that in school? Another colossal flame writhes into the air and Russell shakes his head in disbelief, feeling as though he's privately observing some magnificent, unknown phenomenon of the natural world. At the same time, he feels like an idiot; his thoughts, he knows, are idiotic. Not just that, they're insensitive, at best. Lives are at stake, maybe Andrew's among them—this is the only thing that matters. Russell nears the end of the exit ramp, wishing he were clearheaded. The fire burns just in view, and at last he thinks to try Andrew's cell phone. Straight to voice mail. He calls five or six times before he gives up.

He sits up higher against the wall now, rubbing his eyes, clearing the episode from his mind. So often it feels as if his memories of that morning require some kind of verification, as if they're things he's been told, things he's overheard. And his relationship with Andrew, his great, brotherly love for him, his concern about him during the explosions—Russell's been trying his best to will it all completely from his thoughts. Their decades-long relationship seems no more than a pinpoint in the expanding dimensions of his past, as distant as a star.

The woman is still talking, still on the floor. Maddie's nodding her head, and Russell can tell it isn't an act. She's really listening.

•

When it's dark and late, they step out the window to the balcony and stand in a row against the balustrade. The woman says, "What a fine thing this is to do!" The unlit building across the street has no visible sign or entrance. An insect chitters noisily and the air smells of damp sagebrush. Up above, flat clouds are barges in a blue-black ocean of sky. Russell opens his hand to reveal the impeccably rolled blunt he's decided, against his better judgment, to put forward for evening recreation.

"I shouldn't be doing what I'm doing," he says, looking at Maddie.

"You're offering us your doob? Are you for real?"

"Seems like the right moment for it," Russell says. "Set and setting, that whole thing. Don't they say that at your school?"

"It's pretty gloomy out here, on second thought," says the woman, her mouth twitching the way it did during dinner. "What's that, a Dutch Master? My great-grandfather used to smoke those on his porch before it burned to the ground."

"It's just an idea I had," Russell says. "I thought it might be fun. No pressure."

Maddie shrugs. "What the hey. I could use some fun. Fun sounds good."

He touches his forehead to hers. "Listen—nobody back home ever knows what we're about to do. Is that understood?"

"Why is everyone in my life trying to get me to smoke something?"

He takes a step back. "You stay away from those cigarettes. I don't know what was going through your mother's brain. And tonight's the only time you're ever doing *this*. It's a one-time deal, no discussion."

"That's the same thing my mother said."

"The house itself survived," the woman says. "So did my great-grandfather, until he died three days later."

Russell lights the blunt with his Bic. "I do hope this is your first—"

"Just give it to me," Maddie says.

He passes her the blunt and she tokes on it hard.

"Hey," Russell says. "Take it easy."

She coughs enormously: a tailpipe expelling a cloud of exhaust. A window slams at the other end of the balcony.

"Take it easy yourself. I know what I'm doing."

Already he regrets his decision. "This isn't the nineteen-seventies. That stuff's genetically engineered. That's twenty percent THC."

"Hoo-wee," Maddie says, her eyelids sagging a little. "Howdy-do."

"Sinsemilla," he says. "Capeesh?" He doesn't know what's worse: sharing his weed with Maddie or sharing it with a person whose mental faculties are, by anyone's standards, uncertain. He takes back the blunt, then holds it out to the woman halfheartedly. "You don't have to smoke this, but it's here if you want it. It's marijuana," Russell says.

"Do I look like I was born thirty-five seconds ago?" She lifts an eyebrow. "I have never tried the likes of illegal drugs in my entire life, and I do not intend to begin out here on this balcony."

"We can go inside if you want," Maddie says, laughing through her nose.

"That's exactly where I'll be," the woman huffs, and climbs back into the room.

Maddie looks over the balustrade at the shadowy sidewalk below. "Is it weird that we just go around trusting maps? I mean, what if the world looks nothing at all like our maps say it does? How we would ever know? Is somebody gonna fly all over the place in a helicopter and check? Is that what you expect me to believe?"

Russell tokes on the blunt. "Nobody's asking you to believe a thing. You are hereby free to decide whatever you want about the world."

She reaches into a pocket of her shorts and brings out a roll of Certs, picking at the wrapper for a second, then giving up and tossing the roll through the open window. Russell feels genial, optimistic. He can see, with a euphoric clarity, the half-finished arc of his own life, like a time-lapse projection on a screen.

"Some man was in front of our house a few weeks ago," Maddie says.

"What do you mean?" He takes another toke. "What man?"

"I don't know. A man. Sitting in his car, parked in front of the house. Just kind of staring at us when we pulled up."

"Did you talk to him?"

"No. My mom tried to, but he drove away. I think he's been taking care of the place, is the strange thing. Mowing the lawn, cleaning the pool. Trimming trees and stuff."

Inside, the woman hums loudly from one of the beds. Russell leans into the room, giving her a wave, and gets the pink bakery box from atop the radiator. Standing against the painted brick wall, looking out at the plane-bottomed clouds, he and Maddie eat the macarons and the biscotti, every last crumb, and then he crouches before the window and sets two of the cranberry scones on the sill and balances a third on top. He stands up, riding a leisurely wave of self-possession. "Look," he says. "Sconehenge."

Suddenly, though, his state of mind hardens. He's gone an hour or so without thinking about them, but now Emma and Andrew are back in his head. Did Juliet ever catch Andrew deleting the recent-calls log from his cell phone, as Russell caught Emma doing once? Does Juliet know that Andrew had fallen out of love with her long before he died? He'd still cared deeply for her, and he'd had no intention of subjecting Maddie to the misery of a divorce, but several times, over drinks at the All or Nothing, he'd confessed to Russell that he'd outgrown his marriage.

A scream builds up in Russell's throat but he keeps it from escaping, walking a heavy-heeled lap around the balcony. He is a childless, cuckolded, soon-to-be-divorced career bartender. His forty-plus years on the planet have amounted to nothing more than this. To make matters worse, he went so far as to contemplate, if only for a second, putting a gun to his head and pulling the trigger. His unease about leaving town with Maddie, about the fact that they still haven't spoken to Juliet, seems a trifle in comparison.

They eat the scones and apple turnovers too, chewing hungrily, standing at the balustrade, and then they're looking carefully at one another and Maddie gives Russell a smile, lengthy and sugges-tive, that makes his stomach crumple. She seems to be holding her breath. She takes his hand—there's an air of predetermination about it, as though it was certain to happen—and Russell feels the warmth of her fingers, her skin. Her thumb, in his palm, brushes back and forth and in circles, resulting in a frightful exhilaration. He closes his eyes. His stomach feels hollowed-out like a tunnel. He hears Maddie say, "Russell." Barely a whisper.

When their lips finally touch, he can taste the sugary tang of her breath. He cannot hold back—he cannot stop doing it, this terrible, inconceivable thing. This thing he shouldn't be doing.

Their noses are touching as well now. Their chins. For a few dizzying moments, the tips of their tongues.

"Good night, you moonlight ladies," the woman sings tunelessly from the room. "Rock-a-bye, sweet Baby Jane."

Russell steps away, shaking his head, and they go back inside. The woman stands up from the bed and says, "They call Santa Barbara the American Riviera, and I'm going there, and if you don't believe me, just wait and you'll see."

"You must be excited to see her," Maddie says.

"Excited as a person can be. Good old Jane."

"I'll take the floor," Russell says, tugging the air mattress from its nylon sack. He can't believe what he's done. He's frightened and confused, deeply concerned about Maddie, furious at his own... *what?* What to call it? What is the word for such abominable judgment, such a flagrant violation of decency? What came over him? He's stoned, sure, high as a kite, but of course that's no excuse. He's been getting stoned since the seventh grade and never has he done something so heedless, so selfish.

"You remind me of someone," the woman says to him. "You remind me of me."

"The moment has come," Maddie says, "to document this magical evening for posterity." She's holding a disposable camera, one of those plastic Kodak jobs, an anachronism. "Picture time, everyone!"

They sit down side by side on one of the beds, Russell in the middle. Maddie holds the camera out in front of them and takes the picture.

"We should have said 'Cheese,'" the woman says. "You're supposed to say 'Cheese.'"

"Cheeeeeese," Maddie says, lying back on the quilt. "That sounds delicious."

The woman rises quickly to her feet. "I lied," she says. "I hope you can both forgive me for it. I hope this doesn't get your goat."

"About what?" Russell asks her.

"My name," she says, taking off her helmet. "It isn't really Latifah. That's just something I like to tell people."

Emma

Four days after her visit to his church, Marcus Bauerkemper shows up at the Bora Bora in a plaid bucket hat that is too small for his head. The brim, attached to which is an array of polychromatic fishing lures, scarcely extends to the tops of his ears. As a teenager Emma had a fondness for the show *M*A*S*H*—her grandmother let her watch it on Monday nights if Emma's homework was complete—and he reminds her of McLean Stevenson as Lieutenant Colonel Henry Blake, until she notes his outfit: creased blue jeans and another of his tuniclike shirts, this one the bold, synthetic green of a Little Trees car freshener. She's just finished a midweek graveyard shift, eight leg-stiffening hours of blackjack and roulette. She's walking from the pit to the dressing room as he marches over to her, waving.

"Get changed," he says. "Let's go for a drive."

The slot machines ring all around with their relentless issuing of coins.

"A drive?" Emma asks.

"It's a perfect day for what I have in mind."

"How'd you know I'd be at work this morning?"

"I've been coming to this casino for a pretty long time," he says.

Even so, is it odd that he's taken note of her schedule? She notices for the first time that he isn't wearing a wedding ring. "I don't know."

"You can trust me," Marcus Bauerkemper says, placing his hand on his heart. "You won't be sorry."

She changes into shorts and a V-neck top and meets him fifteen minutes later in front of the casino. It's eight thirty in the morning, Fremont Street as quiet as it's ever going to be. A few twenty-something guys teeter drunkenly down the pedestrian mall, waggling plastic yards of ale, but the block is otherwise lacking in its usual revelry. The air is warm and still. Beyond the great half-cylinder screen up above, the sky is a thick and heady sapphire.

"I kind of need to sleep," Emma says. "I've been up all night."

"You can sleep on the way."

"The way where? Where are we going?"

"That's a surprise. 'An unexpected or astonishing event, fact, or thing.'"

In front of the Pioneer Club, he stops and looks up at Vegas Vic. The neon cowboy towers over them in his yellow shirt and cuffed blue jeans, a cigarette resting coolly between his lips. A red bandana, tied at the neck, opens across his chest like a bib. His hitchhiker's thumb no longer waves. He no longer greets passersby with a loud *Howdy, podner!* And his Stetson has been cropped a number of feet to make way for the screen, which at the moment displays an aerobatic squadron of F-16s—the Thunderbirds, based out at Nellis—Kenny Loggins's "Danger Zone" booming from every direction.

"What's going on?" Emma says. "What is it we're doing?"

"You could make a fortune in this city," Marcus Bauerkemper says, smiling wistfully. "Or you could lose it all, the whole shebang, everything you've got." He gnaws at his lip. "All that and more."

•

He drives a black Nissan Maxima, sleek as a gumball, with tinted windows, leather seats, a moonroof, cherry-wood trim. They head east on Stewart Avenue, out of downtown and across the sun-kindled city. Everything is catching the white sun's light, everything glowing like a flame: automobiles and road signs and storefront windows. She stays awake, a little bubble of excitement floating through her. He still hasn't said where they're going, but soon they're on Lake Mead Boulevard, and Emma's pretty sure they're bound for Las Vegas Bay. Certainly the bucket hat with the lures reinforces this theory. She keeps it to herself, pretending interest in the nearby mountains, which stretch to form a collar around the valley.

He sought her out after the service and they talked for five or ten minutes by the table of cookies in the vestibule of the church. When he asked if he could put her on the mailing list, Emma wrote her contact information on a piece of paper beside the coffee urn. She met Marcus Bauerkemper only six weeks ago, but by now Emma feels, somehow, that she knows him. Knows him enough, that is, that she's relaxed in his company, telling him, during what's amounting to a forty-five-minute journey, about her nightlong shift, her aching legs, Ed Logan's chronic irritability. Marcus Bauerkemper nods. He shakes his head when he's supposed to, and Emma tells him about her parents and her grandmother, and then about Russell. She tells him about Andrew's death, about Russell leaving town with Maddie. He is, Emma can tell, genuinely absorbed in what she's saying, how-ever tedious it happens to be, as if she's shared with him not the many particulars of her troubled life but something amazing—that she's won a lottery, climbed the Seven Summits, donated a kidney to a dying stranger.

She doesn't tell Marcus Bauerkemper everything. She doesn't tell him about the affair.

"How long have they been gone? Your husband and this girl." He's done away with the stately, stagy, preacherly voice Emma has come to expect of him. He sounds like a poised and sympathetic friend.

"Eleven days now," she says. "I know the whole thing's perfectly innocent. I just miss him, that's all. I just want to hear from him."

"Why do you think they left?"

Emma runs her fingertips over the glossy trim surrounding the car's black Bose stereo. "So much for the vow of poverty."

He smells warmly of fabric softener, and rubs his thumbs against the wheel, whose dark padded leather resembles the grip of a tennis racket. "'He who has a slack hand becomes poor, but the hand of the diligent makes rich.' Proverbs Ten, verse four."

She wants to remind him that, according to the Bible, it's easier for a camel to pass through the eye of a needle than for a rich man to enter the kingdom of heaven. You don't have to be a Christian to know that one. She wants to tell him that his fancy car makes him seem like a fraud—and in one respect, at least, he *is* one. When Emma returned from his church the other day, she looked up the psalm he'd discussed in his sermon, wanting to read the verse for herself, wondering what else it might say about the subject of happiness. She googled "joy" and "happy" and "Psalm 126," and among the many search results, halfway down, was a website called SermonCentral.com. Emma clicked on the link and up came the sermon, excerpted from a book called *Journey to Joy: The Psalms of Ascent*, by a Pastor Josh Moody. Marcus Bauerkemper had made adjustments to the wording, but he'd more or less plagiarized what he'd said to his congregation that day, and if she wanted to, Emma could call him to account. She could humiliate him, expose him as the charlatan he is. She could, but she doesn't want to. She is falling for his tricks, the force of his transparent personality. Emma knows it, but she doesn't care.

●

When they reach the bay, he parks in a large, sandy lot and goes around to the trunk. He takes out a green Stanley thermos, a plastic food container, two stainless-steel mugs, two fishing rods, and a tackle box. He hands her the thermos and the mugs.

"Are we seriously going fishing?" she says. "The hat would have given it away, but I thought you were only wearing it because you're a little—well, you know. *Unconventional.*"

"A person could not ask for a more splendid morning!" Marcus Bauerkemper sings.

"Get in a car with a relative stranger and no idea where you're going, and this is what happens, I suppose."

He gives a tight-lipped smile. Before them the lake is calm and narrow, held in by scores of jagged mountains, sunlight warbling on the surface. A few white clouds idle in the blue, blue sky. At the shoreline, he baits their hooks with live worms from the tackle box, tugging at one of the lures on his hat. "These are just for show," he says with a wink.

Emma's been fishing only once in her life, on a campus-recreation trip during college, and so Marcus Bauerkemper reminds her how to cast, how to reel in her line. They're hoping, he explains, for striped or largemouth bass. She's seen on the news that Lake Mead, via Las Vegas Wash, contains trace amounts of ammonium perchlorate from the WEPCO plant, and she wonders if the fish are safe to eat.

In the food container are four enormous gingerbread muffins, which Marcus Bauerkemper claims to have baked himself. He presses the mugs into the rocky dirt and pours them black coffee from the thermos, and they eat the muffins and sip the coffee while they fish, the only people there. Midges scurry around their lines, which angle gently into the lake, gray birds freewheeling overhead. A pair of boats dash by, making waves. Several yards out, to the left and the right, Emma can see a swaying in the water, grasses tendriling up from the murky green depths, and she's careful not to let her hook get caught.

"We're a lot later than we ought to be," Marcus Bauerkemper says. "They bite best around dawn."

"Maybe we should offer them some of these muffins." She swallows an especially moist and gingery mouthful. "They're delicious."

She feels every bit as out of place—and silly, and confused—as she did at his church. She hasn't the foggiest idea what his intentions are. Why on earth would he take her fishing, of all things? Why did she follow him to his car and allow him to drive her all the way out here? It doesn't matter. She has to go with it now, and that's perfectly fine— perfectly suitable, actually—because being here at the bay is taking her mind off Russell, and Emma needs a break from dwelling on him.

She knows, of course, why she went along with Marcus Bauerkemper today. Emma's lonely, as lonely as she was back when she was single. She has friends, sure, but no one she's all that close with, no *best* friend other than Russell. She's too depressed to reach out to anyone anyway. She feels codependent, pathetic, each day unfolding with the unreal inertia of a dream. The house seems forsaken without him, tainted by his absence, and sometimes it feels as if Emma has walked into it, that quiet, lonely place, by mistake. As a means of coping—of comforting herself—she imagines Russell day and night, in various situations; many times, though, he is only sitting with her on the couch in the living room, talking about the tavern, or some news story he's heard, or a movie he wants to see. It's as though he is right there with her, so vivid, so powerful, is Emma's imagination.

Loneliness. That terrible emotion. It's been dogging her for most of her life. She was an outcast as a child. Her classmates thought it peculiar that Emma lived with her grandmother, who spoke slow, choppy English, and they were disturbed by the fact that her mother and father had been killed in a horrific automobile accident—rendered unrecognizable, rumor had it, and it was true. Her classmates were not openly mean, not exactly. They merely pretended she didn't exist, avoiding conversation with her, eye contact, and by the time she entered middle school Emma had come to feel as if she were a carrier of some shocking disease—or of some curse, as if looking upon her for more than an instant would cause one's own mother and father to be killed.

She doesn't like thinking about her unhappy childhood or the self-consciousness that still presides over her personality. *Stop it*, Emma tells herself, looking out at the sky and the mountains and the lake. *Quit your moping and try to appreciate, for one single second, what's right here in front of you, right now.*

•

"The Gospel According to John," says Marcus Bauerkemper, reeling in his line. Some animal is making a noise like a playing card wedged between the spokes of a bicycle wheel. "Are you familiar with it?"

"I can't say that I am, no. I'm what you might call 'culturally Christian.' Which means I've never read the Bible and I don't go to church."

Emma reels in too. Neither of them has gotten so much as a nibble. He rebaits their hooks with fresh, fat, dirt-coated worms. That desperate wriggling of theirs—it saddens her, the worms' hopeless determination.

"New Testament," Marcus Bauerkemper says. "Deals mainly with the Crucifixion and the Resurrection."

"I've heard of those."

They both cast.

"I imagine you're wondering why it is I brought you here," he says.

"I don't want to sound like I'm not enjoying myself. But yeah."

"You seem…How should I put this? You seem like you need to be lifted up a bit, if you don't mind the observation. I took it as a sign that you came to our service this past Sunday. I figured I should do my duty as a clergyman, make a special effort. Go out of my way. My job, if I'm doing it correctly, is about more than just performing services at a church."

"So why fishing?"

"The Gospel of John," he says. "That's the reason we've come here today." He's speaking with his stagy voice again, his pulpit voice. "John 21, to be specific. 'A Breakfast by the Sea.'"

"You're a riddle wrapped in a mystery," Emma says. "Inside an enigma." She gives him a playful look. "That's something Andrew used to say. The friend I told you about, who died in the explosions."

Marcus Bauerkemper nods consolingly, then turns his gaze back to the lake. "Simon Peter, Thomas, Nathanael, the sons of Zebedee, and two more of Jesus's disciples were fishing in a boat in the Sea of Tiberias," he says. "They fished for most of the night, without any luck. When morning came, Jesus was standing on the shore. He called to them, asking if they'd caught anything, and they answered that they hadn't. Jesus told them to cast their net on the right side of the boat, and the disciples did. Lo and behold, they couldn't even pull the net in because of the great multitude of fish."

"One thing you can say about Jesus: he wasn't subtle."

He gives her a stony look. "When they reached the shore, they saw a fire burning, with bread and fish laid over it," he says. "Jesus told them to bring over what they'd caught and have breakfast with him. They dragged the net to the fire, and Jesus gave them the bread and the fish and said to them, 'Follow me, for I am the Son of God.'"

"You gotta love a name like 'Zebedee.'"

"That's an abridged version, paraphrased. But the idea is simple: We must devote ourselves to the Lord if we expect our lives to be fruitful, Emma."

Something plucks at her line, as though cued by his explanation of the story. She calls out, reeling in like crazy. On the hook is a very small multicolored fish, about the size of a spinach leaf, its rubbery fins infused with sunlight.

"Little bluegill," he says, snickering. "Serves you right for making jokes." He wrenches the hook from the fish's lip, cradling the tiny animal in his hand.

"That doesn't hurt him, does it?"

"He's okay, aren't you, fella?" He holds the fish at eye level. "I'd have thought you were the white whale itself, the way she pulled you in."

"Hilarious," Emma says. "Where's the Lord's generosity when I need it?"

Marcus Bauerkemper squints. "You haven't asked for it yet." He crouches down in the dirt, his blue jeans stretching audibly, the back of his bright green shirt saturated with sweat. "Thank you," he says to the fish, setting it back in the water, "for illustrating my point."

The bluegill flicks its tail and is gone.

•

It's so sunny today, so warm. *Too* sunny and *too* warm, Emma thinks as Marcus Bauerkemper drives them back to the city. Sometimes she longs for the elements, these days in particular. The climate in the valley is so predictable: sunny and warm, or else sunny and *hot*, nearly always. It's difficult to be truly unhappy in such a place. It rains here—a lot recently, in fact—but it's uncommon. Nine times out of ten the simple presence of the sun keeps you in a positive mindset. Once, Emma was stopped at a light on a showery winter day that, despite the rain, despite the season, wasn't quite cold enough, and she turned on the air conditioner and breathed into her hands and imagined she could see her breath—she looked out at the kettle-gray sky and pictured herself living grimly in some dank northeastern locale. (She's always had such a romantic attitude toward sorrow.) Now her life really is grim, and Emma wants the weather to match her mood. Or rather, she feels her emotional state improving but prefers to toss and turn in the misery she knows she deserves.

How skillful she and Andrew were in their deception, at keeping things hidden. Yes, she deserves whatever else might come her way. They were so cunning. She didn't allow herself to acknowledge it at the time, not fully. The use of voice mail and email was strictly forbidden, and if they found themselves on a double date, they avoided eye contact as best they could, avoided responding with too much enthusiasm to each other's remarks. She always brought her own gym towel when she worked out in Andrew's spare bedroom, and meticulously wiped any perspiration from the equipment when she was finished, never showering there. They promised each other not to get greedy with their rendezvous: once or twice a week would have to suffice.

They had no intention of leaving their spouses and running away together, as people are always doing in the movies. And so they were careful, always careful. Their skill at managing the affair made Andrew, too, feel especially bad, and there were days when Emma wondered if they would ever talk about anything but their regret and their immorality—days when she wondered if these two things above all were what united them as lovers.

She lowers her window now, trying her best to embrace the weather, letting in the sunlight and the warmth, the road winding north through desert hillocks and flat stretches of flowering creosote. Marcus Bauerkemper turns off the air conditioner. He has a reflective look on his face, and says, after a lengthy silence, "I've made some poor choices in my life. I'm realizing that now. I don't need to go into detail, but maybe this excursion was as much for me as it was for you." He sighs, sounding the way he did back on Fremont Street, in front of the Pioneer Club. "I don't know. I needed a little break, I guess, even for a couple of hours. It was nice doing this with you, Emma. Thank you for coming."

She smiles at him. "You're not alone," she says, "if it makes you feel any better. I've made some pretty poor choices myself."

"I was right, then. You do need lifting up."

A couple of minutes later she asks him, "Do you ever, like, take confessions? I know you're not a priest."

"The sacrament of reconciliation isn't something we practice at our church," he says. "But I'm all ears."

She doesn't say anything for a while. Then she says, "Okay, here it is: I had a relationship with another man. The man I told you about. Andrew." It feels good to admit it to someone other than Russell. He and Marcus Bauerkemper are the only two people she's ever told.

"I see," he says.

"He was Russell's best friend. Doesn't get any worse than that. I mean, I could *murder* somebody."

"The Lord forgives. The fact that you're able to own up to it counts for a lot."

"Tell that to my husband."

The wind stirs Marcus Bauerkemper's silvery semicircle of hair. He irons it with his hand, adjusting his glasses. "There's more to you than a single bad decision," he says.

"Your turn," Emma says. "What's your story?"

"Like I told you, there's no need for me to go into it."

"That's super fair. Thanks a lot."

"It isn't my job to burden other people with my own problems."

The Maxima hugs a bend, gliding along like a luge. He smiles meekly, and then something catches Emma's eye, something at the edge of her field of vision. It happens so fast she might not have seen the blur of movement at all: a bird comes flying through her open window and slams into the steering column, as if shot from a bow. It's leaping around and is in her lap now, a coot or a merganser or something—something with webbed feet and a spiky crest. There are feathers everywhere, as though a down pillow has burst apart, and the bird screeches and beats its wings. It continues leaping hysterically, and for a second, as it hovers beneath the car's sun visor, Emma is face to face with it. She sees a small, watery eye, yellow and hooded. Marcus Bauerkemper is shouting, and the Maxima swerves, and swerves again. The bird strikes out at her with its beak, nipping Emma's forearm, and she swats its head in defense. Marcus Bauerkemper veers toward the shoulder. As the car comes to a stop, Emma throws open her door and the bird flutters out, landing in a patch of dry red brome. It stands for a minute, collecting itself, before flying away.

The slick brown plumage is all over the dashboard and the console and Emma's clothes. Marcus Bauerkemper is still shouting— "Jesus fucking Christ!"—but Emma can't get herself to speak. The individual parts of her body feel incredibly heavy: her eyelids and her jaw and her limbs. There's a contracted feeling in her head and chest.

Marcus Bauerkemper turns off the car and they both sit there, breathing.

"Are you okay?" he asks her. He puts his hand on her shoulder. "I didn't mean to overreact. I'm sorry."

Emma brushes some of the feathers from her lap, pulling her door closed, wondering if they've been killed and simply haven't realized it yet. "You took the Lord's name in vain," she says absently. "What kind of a minister *are* you?"

Simon

The third time he follows her to the Guardian Angel Cathedral, one of the doors is unlocked and Juliet disappears into the church. Simon sits in the darkness of his pickup, parked, like last time, in front of the gift shop next door. He hasn't spoken with her since she took her shirt off in her living room and then asked him to leave, three days ago. She's on his mind more than ever. Simon can't keep himself from thinking about her, her shoulders and her breasts and that black sports bra.

Getting out of the house wasn't a problem. Things with Rebecca aren't good, which allows him a fair amount of freedom. She's giving him the silent treatment, still angry that he quit his job before conferring with her, that he assaulted her water bottles with Daniel's bat. Tonight she made dinner for herself—nothing for him—and ate it alone in the den. He wonders if his unemployment is a false excuse for her anger. There's a rift between them that seems unprecedented, unjustified, as though some fault in their marriage has finally ruptured, independent of the big argument they had. He's terribly sad. He didn't say where he was going. He simply left.

A pale sliver of moon sits low in a corner of the sky, traffic inching by on Las Vegas Boulevard. Ten minutes pass. Fifteen. Twenty. Two hookers are standing beside a light pole on the other side of the parking lot. Simon's never been with a hooker, and he has no plans to engage one now. He can't help looking at them, though, on the rare occasion he sees one, even if it makes him feel glum. Glum not just for the women, most of whom are morbidly thin or bear visible bruises, but for himself as well.

He can see that one of them is a man in drag—Hispanic, rangy. The man has on a tight red dress and black stilettos, and starts to lurch around like a peacock, head lowered, as though he's dropped a contact. The other hooker is Asian, short and busty. A woman: somehow Simon's sure. She wears big hoop earrings, a sequined tube top, a purple miniskirt. When they see Simon watching them, he looks quickly in the opposite direction. The man in drag comes over anyway. Simon keeps his window down—some combination of manners and subservience.

"Hey, baby," the man says. "What's the word?" His voice is deep, gritty, orange lipstick smearing the borders of his lips. Eyeshadow blackens the bags beneath his eyes. He seems to scrutinize Simon, as though they've met somewhere before but the man can't quite place him. "Little company?" he says.

The other hooker comes closer, tilting her face and scratching at her ear. Simon sees himself in a bath with her at some run-down hourly motel, half-clothed with her in the front seat of his pickup, under the covers of his bed with her while Rebecca is out of the house somewhere. Then he realizes that she, too, is a man.

"I'm good," Simon says, and smiles. A sense of desolation comes over him. "All good."

It's the kind of scene people always imagine when they think of this place. The sex trade, recreational risk-taking, bad behavior. The negative perceptions bother him. In spite of what most tourists believe, this isn't the real Las Vegas. (*Where do you live*, outsiders like to joke, *in a hotel? What's your wife, a prostitute or something? A showgirl?*) Saying the Strip is Las Vegas is like saying Bourbon Street is New Orleans. Vegas is tract homes and strip malls, Taco Bells and Targets. It's minivans and station wagons, little girls with sidewalk chalk, boys on BMX bikes. It's Scouting and Pop Warner, and churches of all denominations. It is, more or less, every other city in America, and its individuality, Simon thinks, lies not in the Strip or Fremont Street—not in gambling or vice—but in the desert, the Mojave, where kids catch whipsnakes and lizards, where there's beauty and mystery, the wood-tar fragrance of creosote, the trifold chirrup of katydids. Simon wants to walk with Juliet out there, hand in hand in the magnificent desert, to the mountains and beyond.

The two hookers are back beside their light pole. Juliet is still in the church. On the sidewalk, a woman hobbles by in a white T-shirt and sweatpants, pushing a shopping cart filled with garbage bags. A dumpster diver. A down-and-out. Horrible, Simon thinks. He doesn't have any cash on him. He searches his pockets for loose change. They're everywhere in this part of town, the dejected and itinerant, sharing real estate, he assumes, with the hookers and the junkies.

Sometimes Simon thinks of Andrew Huntley as dejected and itinerant in whatever afterlife he's part of now, roaming by himself from one metaphysical plane to the next, waiting to be delivered.

●

When Juliet comes out, a good thirty minutes from when she arrived, Simon follows her back to Bighorn Heights. He doesn't turn into the subdivision. He keeps going, driving around for a while; he'll give himself away if he shows up too soon. When he finally rings the bell, Juliet opens the door quickly and says, "Still at it, huh?"

"How'd you know?" He laughs, embarrassed. A little afraid.

"Don't treat me like I'm a moron."

"Maybe I'm your fairy godfather," he says. "Maybe I'm supposed to protect you, bring good luck. It's a remote possibility, but—"

"You gave me your word. It's weird, Simon."

"There's nothing threatening about it. You know that, right?" He shrugs. "I'm as harmless as they come."

She rubs at the back of her neck, wearing a low-cut tank top and jeans. "I'm not sure I believe that." She seems to reconsider. "But I guess I don't really mind anymore," she says. "I've come to accept it—*expect* it—you being around all the time, out there somewhere." She leans against the half-open door. "Really, though. What if Maddie were home right now? You just showing up like this."

"You think I'm crazy, I know. I probably am."

She looks down at her flat-soled shoes. "In a good way," Juliet says, granting him a smile.

Simon feels a twirling in his head. "Can I come in?"

"Is that such a good idea, do you think?"

"It isn't," he says, "no. I only thought we could—"

"Stop yapping for once," she says, and opens the door all the way.

•

They sit on barstools at the kitchen counter and she pours them red wine from a box. Once again, Maddie is the topic of conversation. She and the bartender are still off camping together, somewhere upstate. Juliet sighs, lights a cigarette. She raises her glass to toast, then sets it back on the counter and shakes her head. Simon takes a sip of the wine, which warms his mouth and leaves a vinegary coating along his tongue and lips. Juliet takes a sip too, scrunching her face. The kitchen is compact and slender, with a built-in butcher block, a smooth-top range, a black refrigerator that's all nicked and scratched. Simon glances around for a cat. The range, catching light from the overhead bulbs, is buffed to perfection.

"She's seventeen," Juliet says. "She wants her freedom, and she's in a lot of pain right now. I get it. But she still lives under this roof. Who's ever heard of such a thing—leaving without even asking me? And to put me through this right after her father dies." She takes a drag on the cigarette, drawing a finger around the lip of her glass. "And *Russell*. He's a family friend, we've known him since forever. But goddammit. How could he do this to me?"

"It isn't right," Simon tells her. He imagines Michaela in the same situation: away somewhere, as a teenager, with a man more than twenty years her senior, family friend or otherwise. Simon imagines his own worry and rage. He'll see her in just a few days. With classes out until the end of August, she and Daniel are coming home for a week. Simon can't wait. "He should know better. They both should."

"It's like he abducted her or something, never mind what the police want to call it. That's how it feels, at least. I don't even know where to look for them. Maddie says they're still in Nevada, in these emails she keeps sending, but God only knows what town."

She waves her cigarette in the air, silent for a moment, her lips stained with wine. It looks like eyeliner—like crusted makeup—and reminds Simon of the Hispanic hooker from the parking lot.

"I've got news for them both," Juliet says. "I'm in a certain amount of pain myself."

There's something so attractive about her widowhood. It makes her stand out, makes her seem so human, her close association with grief, even if she *didn't* love her husband.

"Someone keeps leaving pecan Sandies by Andrew's headstone," she says. "You know, the cookies? He used to love those."

"Hmm," Simon says. "That's kind of sweet, whoever's doing it. No pun intended."

She smiles with the corners of her eyes, blowing smoke over her shoulder. "I assumed it was Russell at first, but it keeps happening." On the counter is a glass ashtray from the old Castaways hotel, and she taps her cigarette on the scalloped rim. "It *is* sweet," she says. "You're right. I'd just like to know who's responsible for it."

"How come you've been going to the church?" Simon asks, changing the subject. "The cathedral," he says softly. "You keep going back there."

Her eyes are all over the map.

"I'm sorry," he says. "I shouldn't have asked."

What he really wants to bring up is the sports-bra incident. What is he doing here, in light of it? Are they seeing each other now?

Of course not. She didn't even want to let him in the house tonight. No. They've simply been spending time together—a more accurate way to put it. A way that doesn't make it sound like he's having an affair.

"It's difficult to explain," she says. "Or maybe it isn't. It's like I keep thinking he's going to show up there, come looking for me or something." She wipes her eyes with the ball of her thumb. "Remember when you were a kid, and you were in some crowded place with your parents? If you got lost you were supposed to meet them at the drinking fountain or somewhere, right?"

Simon nods.

"It's kind of like that," she says. "Like we've gotten separated and I keep returning to the last place I saw him. Except that he was never even there! His body, I'm saying. It was just the casket. But if he…if Andrew could only find his way to that church, you know? His *ghost* or whatever. Who knows what I'm even talking about. Now who's the crazy one?" She drinks from her glass, puts her cigarette out in the ashtray. "Tonight I just sat there in one of the pews, waiting like some kind of lunatic. It's funny—I've felt closer to him since his death than I ever did when he was alive. He wasn't a faithful husband. Somehow that doesn't matter anymore." She raises an eyebrow, then says, "When I try to think of the years before Andrew and I were together, I can't. Not really. Isn't that odd? I mean, who was I back then? Did I ever not know him?"

Little worlds inside us, Simon thinks. *Little worlds inside us all.*

"Now it's *my* turn to ask an uncomfortable question, one you never seem to answer," Juliet says. "How come you're not at home with your wife?"

●

Then they're in the backyard, standing on the patio beneath a wooden pergola overgrown with honeysuckle vines, sipping their third sour glass of red wine, looking up at the moon, which is higher now, thinner, and Juliet sets her glass down on the table and takes hold of his shoulders and kisses him hard on the mouth. She uses her tongue. She grabs his ass, tugging at his belt. An inner voice tells him to get away, get away now, as quickly as he can. Simon sets his glass down next to hers, trying not to think about what's happening.

Don't think, he thinks. *Let it happen.*

He shuts his mind off, powers it down. A second later it's up and running again.

He hasn't kissed any woman but Rebecca in more than twenty-five years, but it feels so natural, so inexorable, that Simon soon finds himself proceeding with an unexpected confidence, returning Juliet's favors: pushing his tongue into her mouth, holding her ass. She tastes like fermented grape juice and lip balm and tobacco. He wants to lick those tastes right off her lips, right off the inside of her mouth—he *is* licking them off. Her house is at the very edge of the subdivision, the yard enclosed with a cinder-block wall. A wrought-iron gate leads to the desert on the other side—he replaced the latch a few weeks ago, when the gate wouldn't stay closed—and Simon can smell the creosote, blended with Juliet's lemony perfume. He can hear those high-pitched katydids. He's a married man with two kids, and this is possibly the worst thing he has ever done. Worse, maybe, than leaving Andrew Huntley to die. At least that was an act of survival. But this, this is nothing more than sleazy self-indulgence. Already the guilt is scrabbling around inside him, building its nest. Juliet unzips Simon's khakis, unbuckles his belt. She kneels on the concrete and yanks down his boxers and takes him in her mouth. He can hardly contain himself; it's been the longest time. Rebecca never does this sort of thing, not anymore.

   …Rebecca.

Don't think!

A floodlight hangs in a corner of the pergola, hosting a dizzying swarm of moths, and Simon watches them circle and dart amid the straggly vines. He takes Juliet's hands and brings her to her feet. He pulls up his boxers and his khakis and leads her across the yard, through the grass and around the pool and past the old dogwood tree, through the gate and into the darkness of the Mojave. A startling darkness, in spite of the floodlights on the pergola and the warm, buttery glow of Bighorn Heights. "What are we doing out here?" she says, and Simon says, "Stop thinking and let it happen."

   A margin of bare dirt runs the length of the wall, which surrounds the entire subdivision, and he leads her past it, through the shapeless silhouettes of shrubs and large rocks. "Be careful where you step," Simon tells her. When they come to a clearing, a dozen or so yards from the gate, he lifts her arms above her head and takes off her tank top. He takes off her bra and unbuttons her jeans. "Simon," she says. He pushes down her jeans and her underwear, and kneels in the coarse dirt and kisses her thighs. "Snakes," Juliet says. "There might be snakes." He kisses her navel and her wrists. He stands up and kisses her shoulders, her breasts, and then he slides two of his fingers inside her, feels her rise onto her tiptoes. Feels her breath in his ear.

Then his khakis are around his ankles, and Juliet is on her hands and knees in the dirt, and Simon's behind her. Her head falls forward. "Simon," she says. Crying as she says it. He thinks so, at least. "Fuck," she says. Yes, crying for sure. "*Fuck, fuck, fuck,*" she says, and Simon feels the earth against his legs. He smells the creosote, hears the katydids. He sees the thin, pale moon in the sky.

Maddie

The woman's real name is Paula Toms. Since the age of twelve she's been in and out of group homes, foster homes, mental-health centers, and she now lives in an adult-care facility in Duluth. She's on a kind of leave, she explained: she's been granted special permission to travel to Santa Barbara. Due back at the end of July, she suffers from a rare disorder her great-grandfather used to call "Spaghetti Brain."

"I'm all mixed up," she told them, earnest-eyed, the night before last at the Overland Hotel. "Like a bowl of spaghetti." Maddie laughed, stretched out on one of the beds—high as could be—Paula Toms sitting atop the cast-iron radiator. Russell lay on the air mattress with his eyes closed. "It's a chromosome thing," the woman clarified. "You know what a chromosome is, Goldilocks?" Maddie's stomach seesawed from the heavy mixture of baked goods and marijuana—she'd never smoked pot before.

She doesn't believe a word the woman says.

•

Now Paula Toms is twitching her mouth and examining a display of little plastic snow globes, intricate scenes of mountain ranges, rodeo riders, covered wagons. They've stopped in a small general store in a town called Genoa, just east of Lake Tahoe, off Route 206—the oldest settlement in the state, according to a Nevada guidebook they picked up back in Ely. The shelves hold bushel baskets of licorice, caramels, taffies, and chocolates, of toy six-shooters in carved leather holsters, of tomahawks and Native American headdresses, the rear of the place designed after an old-fashioned soda fountain. You can tell that nothing in the store is as old as it's pretending to be.

Paula Toms wants to buy a gift for her sister. In faded red culottes and a man's white undershirt, she looks blowsy and tired this morning—looks every bit as off-kilter as she is. She left her safari hat in the car, her hair in a great knotted heap that reminds Maddie of one of those stainless-steel scouring balls. Maddie stands behind her as the woman picks up a boot-shaped coffee mug that reads GREETINGS FROM HISTORIC GENOA, NV. She turns the mug around in her hands, then throws her head back and shouts, "Classic!" Russell sits at the counter sipping a root-beer float, watching Paula Toms with a kind of spellbound affection—baked, Maddie figures, though she hasn't seen him smoke today. It isn't even noon.

Maddie walks down an aisle of arrowheads and bright polished stones. Most of the merchandise is covered in dust, and she wipes the arrowheads and the stones on the front of her pink button-down before inserting them into the pockets of her shorts. The gray-haired clerk who made Russell's float is oblivious, replenishing a barrel of Whirly Pops at the front of the store, an untied apron swinging from his neck. With a brazen assurance, Maddie shoves a tiger's eye the size of a jawbreaker into her left front pocket, the leg of her shorts bulging like a cheek. She goes over to Russell.

"That woman," he says in a spacey sort of way, nodding at Paula Toms. "God bless her."

Maddie feels bad about laughing at her in the hotel room the other night. She didn't mean to; she's blaming it on the pot. She likes that Russell's so nice to Paula Toms, so respectful of her, even though she's shown herself to be somewhat abrasive. His kindness aside, Maddie can't seem to turn her attention away from him. There was a moment that night at the Overland, just before they kissed. They were standing on the balcony, and Russell was fingering the tiny whiskers at the end of his chin—he hadn't shaved in days—and Maddie felt this tremor of arousal that startled her. She had no idea how to interpret it. The next thing she knew he was kissing her. Or she was kissing him. She isn't entirely sure how it started. And now, whenever he says anything, anything at all, she's filled with this unknown warmth, followed by a prickle that stems from her neckline and flowers in her ears. She grows almost dizzy, as if she's fallen into some sort of swoon, like the women in the romance novels her mother reads—not to be confused with the strange, detached, inhibited feeling of being stoned.

She feels it right now, that warmth and prickle. That almost-dizziness. It's more than being turned on. Maddie is overwhelmed by it, the big, happy feeling inside her.

They haven't discussed the kiss even once, though Maddie tries at every turn to express her affection for him, taking his hand, caressing his back. It happened too quickly, too carelessly, both of them wasted, but she doesn't blame him for it. She was a willing participant, even if the whole thing is a bit of a blur.

Last night they camped in an RV park in a town called Dayton, and Maddie awoke at three a.m. to a chill deep in her bones, the sleeping bag unzipped, the tent dark and still, Russell asleep beside her. Paula Toms was in the backseat of the Corolla with one of the falsa blankets. Maddie sat up and watched the small movements of Russell's eyelids, staring for a long time at his face, which, in spite of the stubble, looked so youthful, so vulnerable, without its thin-rimmed glasses, as though he were a boy who'd been dressed up as a man. She wanted to touch her fingertips to his forehead, his nose, his lips. She reached out her hand, pulling back at the last moment, a slick, shivery urgency between her legs. She thought of the only time she's ever had sex, when she lost her virginity to Darin Swordoski in the wooden shed behind his house.

They were on the swings in Darin's backyard, twisting them around and letting the swings spin free, and after a while he tipped his handsome face toward Maddie and kissed her, more intensely than he usually did. Darin's parents were asleep in their bedroom, and he took her hand and guided her coolly to the shed, where no one would see them, no one would hear. He opened the door and switched on a battery-powered light in the same unworried way, as if showing her to a honeymoon suite, his smile suggesting the keenness and assurance of a young leading man—a Daniel Radcliffe, an Ezra Miller. He got a couple of lounge-chair cushions from the corner, dusted them off with his hand, and arranged them side by side at Maddie's feet. She'd never wanted anything more... and then, suddenly, she *didn't* want it. But it was too late, it was already happening. "Swords," she said. "Swords." Maddie wanted her father to come rescue her. She heard the noisy trill of summer insects outside, the screech of an owl. After that everything sounded muffled, as though her ears were stuffed with cotton. At one point, Darin's heel hit the door and the door swung open and Maddie looked out at the black granite sky, star-flecked and glinting. When it was over, he sat up against a wall of the shed and pulled her into his arms. She looked down at her shirtless chest. The skin looked rubbery, embalmed, in the blue fluorescent light; her nipples, shriveled inward, were the color of Silly Putty. She folded her arms, closed her eyes, feeling the winglike motion of Darin Swordoski's eyelashes against her neck.

What would it be like to have sex with a man who's so much older than she is—who's practically her uncle? At one time the idea would have grossed her out, made her gag, made her hurl. But now...

What would it be like, Maddie wonders, to have sex with someone she really cares about?

She sits down on a stool next to Russell, savoring the smell of his unwashed skin. He slurps the last of his float.

"Breakfast of peons," he says, getting up from the counter.

He buys some granola bars, a packet of beef jerky, some bottles of water. They plan to hike in the woods around Lake Tahoe, at a place called Zephyr Cove, then camp there for the night.

Paula Toms is taking forever to find a gift for her sister. A few minutes later she walks up to Maddie holding a toy sheriff's badge and says, "This'll do just fine."

•

At the campground, Maddie and Paula Toms wait in the Corolla while Russell goes inside the office and pays for the site. Maddie stuffs the tiger's eye into the glove compartment. When he comes back, they drive through a sprawl of tents and motor homes and

SUVs, slender conifers sprouting up from the needle-packed earth, lining the road like the balusters of a staircase. The campsite has its own parking space but not much else. A fire ring with a cooking grate. A large green container—a bear-proof food locker, Russell explains—that resembles the old steel desk her father used to have at the WEPCO plant. They get out and stand by the front of the car. Paula Toms seems offended by the concept of a hike, narrowing her eyes and pointing her chin as Russell explains how they're going to walk through the woods and along the lake. "What for?" she asks. "Why would anybody want to do that?" He responds that people like hiking for a variety of reasons. As a means of soaking up sunlight and warmth on a beautiful day, for instance. Of connecting with nature. Of getting some exercise.

"I'll be right here in this automobile," Paula Toms says, knocking on the hood, wearing the safari hat again. They had lunch at a deli in Genoa, and a caraway seed has lodged itself between her two front teeth.

"We won't be back for a while," Russell tells her. "You're going to just sit here?"

"You've got that perfectly right, Mr. Walk Around A Lake For No Reason At All."

"We're not going to walk around the entire lake. We're only— look, why don't I put up the tent first," he says. "Then you can at least take a nap or something."

"The backseat of this car suits me good and dandy," Paula Toms says, getting back in the Corolla. "This is a real blue-ribbon vehicle you've got here. Stop pretending it isn't."

Maddie and Russell walk down to the cove, which looks as if it belongs in the Caribbean. It seems like a mirage after their twelve long days in the desert, the sand whitish, fine-grained, the water so clean you can see directly to the bottom. People swim, or skim Frisbees, or lounge on beach towels beneath enormous umbrellas. The sun shines warmly on Maddie's shoulders. They find a trail that begins at the shoreline, winding into the thin green woods. Russell wears boots and jeans and a soiled purple T-shirt, Maddie her Jack Purcells, her shorts, her button-down. The needles on the trail are spongy beneath their feet, and the surface of the lake sparkles between the trees.

The day grows cloudy but it's still warm, still dry, and during the hike they swig from the bottles of water until they've drunk it all—Maddie in front, acutely aware of Russell's presence behind her. She wishes she were wearing some type of ankle-length dress, something matronly to hide her legs and her butt. She doesn't like her legs, which by nature are pale and, despite three years of long-distance running, muscleless, and she hates her butt, which is too wide and too soft, squashy as ground beef in plastic wrap. Her short arms are out of proportion to the rest of her body, and her eyes are too dark, too small, too far apart, and she resents her hair for its floaty indifference and the fact that it seems to possess no true color, sometimes blond, other times brown, other times a sort of yellowish-orange, depending on the season or the time of day. And oh yes, her breasts. Her breasts might as well be nonexistent, each one reminding her of a little plastic top, the kind you might find in a Happy Meal or a toy-capsule vending machine, the kind you could fit in the coin pocket of a pair of Levi's. Guys rarely ask her out—not, Maddie is certain, because of her superior intellect, not because she's on course to be valedictorian of her class and they therefore think her intimidating, but because of what Frank Harris, the fastest member of the men's cross-country team, once called her "itty-bitty titties." She was wearing a form-fitting tank top at the time, and he went on to say that Maddie was in fact the *head* of the Itty-Bitty-Titty *Committee*, and when she responded that committees don't have *heads*, they have *chairs*, Frank Harris and his teammates, stretching near the faculty parking lot before practice, erupted in laughter. Throughout her childhood her father told her she was beautiful, a princess, destined to break a multitude of hearts: what fathers are supposed to tell their daughters. For a time, she actually believed him.

They stop to rest at a bend in the trail. Maddie leans against a boulder nestled between two ponderosas. Beyond the trail is a wide gap in the trees, and the lake, improbably blue, stirs with whitecaps. She looks up at the two slender pines.

"Did you read about that tree-killer guy?" she asks, making conversation. She's so nervous around him now. "Back in Vegas? The one who got thirty years for killing like five hundred trees?"

"I haven't," Russell says. "No."

"He lived in this retirement community up on a hill, and he was angry that some oaks I guess the city had planted were ruining his view of the Strip. From his back deck or something. He was in his sixties, I think, and he files some complaint and gets no response, so he decides to solve the problem himself. He chops off the tops of all the trees."

"You and trees." He leans beside her against the boulder. "Just like your dad."

Russell's right. Since elementary school she's had a deep affection for them: the mesquites and acacias that grow shaggily along the avenues of Summerlin and Green Valley; the piñons, junipers, and white firs scattered throughout the wilderness of Mount Charleston, where Maddie and her parents used to go for weekend picnics when she was a girl; the ancient Chinese elms that shade the residential streets of central Las Vegas. She has cousins who live in that part of town, and Maddie's always taken by the impossible heights of the elms, which tower forty, fifty feet over streetlights and houses, some of the trunks as big around as a tractor tire. On a windy autumn day, the leaves high above will ruffle among the knotty branches before drifting in large groups, snowlike, to the ground. She might bend down and look closely at one, examining the midrib and the lateral veins, the serrated margin and the apex, the apple-yellow hue—units of its beauty. In what little spare time she has, between student-council meetings and band practice and cross-country practice and the nightly hours she devotes to her homework, Maddie reads about trees of all varieties, memorizing bark surfaces, the shapes of leaves, canopy sizes, growth rates. She attributes her interest to her father, who was himself fascinated by them. Like Maddie, her father studied them as a side interest, collecting numerous books on forestry and arboriculture, and she strives to match his impressive knowledge of their particulars.

"So this guy," she says, "he doesn't really chop the trees *down*. He just kind of cuts them in half so he can see the Strip again, you know? But he doesn't stop with the ones behind his place. He keeps going, chopping trees in half all over the city. Some of them he just carves up, enough so that they'll die a slow death. No one knows who's responsible, but then one night a retired cop's driving down Green Valley Parkway and spots him in the act. The cop gets out with a golf club and chases the guy, and when he catches him, this old man, a pruning saw falls out of the guy's jacket." She watches as a breeze tousles Russell's hair. "When the police searched his place, they found like a ten-page manifesto or something, all about ridding the world of trees forever."

"Arboricide," he says. "Is that a word?"

He smiles, and Maddie leans in and kisses him.

"Whoa. Hey, hey, hey." Russell pushes her off, stepping away from the boulder. "Maddie. Sweetheart."

"What?"

"We need to talk," he says.

She looks down at her tennis shoes. She wants to run. Run back to the campsite. Run all the way back to Las Vegas. "I just—I thought we—" She folds her arms, angry now. "It's not like I'm some little girl."

"Look," Russell says softly. He leans beside her again, taking her hand.

"Don't touch me," Maddie says, and jerks it away.

"Maddie."

"Why do you have to be such a loser?"

"Excuse me?"

"You're a fucking loser. I don't even like you anymore, okay? I only kissed you the other night— I don't even *know* why."

"All right," Russell says, his voice leaden with sadness. She's hurt him. Good.

"Fuck off," Maddie says. She starts to walk back down the trail.

"Hey."

She turns on her heel. He's come around to the other side of the boulder, hands on his hips.

"This is a difficult time," he says. "For both of us."

"You know what people say when the name Russell Martin comes up? They say you're a joke. That's what my father used to tell me, anyway." A lie. "A pothead," Maddie says. "A failure. Just ask Emma. Why do you think she cheated on you?"

"That's enough!"

Russell starts toward her down the trail and Maddie takes one of the polished stones from her pocket and whips it at him, hitting him in the neck.

"Jesus!" he hollers, bending over, his hand pressed to the skin. "What the hell!"

She walks back to him. "I'm sorry. I didn't know what you were going to do."

Russell sits down in the dirt. "I wasn't going to do *anything*."

When he moves his hand away she sees a welt taking shape below his ear.

"What *was* that?" he says. "What's the matter with you?"

"Are you okay?"

"Just back off."

He labors to his feet, the welt the color of an eggplant. "You know what?" He draws in a breath. "It was your dad."

"Huh?"

"The guy. The affair Emma was having. It was your father. You want to say hurtful things? You want to hurt me? There you go. How does *that* make you feel?"

"Are you serious?"

"I wish I could tell you I wasn't, trust me. But yeah. Fucking yeah. The crazy thing is, I always knew. And guess what? Emma fessed right up when I asked her about it, which, to put it all together for you, is why we're here at the moment. So now you know, now you get to deal with that fun bit of news. Like you said, you're not some little girl."

Maddie's stomach lurches. Over the water, a cloud opens wide, letting through a filmy shaft of sunlight.

"How could you do that to someone?" she says. "Even if it's true. How could you say something like that to me?"

She runs off without him. By the time she's made it back to the cove, the clouds have broken up entirely and the day is sunny again. Walking up to their site, Maddie has a spell of dizziness, and she leans against a wooden marker post and vomits into the brush.

Russell

In the spring of 1981, Russell and Andrew found a tortoise in the desert south of their neighborhood. They named him Roger Waters. (Pink Floyd was their favorite band.) They'd met in the fall, and by now their friendship was as important to Russell as anything: his baseball-card collection; his blue Schwinn King-Sting; his beloved copy of *The Wall*, a double album he'd saved his allowances for, its surfaces smudged from wear. They kept the tortoise in Andrew's backyard, feeding him uncooked broccoli and stale Pringles. In the space of a week his shell grew pale, cracking in several places. It smelled like the length of skin between Russell's inner thigh and his scrotum.

Then one of the plates sloughed off into the grass, revealing a yellowish, puddinglike pus, and a white froth began to ooze from the corners of the tortoise's mouth. Lesions marred the soccer-ball pattern of his shell, the plates continuing to decay, dropping off like scabs. For hours he would stand at the edge of the small flagstone patio and look steadily from side to side, as though waiting to cross a highway. He no longer ate.

"We need to put him out of his misery," said Russell one Saturday in April. "A mercy killing. I hate to say it, but that's our only option."

They were walking home from 7-Eleven, down a long block of single-story tract houses. Painted off-white or pinkish-yellow or caramel, each house in their neighborhood resembled a tasty dessert: each one, with its stuccoed walls, appeared edible and sweet, some kind of confection of coconut or marzipan. The sun was veiled in a cottony haze. Driveways were stained with oil, and green tumbleweeds grew in yards of red decorative stone.

"That's cold-blooded," Andrew said. "I worry about you some-times."

"Have you *seen* that animal?" Russell peeled the plastic lid off his San Diego Padres Slurpee cup. He tossed the lid and the straw over his shoulder and drank what was left of the cherry-flavored contents. "It's inhuman to keep him alive."

"Inhu*mane*. And no, it isn't. I'm going to get my mom to take him to the vet. He's just a little sick. It's no big deal."

Rumor had it that Andrew's mother was a gambler and an alky—that she stayed out all night playing the tables downtown, then showed up wasted as Andrew was leaving for school in the morning. She wore cutoff jeans and tight T-shirts, and had the silky, wavy hair of a fashion model. His father had served in Vietnam, and walked with a limp. He tinkered endlessly with the old Econoline stranded at their curb, cursing from beneath the chassis. He never said a word to anybody. It was unlikely that either of them would take the ailing tortoise to a vet.

"His shell looks like a rotten cantaloupe," Russell said.

"You want to club him with a baseball bat? Is that what you want to do? Drown him in a fucking bathtub? He's a pet. He's *our* pet."

"There's other ways." Russell wound up and pitched the empty Slurpee cup at a mailbox mounted on a post. "I don't want him to suffer anymore, all right?"

Here and there the decorative stones spilled onto the sidewalk, and they took turns kicking them into the street. He remembered other reptiles he'd taken from the desert, with other friends. Lizards, mostly—striped or speckled or spiky-skinned. Russell would keep them in Tupperware containers or cardboard boxes, where, refusing to eat the fire ants and grasshoppers he fed them in the evening, they grew dim-eyed and died. Gradually, for one reason or another, those other friendships had died as well, until he'd found himself alone. Then he'd met Andrew.

"What other ways?" Andrew said.

"Suffocation, for one. That wouldn't be too bad. I think it's like falling asleep or something. Like one of us could pinch his little nostrils shut for a minute or two, and that'd be it. It'd be all over. He wouldn't even put up a fight—he's a turtle. What defenses does he have?"

"He'd pull his head back into his shell, Professor Genius. That's what they do. Why do you think he carries that thing around all the time? Besides, he can breathe through his mouth like we can."

"I surrender," Russell said. "You know it all, as usual."

Andrew took a pouch of Red Man from a back pocket of his shorts. He'd stolen it from his father's reserve in the crisper drawer of their refrigerator. "You don't have to be a cock-munch about it," he said, tucking a dark lump of chew between his cheek and his gum.

"The bathtub idea's not such a bad one," Russell muttered.

As they neared the end of the block, Andrew flattened a Coke can with his tennis shoe, singing a rhyme that was making its way around the neighborhood:

"You motherfuckin' titty-suckin' two-balled bitch!
Your mama's in the kitchen cookin' red-hot shit!
Your daddy's in jail
Raisin' some hell!
Your sister's on the corner sayin', 'Pussy for sale!'
You go downstairs to get a drink
And smack your balls on the kitchen sink!
You go outside to cool 'em off
But a goddamn neighbor bites 'em off!"

Russell rolled his eyes. "That song makes no sense."

"Neither does your plan to kill Roger Waters."

"We can always just let him loose in the desert. Put him back where he came from, let him sort things out on his own. At least then he can die with his family," said Russell. "In his homeland."

"His *homeland*?"

"Who knows—maybe he'll get better if he's back in his natural environment."

Andrew spat. "It's a thought," he said.

Around this time Russell and Andrew had started seeking out dark, enclosed places where they could be alone together. The men's room of the 7-Eleven, where they'd turn off the lights and lock themselves in the tiny, reeking stall. A vacant office park near their school, a rear door of which someone had jimmied, breaking off the handle. The back of the Econoline, when Andrew's father wasn't home. Their closets. Their garages. The sessions would last for five or ten or fifteen minutes, sometimes longer. "Trust me," Andrew would say. "It's totally normal. All kinds of guys do it."

Andrew's older sister lived in Tucson with her boyfriend and their three-year-old son, and at the end of the month Andrew's parents drove out for a visit, leaving him home alone for a couple of days. He and Russell had the house to themselves. The place reminded Russell of *The Waltons*. Andrew's mother had a thing for antiques, which didn't seem to jibe with her reputation in the neighborhood as a gambler and a drinker. Everything was from an earlier time, most of it pretty shabby—the furniture, the light fixtures, the doorknobs. White lace curtains covered the windows, at odds with the brick-patterned linoleum in the kitchen. Pewter candleholders decorated the mantelpiece. An old-fashioned record player, a Victrola, stood against a wall in the family room. Andrew put on some music: Mendelssohn's "Violin Concerto in E Minor," he explained. "Listen to the final movement," he told Russell. "It's fucking amazing."

Russell sat down on the wooden-armed couch, its cushions stained and ragged, his Adidas propped up on a coffee table that looked as if it had been around since Napoleon. He didn't know who Mendelssohn was, or what Andrew meant by "the final movement." The Victrola had a beautiful, rose-colored finish but was coated with dust, cobwebs netting the corners of its open top. As the notes rose and fell, Andrew talked about the "timbre" and the "coda," calling them "transcendent," closing his eyes as though savoring something delicious. He was a talented musician—he played guitar, piano, and violin, and had even written a few songs of his own—but Russell had never heard him talk this way before, never heard him use such big words. It didn't even seem like Andrew anymore. They went to a public school and lived in a solidly working-class neighborhood, and years later it would occur to Russell that Andrew had hidden this aspect of himself, stowing it away like a scandalous secret.

"The final movement, huh?" Russell said. "Sounds more like a *bowel* movement to me."

But Andrew kept his eyes closed. On the coffee table, next to its case, sat his violin, reddish-brown with an inky trim. Like everything else in the room, it bore an old-world shabbiness and looked out of place in the seventies-era house.

When the concerto was over, the arm lifted from the record and settled beside it with a series of noisy clicks. He put on Mozart next, then some guy named Kreisler, then Billy Joel's *Glass Houses*, and then he drew the curtains and turned off all the lights and sat next to Russell on the couch. The room was still perfectly bright, and Russell saw the embarrassment on his face as Andrew reached over and unzipped Russell's shorts.

Since the age of seven or eight Russell had had an acute, nearly debilitating awareness of himself, but he was twelve years old now, almost a teenager, and he kept waiting for it to go away. He felt dizzy and shaky, ugly and incompetent. Whenever they did this he couldn't stop doubting his appearance, his intelligence, his general personality, replaying in his mind every word he'd spoken over the past hour or so. He didn't know exactly what to call it or how it had come into being, this constant self-assessment, which was only worsening the older he got. He could no longer remember when he'd moved freely and comfortably through the world, unimpeded by his thoughts.

With a tentative hand, he unzipped Andrew's jeans, "Don't Ask Me Why" blaring from the record player. Andrew was diabetic, and when he was younger he used to get up once or twice a night for a drink of water. The bathroom faucet would always wake his father, and so his father had taken to sealing all the faucets in the house with duct tape before he went to bed each night, leaving Andrew to suffer his thirst until morning. Strangely, it eased Russell's discomfort to think of this, and soon he was able to relax, his head falling to one side. Then the song ended and their hard breathing was the only noise in the room. Just when he thought he was going to burst with pleasure, a rasping, whistling sound came from the backyard, and they looked over to see Roger Waters standing at the patio door, his brown beak pressed to the glass. His mouth—that of an old man without his dentures in—was half open and frothing.

"Goddammit," Andrew said. "I was right where I needed to be. I'm gonna kill that fucking turtle."

"I'm glad we finally see eye to eye."

They zipped themselves up. Andrew got up and turned the lights back on, opened the curtains. Russell watched the tortoise from the couch, the raspy whistling growing louder. They decided then and there to put him to death.

They filled a bathtub with water, and Andrew played "Goodbye Cruel World" on the Victrola. But when they went outside, Roger Waters was already dead, splay-legged at the edge of the patio, a green fly buzzing around his shell.

●

Now Russell sits up in the tent and runs his fingers through his hair, his own legs splayed out in front of him. A riot of silhouettes plays across the polyester dome, branches swaying in the wind. It was the slam of a car door that woke him. The woman, Paula Toms, is spending the night alone in the Corolla again. Maddie's huddled in the sleeping bag. She went to sleep with her back to him, still livid—justifiably. How could he have been so callous, so rash?

Russell was dreaming. In the dream, he was at the wheel of some unknown car, speeding down a highway in an unknown city. He remembers the narrative, such as it was, in its entirety. The car shook as the tires rode the pavement markers that divided the lanes, joggling along for what seemed like hours. Then he drifted fully into the adjacent lane, and a horn was blaring, and he saw a car whose windows were mere inches from his own, a car he was about to sideswipe. Andrew was driving it, and then it was Emma, then Maddie, the three of them sobbing in turn. Then the horn was overpowered by the sound of steel scraping steel, the two cars fender to fender, angling toward a concrete barrier that ran down the center of the highway.

Then the dream proceeded quickly, in unfocused fragments. The car Russell drove was lifted into the air, turning upside down as it soared over the barrier, the other car spinning into traffic. And then Russell was lying in a bed in a very white room, the movement of his lungs resulting in a pain unlike any, each breath an agonizing effort. His head, too, was a source of extraordinary pain. Everything slowed back down. The darkened screen of a suspended television watched him from across the room as he wondered if Andrew/Emma/Maddie had survived. He suffered in the bed for months, and no one ever checked on him, no doctors or nurses. Nobody came.

At last the door of the room opened slowly and in wandered Roger Waters the tortoise, munching on a Pringle—his mouth free of froth, his shell returned to its original condition. He stared at Russell with his small, black-bean eyes as he finished the chip. Then the tortoise smiled freakily, showing his ridgy green gums. That was when Russell woke up.

●

At present, he pulls on his boots, fishes the flashlight out of his backpack, and crawls out of the tent. The night is exceptionally dark—he can't find the moon, and the misty white belt of the galaxy crosses the sky overhead—but here and there yellow lights shine down from tall wooden poles. The silence is spooky; he doesn't even hear any insects. Somehow the swaying branches make no noise at all. He imagines being attacked from behind by a bear, and considers crawling back into the tent to get the Ruger from his backpack.

He shines the flashlight into the Corolla. The woman's helmet is on the console, wedged between the two front seats, but she herself is gone. Russell walks around the campground. Nothing stirs but the wind. Everyone is asleep.

He goes behind a tree and takes his one-hitter from his pocket and gets high. He feels the tender lump on his neck. He can't believe what he said to Maddie today, or how he felt when they kissed on the hotel's balcony: invigorated, alive with desire. For dinner last night, they ate hot dogs and baked beans in front of the fire—Maddie refusing to speak to him, the woman talking nonstop as she devoured three of the charred dogs in rapid succession—and Russell caught himself glancing at Maddie's breasts, which stood out whenever she sat back in his lawn chair. He feels so lecherous. His love for her is ample and pure; he's known her all her life. Now he can't allow himself to even look at her.

Why are they still traveling together? Why, under the circumstances, hasn't he taken her home? The morning they checked out of the hotel he used the computer in the reception area to google the age of consent in Nevada. If what he'd done was a crime—if he was guilty of some kind of sexual misconduct—he would turn himself in and accept the consequences. But he's broken no law. The age of consent in Nevada, as in most states, is sixteen. Even so, what he did was sickening, wrong. He tries to clear his mind but cannot erase the memory of Maddie's lips pressing softly against his own.

He walks around some more, shining his flashlight over the tents and motor homes, searching for the woman. Then he hears something—footsteps—down one of the trails that begin at the campground. The trail disappears into the woods, and Russell nerves himself to follow it. The beam is a tunnel through the conifers, which smell extra piney, he thinks, in the absence of sound and natural light.

"Paula?" he whispers. "Is that you?"

"Right here!" the woman cries, suddenly appearing in the tunnel of light, turning around to face him.

"Shit!" Russell says. "You scared the hell of out me. Where are you going?"

"It isn't so easy to sleep in that car of yours, you know." She waves her arm, shooing a mosquito.

"I wouldn't guess it is. Do you want to come in the tent? We can all squeeze together."

"I liked it better when it was dark."

"Sorry," Russell says, turning off the flashlight. They stand opposite each other in the middle of the trail. "What are you doing out here?"

"Walking around."

His eyes adjust, and he can just make out the melancholy look on her face. Maybe it's only drowsiness. "You all right?"

"Sometimes I don't even know where I'm going," the woman says. "I just start walking, and I don't even know where I'm gonna end up."

"But a hike," he says, "that seemed crazy to you."

She shoos another mosquito. "I stayed in this place called Quakertown once. A bunch of wagons that were carrying the Liberty Bell stopped there during the Revolutionary War, and this man named Evan put the bell behind his house for the night, and all the guys that were taking the bell from this one city to this other city slept at some hotel called the Red Lion Inn." She stares at him. "Before it cracked. Way before."

"Right."

"See all those stars?" She points into the sky. "I'll tell you something about them."

"I'm listening," Russell says.

"That's where she lives now—Janie. That's where she is. Way up there."

"Your sister."

"Little Jane," the woman whispers. "She died, you know. She's not in Santa Barbara. That's something else I lied to you about." She blinks her eyes slowly at him. "Don't tell the other one. The girl."

"Maddie."

"Yes."

He nods. "Our secret."

"She died," the woman says again, still whispering. "She was just a little thing, with her pretty yellow hair. Pretty little Jane."

"I'm sorry," Russell says.

"Oh. I didn't realize that," says the woman, with great disappointment in her voice. "I didn't realize you were sorry."

He walks her back to the Corolla and they sit in the front seat with the windows down. Her sister drowned, she explains, in 1974, during a family vacation at the beach. Jane and their father were playing in the surf when out of nowhere a large wave crashed down on them, pulling her out. The woman—seven at the time—watched from their blanket in the sand, their mother at a snack bar getting the two girls ice-cream cones. By the time their father got to Jane, it was too late. The doll the woman carries in her duffel bag was her sister's favorite. It was with them at the beach that day, and the woman is traveling to Santa Barbara to return it.

"A pilgrimage," Russell says.

"It's something I need to do. Can you understand that? Can you appreciate a thing like that?"

"I think so," he says.

"Are you still sorry?"

"I am." He peers at her in the darkness. She wears the same oversized T-shirt she had on earlier today. "Of course."

"Have faith," she tells him. "Say your prayers. Try to understand."

Russell smiles.

"That's what my great-grandfather used to say. He was the smartest person I ever knew, and he spent a lot of time in India and this place called Chad, which is this country with a person's name, and he's gone now too, just like Jane." She looks out her window.

"You must have really loved them," Russell says.

He wonders about her parents, whom she hasn't mentioned before tonight. Are they dead? He wonders if her helmet once belonged to her great-grandfather, and why the man spent time in Asia and Africa, and how likely it is, given the unquestionable age difference, that the woman knew him so well. Russell can't see how she'll ever make it back to the beach where her sister died almost forty years ago. Is the story even true?

He thinks of his dream again—what does it signify?—and that poor desert tortoise, which he and Andrew snatched from its natural habitat and then killed by way of their stupidity and neglect.

Andrew. The remains of a seventh victim have been unearthed at the WEPCO site. Russell read about it at the campground's office, in the *Tahoe Daily Tribune*. Andrew's body is the only one that has yet to be found.

Russell thinks of Emma now, missing her more than ever.

"I know what that's like," he says. "Losing someone you love."

"You're always saying things, aren't you?" the woman says. "You're always saying that stuff that comes out of your mouth."

Emma

"Seven o'clock," Marcus Bauerkemper tells her, his full-bodied voice resounding through the receiver. "Say you'll be there."

"Should I bring a boom box and a Rubik's Cube? I haven't been to a spaghetti feed since Reagan was president," Emma says. She stares out the living-room window, curled up in Russell's La-Z-Boy, sunlight canting through the tilted blinds. "I didn't know they had them anymore."

"They do. *We* do. It's the church's annual fundraiser."

"What ever happened to a good old Friday-night fish fry? Now I'm craving haddock and cod."

"It isn't Lent," he says. "It isn't Friday. Besides, we leave the fish fries to the Catholics. Come on, tell me you're coming. You'll have a wonderful time."

Emma thinks back to the congregation at his church. Nobody there seemed like the kind of person she normally takes an interest in. Then she remembers how lonely she is. She's hung out with her friend Charlotte, the slot attendant from the Bora Bora, a couple of times after work, but all Charlotte does is talk about herself or the casino. Emma can never get a word in. Maybe stepping out of her comfort zone again isn't such a bad idea.

"Emma? You still there?"

"Still here," she says. "Do you always put so much time into recruiting new members?" She's playing hard to get. She likes his open, avuncular way of listening to her—of cheering her up.

Marcus Bauerkemper laughs heartily. "Like I said, I'm making a special effort. I believe that you and I met for a purpose, Emma. Besides, I wanted to see how you're doing. After what happened to us the other day—that bird."

"A fortune-teller told me to expect an event that would alter my life. Maybe that was it. I don't feel any different, if it was," Emma says. "I can't afford to make some big donation, if that's what this is about."

"Five dollars, all you can eat. I've got you covered, though. All you have to do is show up."

"Well, I suppose I—"

"Don't be late!" Marcus Bauerkemper says with a thundering excess of glee. "And hey, do yourself a solid: have a blessed rest of your day!"

A spaghetti feed? Did she just agree to go to a spaghetti feed? She's so lost, groping her way toward…what? What salvation are some quirky pastor and his caricature of a church going to provide? Her loneliness, needless to say, is only an extension of the real issue. Nothing can straighten out her life but Russell's return.

She sits there for a while with the phone in her lap, the recliner giving off the funky, hempy odor of his clothes. Despite her aversion to his habit, Emma keeps worrying that Russell has run out of his weed. She hates to admit it, but she knows he really does depend on the stuff for a balanced state of mind. Without it he's a squirrelly mess, especially, of course, during times of trouble.

Emma hopes Russell is as calm as he can be. Perhaps he's even managed to enjoy himself. Perhaps he's even forgiven her.

•

When she arrives at the church that evening, the parking lot is empty except for Marcus Bauerkemper's Maxima. She goes inside to find the lights dimmed in the vestibule, a white candle burning on the card table. Beside the candle is a ceramic vase that holds a long brown feather, like the ones from the bird that flew through her window. She can smell something cooking down a hall to the right of the nave, and hears noises coming from what has to be some kind of kitchen. Then Marcus Bauerkemper appears in the hall wearing an apron and an oven glove.

"You're here!" he booms, walking toward her. "Don't be mad. Give me a chance to explain."

"You've got one minute."

"I wanted to have dinner with you," he says. "I admit it, I'm in the wrong. I knew you'd never go for it, and the spaghetti feed was the only thing I could come up with." He smiles at her. Beneath the apron—which reads *Shiitake Happens* around a cartoon image of a dancing mushroom—he wears his creased blue jeans and a black band-collar shirt. "I was hoping you'd think the whole thing was…I don't know, sort of thoughtful, I guess."

"You *lied* to me?"

"The fundraiser was a few months back. So it does exist, at least. Not a total lie."

"I'm not quite sure how to react right now."

"Say you'll have dinner with me. Say you'll stay." He takes off the oven glove and sets it down on the table. "We have a connection, am I wrong? You feel it too," says Marcus Bauerkemper. "It isn't the kind of thing we can easily ignore." He takes the feather from the vase. "See this? It represents something. Would you like to know what that is?"

"I don't know that I do."

"It represents the future, Emma. This feather here is a remnant of what happened to us. Our near-death experience, let's call it, which changed the way I think about the world, and about God. And most importantly, about you." He waves the feather like a small flag. "You said it yourself: it was life-altering. Just think of the probability of such an event. *The physics.* I believe that bird was a sign, direct from the Lord above."

"I thought we had a connection too," she says. "Turns out I was wrong. I'm a married woman. I have a husband. Am I some kind of tramp in your eyes?"

Marcus Bauerkemper slides the feather behind his ear and says, "Don't move!" He goes into the nave and comes back promptly with two of the padded folding chairs, opening them like the fawning proprietor of a restaurant, extending a hand over the table. "Sit," he says. "Let's eat."

"There isn't going to be any dinner," she tells him, heading toward the doors, feeling more alone than ever.

"Emma," he says. "I made haddock. You said you were craving it."

She turns around. "I was obviously—are you *crying*?"

Marcus Bauerkemper shrugs. "I apologize." He wipes his eye with the hem of the apron. "It's just…I'm in a bit of trouble, you could say. I'm telling you the truth, all right? I'm coming clean. I'm ready to talk about it now." He has a frightened look on his face. More bullshit. "I thought you might be able to…" Clearing his throat, he takes the feather from behind his ear and places it back in the vase. "Maybe I could ask you a favor."

"A favor."

"I lost some money," he tells her. "A lot of money. Money that doesn't belong to me."

"Who does it belong to?" Emma says, though of course she knows. "Forget it. Why would I care?"

"Because you're a good person, Emma. I realized that the instant we met."

"You stole from your congregation," she says. "Is that it?"

He adjusts his glasses. "I've been thinking that maybe if you and I, I don't know, collaborated. At the Bora Bora, I mean."

"Are you saying what I think you're saying? Am I on *Candid Camera* or something? Please tell me."

"You occupy a unique position at that casino, Emma. An advantageous one. Wouldn't you agree?"

His tone has turned villainous. What sort of person is she dealing with here? She wants to bolt for the parking lot, but she has to be careful, she decides—be on the safe side. Stop insulting him and finesse her way to the refuge of her Civic.

"What you're referring to," she says. "I wouldn't know the first thing."

"It can be done," he says, "in a whole host of ways. Careful, artful ways." He winks, regaining his composure. "Ways that carry almost no element of risk."

"Your dinner smells delicious. I'm sure you put a lot of work into it, but I'm not the right person to—"

"Ways that are *gentle*," he says, placing a low-voiced emphasis on the word, making it sound slimy. "'Moderate in action, effect, or degree.' I'm not talking about robbing Fort Knox. What I have in mind—well, let's just say that if it's done correctly no one will ever even notice."

He comes over to her and takes her hand, letting out a long, contemplative breath. When Emma tries to take her hand away, Marcus Bauerkemper tightens his grip—not menacingly (though Emma's pulse is beating in her face, a tiny ball being dribbled against her forehead) but in a way that suggests foreknowledge and confidence. And so she opens her mind to it, the notion of scamming the casino, a notion she has never considered, not once, in all the years she's worked there. She thinks of her earnings relative to the physical and mental demands of her job. She thinks of all the bad tippers, of Russell's hourly wages, the low balance of their checking account, their nonexistent savings, their credit-card debt and the bank's recent threat to foreclose on their mortgage. The possibility of financial freedom sends a corkscrew of excitement up her spine. It would take time: weeks. Months, perhaps. It would take patience and guile. It would take great caution. But what if she got them back on their feet? What if she tracked Russell down, wherever he is, and told him their worries about money are over? What if he forgave her as a result? What if Russell came home?

Has she no moral compass at all? And what would happen if she and Marcus Bauerkemper were caught? A class D felony charge, Emma knows. Prison time if they were convicted.

Still. She's grown to hate her monotonous, dead-end job. What might she have done in her life had she not chosen it—by process of elimination—shortly after college, over twenty years ago now? What is she even doing in a city like Las Vegas? Why was she born and raised in this breeding ground for excess and iniquity? Why has she stayed? She majored in finance at UNLV. Working tables at a sawdust joint on Fremont Street was the least of her employment options, the pay abusively insufficient. She could have been a casino executive of some sort. A financial planner. An investment banker in a big city like San Francisco or New York. She has the intellect for it, a mind for numbers. But she lacks the confidence to challenge herself in a more engaging line of work. (Isn't this the reason she went back to school to become a dealer?) Not that there's anything wrong with making your living on the floor of a casino, and not that Russell, who has a degree from UNLV of his own, has done anything particularly impressive with *his* life. It's simply that Emma is selling herself short. She knows she is capable of so much more.

She's trained to spot scam artists, to control a table so as not to be taken advantage of. Emma lied to him: she knows all the schemes, the sleights of hand. Every dealer does. But despite her training, despite the vigilance of the pit bosses, despite the state-of-the-art surveillance and the undercover cops, casinos throughout the world lose huge sums of money every year to cheaters. There's always a chance of getting away with it, especially for those in the know.

"Both of us can come out ahead, my dear. Both of us," Marcus Bauerkemper tells her, nodding conclusively, "can benefit."

Simon

There are two kinds of people in the world, Simon thinks. Those who know themselves, whose character is immutable, and those who don't—those who change fundamentally, curiously, from one moment to the next, depending on the surroundings, the circumstances, the company.

Know thyself: the most quoted of the Delphic maxims. He minored in philosophy at Western Michigan, where he wondered for eight consecutive semesters who exactly he was. *Who is Simon Addison? What is he made of?* Nearly three decades later, he still can't say.

Could he have guessed, in his early twenties, that one day he would leave a man to die in order to save his own skin? That he would be an unfaithful husband? A person who lies without hesitation?

His twenties. He should have sewn his wild oats back then. Simon regrets that he has no memories of a hedonistic bachelorhood. He thought at times about leaving Michigan, moving in search of thrills from one big city to the next: Los Angeles, San Francisco, Chicago, New York. He imagined himself working odd, minimum-wage jobs, carousing until the wee hours, spending all his money on rent and booze and savoring his unrestricted life as a nomad. He did nothing of the sort. He settled down early, got comfortable, and the old, compelling voice is still there in his head (he always assumed it would fade away): *Anywhere*, it whispers, *is better than where you are now.*

Sometimes Simon can't believe Rebecca has been his wife for so long. He still loves her, even though he has now had sex with another woman—which has happened three more times over the past few days. One of the times Juliet was going down on him on the couch in her living room and the two of them did something he can't stop remembering, something he's never done with Rebecca. He came in Juliet's mouth, and instead of swallowing it or spitting it out, she brought her face up to his and kissed him, passing it to Simon, and then Simon went down on her in return, fingering her while his own semen dribbled from his lips. She clenched his ears and locked her sturdy legs around him and screamed. It was several minutes before she caught her breath. They lay voiceless on the carpet for several more, the sharp taste lingering on Simon's tongue.

It's bad enough that he made no effort to save Andrew Huntley on the day of the explosions. Now he's treating himself to Huntley's wife, making love to her on the man's furniture, in his pool, against his washing machine—everywhere is fair game but the master bedroom. Each time, when Simon returns home to Rebecca, he feels the way he did atop the desert bluff that morning in May. Sourmouthed. Tight-throated. Sick to his stomach. As far as he knows, his wife has no suspicions at all. He wonders how long the affair can last. How long will he let it?

Once, when Daniel and Michaela were little, Rebecca was at a friend's for her monthly book club and Simon put the kids to bed and opened a can of beer and started to watch a Tigers game on television. Halfway through an inning the old voice whispered to him and he had an impulse to leave the house. He turned off the game, locked up, and took a walk around the block. When he got home, fifteen minutes later, Daniel and Michaela were sleeping soundly—everything was fine. The next time the book club met, Simon walked for over an hour. Again Daniel and Michaela were sleeping when he returned. The third time he left them, Rebecca was in Kalamazoo visiting her college roommate, and Simon went to the local bar-and-grill and ate a late dinner by himself. Leaving his children unattended for so long gave him an unexplainable rush. He drove home slowly, and once again the two of them were asleep, perfectly fine, when he walked in. The situation with Juliet is no different. He does what he does, and Rebecca and the kids are none the wiser.

He doesn't want to lose her, the mother of his children—the only other woman with whom he's ever been intimate. What would she do, though, if she found out, if Rebecca followed him, for instance, the way Simon has followed Juliet, and saw him pulling his pickup into some stranger's driveway, saw some woman greeting him at the door? What would happen?

Perhaps nothing. Perhaps she'd bury the information as far down inside her as she could, as he himself tried to do after leaving Andrew Huntley to die. Perhaps she wouldn't confront him at all. Why risk their marriage? (To say nothing of the kids' bright futures. Who knows how Daniel and Michaela, even as adults, might react to the collapse of their parents' relationship?) What is the likeliest result of a divorce? Loneliness. And what is worse than being alone?

●

Simon has been offered every position he's applied for, at Tommy's and Fabulous Freddy's and Circle K. The one he accepted, four days ago, has aroused in Rebecca a vociferous anger—for its low pay, its remote location, its "randomness." He's taken a job at the gift shop of the Red Rock Canyon National Conservation Area. (What is she going to tell people? How can they afford to maintain their current lifestyle?) Red Rock Canyon is a forty-five-minute drive from their neighborhood, west of the city. This is his second day on the job.

He tried to explain that he took it precisely *because* of its remote location: the middle of the desert, the place he so loves. WEPCO was out in the desert too, but this job doesn't require Simon to risk his life. The gift shop is called Elements and is located in the visitor center. Beyond the building are escarpments, cliffs, and ravines, a breathtaking spread of eolian sandstone. Between the mountains and the city are great flatlands of alfalfa, lilies, and marigolds. Yesterday, during both his breaks, Simon stood at the edge of the parking lot with his hands in his pockets, taking long, even breaths—taking it all in.

The gift shop carries clay pots and rainsticks and turquoise jewelry, some Panama Jack merchandise, things like that. Beside him at the cash register, perched on the counter, is a mechanical tortoise named Mojave Max, which sells for $29.99. Mojave Max is the official mascot of the Clark County Desert Conservation Program, and bears a shameful resemblance to Franklin the Turtle. Taped to his shell is an index card that reads PRESS ME, and when you press the shell, the tortoise chirps, "Stash your trash! Keep our deserts clean!" This single nuisance aside, Simon can tell he's going to like his new job. He's had to memorize an exhaustive fact sheet about the canyon—its evolution since the Paleozoic era, the flora and fauna that thrive here—but it took him all of five minutes to learn how to operate the register. It's just the sort of mindless work he's been looking for. On top of that, gift-shop proceeds go to desert maintenance, school field trips, and community outreach. The job matters.

Now, having taken a few bags of trash to the dumpster, Simon stands in the parking lot again. During the summer, the shop stays open until eight. It's half past seven, and a saucer-shaped cloud hovers in the sky. The sun screams light. In the eastern distance, across the city, Frenchman Mountain arches its jaggy spine. When Simon turns around, Rebecca is pulling her Taurus into a space near the doors, Daniel beside her, Michaela in the back.

Simon wasn't expecting his family to stop by. His children call home, on average, three or four times a month, updating Simon and Rebecca on the developments of their lives, but he feels more distant with them than ever, regretting the amount of time he spent at the plant when they were younger. Why didn't he quit years ago? Why wasn't he a more available father? The older they get the farther away they seem to live—Philadelphia and New York might as well be Hong Kong and Shanghai—and the less he recognizes them when they return, Daniel's hair longer now, thinner, browner somehow, Michaela's boyishly short and dyed bright blond (she reminds Simon of Hermey the Elf, from the Rudolph special she used to love as a girl). They flew home the night before. Over slices of apple pie at the kitchen table, Simon informed them of his change of employment, and they stared at him with looks of incredulity and scorn. Even so, it's nice to have the two of them back.

"What a surprise!" he says as his family emerges from the car in T-shirts, shorts, and sandals. Simon is instantly conscious of his own outfit, which looks like a Boy Scout uniform: beige cargo pants and a matching button-down, the latter crowded with epaulets, flap pockets, and colorful badges. He watches Rebecca bite her lip.

"We had dinner at Battista's," she tells him. "The kids' idea. The nostalgia factor, I guess." The restaurant, a local favorite just off the Strip, has been serving its delightful Italian fare for decades. "They wanted to say hello since we were already halfway here. So—hello."

He hugs his children. Not only is Daniel's hair different but he's been lifting weights as well. The breadth of his shoulders makes Simon feel as though he's hugging a stranger.

"Hey, Dad."

Michaela looks around. "There's something so…*Martian* about this place."

"Come on in," Simon says. "We're just about to close up."

His coworker, a semiretired grandmother named Lynne, gives a brief hello before disappearing into the stockroom with an armload of khaki bush vests. The gift shop is empty, and they stand around a table of novelty scalp massagers, one of which is in the shape of a tarantula. Simon picks it up, tapping its hairy metal legs against his hand.

"I know it seems strange," he says, "but this works for me. I like it out here—I like the job. So far, at least. I don't even think about the plant anymore. That was a totally different me back then. That's what it feels like, anyway."

Rebecca sighs.

"I'm a little skeptical," Daniel says, "of this *new* you."

Michaela narrows her eyes. "Will I have to transfer to UNLV?"

"What? No, of course not. Don't you worry, your mother and I have everything accounted for."

Luckily, they have a 529 plan, just enough to cover his daughter's final year at Columbia. The house is another story.

"That's right," Rebecca says. "It's all figured out. Everything but paying for groceries and keeping the electricity on."

"So what's the deal?" Daniel asks. "Is this a rough patch or something? You're, what, fifty now? Life kinda sucks sometimes, Dad. Snap out of it."

"Hey," Rebecca says, cuffing their son on the arm.

"Fifty-*one*," says Michaela.

"Forty-eight," Simon says, "thank you very much. And yeah, maybe this *is* a rough patch I'm going through. I nearly died, Daniel. I almost went right up along with that place."

Because of finals, neither of his children came home in the wake of the explosions. They called him every day for a week, but Simon feels a balloon of resentment inflating inside him.

"You guys sell bottled water?" his wife asks. "We're getting low at the house. You know, after your meltdown." She isn't going to let him forget how he acted. "Listen. We're just a little confused, honey." Rebecca looks him in the eye, penitent. "I guess we're still trying to process things." It's the nicest she's sounded all week.

"Sorry," Daniel says. "Mom's right."

"If this is what you need, Daddy, I'm with you." His daughter takes his arm. "I'm on your side."

Daniel rolls his eyes. He walks a slow lap around the shop, trying on boonie hats and wraparound sunglasses. At the counter, he presses his finger to Mojave Max's shell and the toy tortoise utters its high-pitched appeal.

Michaela picks up one of the scalp massagers, this one made to resemble a tumbleweed. She slides it onto the back of Simon's head. "You get a discount on this stuff?"

As a teenager she went through a phase—to Simon's vexation—during which she wore nothing but black vinyl on the weekends, spending her free time at ninety-nine-cent movies with a bunch of kids who described themselves as "goth" and "steampunk": a fellowship of contemptuous misfits, set apart by their high grade-point averages and leather trench coats and polished brass pocket watches. Years before, she'd lean against the sink on tiptoe while Simon shaved in the morning, identifying the gobs of shaving cream floating in the water: *A hippo! A bicycle! Oscar the Grouch!* He can remember the pink Hello Kitty swimsuit she was in love with when she was two, and rubbing sunscreen on his daughter's arms, the spray of freckles and the fine golden hairs. He can remember her chubby little nose, red as a radish, the morning she was born.

She sets the scalp massager back on the table. Simon feels so sentimental all of a sudden—feels an inward quiver of embarrassment.

"I love you," he says, nevertheless. "You and your brother. I love you both, very much." He looks at Rebecca. "You too," he tells her.

Daniel comes back to where they're standing and Simon remembers other things as well. Holding his son's hand when he was a toddler, the tiny fingers limp in Simon's palm. The odor of his unwashed hair as he climbed into the tub each evening—a kind of dried-saliva smell that overwhelmed Simon with a sadness he could never understand. The time Daniel plucked a silk-swathed moth from a spiderweb in their yard, unwrapped it, and cried when the moth flew away.

"I love you," Simon says to him. He's proud of his boy, the would-be attorney. A grown, confident man.

Daniel looks him up and down, crossing his arms over his newly rounded chest. "Nice getup," he says.

●

Simon is still sleeping in, still skipping showers, eating unwholesome food. The next day, though, he's up early. He washes himself thoroughly, has a bowl of Grape-Nuts for breakfast, drinks a glass of water. He doesn't have to be at the gift shop until noon, and he puts on his helmet and his hydration pack and tells Rebecca he's heading out for a ride.

There's method in his madness. He called Juliet on his way home last night and they decided to spend the morning together—she'd cancel her a.m. appointments.

It's warm and cloudless, and Simon pedals briskly from one block to the next, past a dry wash and a substation and a neighborhood park, through a thick, wailing wind. At the corner of Stephanie Street and Horizon Ridge Parkway, he sees an elderly man he often passed during his commute to the plant. The man—white-haired and, Simon presumes, senile—likes to stand at the curb in plaid Bermudas and a sleeveless undershirt and smile at the daily freshet of automobiles. Simon always tensed when he saw him, particularly if he was driving in the right lane, afraid the man might lean too much from the sidewalk and get hit or cause a collision. Now and then Simon found himself stopped at the light observing the man, whose eyes would bulge as he wrung his hands and waited for the next surge of traffic, his smile never dimming. On one occasion a woman lowered her window and held out a bill, but the man took no notice. In all the time Simon drove past him on his way to work, he never once smiled back.

He turns up Stephanie Street now. In the little circular mirror attached to Simon's helmet, the man grows smaller and disappears. Daniel and Michaela were asleep when Simon left the house. He's glad he wasn't forced to talk to them. A crossness frizzles inside him as he rides. He keeps recalling the way Daniel responded to his new job—his own son treating him like he was some kind of ignoramus.

By the time he gets to Juliet's his anger has settled. They go straight to bed—to the bed she once shared with her husband. It's been understood that this is off limits, but this time Juliet leads him there by the hand, neither of them making mention of it.

Afterward, she gets up and leaves the room unclothed and comes back with an open bottle of George Dickel rye. Eight o'clock in the morning. A weekday, no less.

"What about your afternoon appointments?"

"I'll cancel those as well."

"No cigarette?"

"A gal has to draw the line somewhere."

The lamps are off, the curtains closed. They lie nipping from the bottle, her leg on top of his, the room enveloped in shadow. There are two dressers, two nightstands, an oval floor mirror. Like the rest of the house, the room is stark white, with nothing on the walls.

"So tell me," she says. "What's on Simon Addison's agenda for today?"

He's too prideful, after Daniel's reaction yesterday, to tell Juliet about his job at the gift shop. "Little of this," he says. "Little of that."

She spreads her thighs. "Maybe a little more of this?"

She can be so uncouth sometimes, so juvenile. It turns him on. He has a hard time imagining her at her practice, leading her art-therapy workshops, treating other people's psychological problems. "You're drunk already," Simon says.

Juliet laughs wildly, getting hold of him under the sheet, the bottle upright in the crook of her arm. The feeling is lovely—*better* than lovely. It's sublime.

"I have to ask," he says. "Not to be awkward, but why are we in here? Your bedroom, your bed. It was a little unexpected."

She thinks for a second. "I don't know. Call it closure. It seemed okay. Why, does it upset you?"

"A bit. Well," he says. "A lot, maybe."

She looks at him. "We didn't have a sex life, Simon. We had an *intercourse* life—sometimes. There's a difference." Juliet closes her eyes. "This is just another room to me now."

"What was it like?" Simon ventures. "Your…whatever. Your intercourse life." What is he saying? "Can I ask that?" For some reason he wants to know.

"I'm not sure you can."

"I'm sorry," he says. "I don't know where I'm coming from all of a sudden."

And then, with Andrew Huntley on his mind, Simon wants to tell her: he wants her to know that her husband's death was his fault. This is all he needs, isn't it? To admit it to someone. Who better than the man's wife? It's because of Simon that she's in mourning, in pain.

Juliet smiles at him. "No, we can talk about it."

"Was it anything like this? Like us?"

"Ha! Nothing at all."

"Do you forgive him? The cheating, I mean. You've mentioned it."

"Would your wife forgive *you*?"

"Ouch."

"Yeah. The pink pachyderm. Big fat mood killer."

"You kind of enjoy that," he says. "Putting me on my heels."

"Well?"

"I worry about it, of course—Rebecca. I don't want to talk about that, if it's all the same to you."

Her hand goes loose, and there's a silence, awkwardly long. What an ass he is. She's thinking about Andrew now, her dead, never-to-return husband. Thinking about chance too, perhaps—the unnerving concept of it. Or about mortality, and the whole maddening unfairness of the universe. All things Simon's been musing on, at any rate. He thinks of the elderly man on the corner, who's never mattered to him before today. Simon wishes that just once he could have been friendly enough to smile back at the man. As for confessing to Juliet, he won't do it—he won't complicate her grief for the sake of making himself feel better. He won't allow himself to be so cruel.

"There's nothing to forgive, if you want your answer," she says. "We had an arrangement, this unspoken kind of thing. We stayed together for Maddie, not for us. There was no mystery there."

"I understand."

"But he had it both ways. He could have me whenever he wanted, and I didn't mind that." She runs her fingers along his leg. "It was hot, I'll admit it, the thought of him with another woman. Is this what you wanted to hear? It's the truth, anyway. Sometimes we'd have sex later on, after I was sure he'd been with her. I knew when he didn't have time to shower, and it felt like...I can't even describe it. Like she was there with us, in some crazy way. You know—dirty, and weird, but intense."

Simon can't believe the things she says, this woman who has come so bizarrely into his life. He plucks the bottle from her arm, takes a long drink.

"Have you ever wanted to do that?" she says. "Have a three-some? An orgy or something? That's what it felt like. That's what I pretended was happening."

"So," Simon says, "my kids are back in town," and Juliet gives another wild laugh.

"You're the one who brought it up." She rolls onto her side. "Do I get to meet them?"

"Certainly," he says. "I thought we'd have you over for dinner tomorrow night. How does six o'clock sound?"

She gives him an earnest look. "Have you talked to them at all? Have you told them about it, what you went through?"

"They've got a lot on their minds," he says. "I haven't talked to *anybody* about it, not really."

"Maddie and I haven't connected much either. Not that we've had any opportunity to."

"At least she's still living at home. You're not some retired parent, the way I am."

"I haven't seen her in almost two weeks." She clicks her tongue. "It's all because of me," she says. "I tried to be there for her but I failed. Somehow I didn't give her whatever it was she needed."

"She's a kid," Simon tells her. "Who lost her father."

He puts his arm around her, missing his family now, remembering the day he met Rebecca—at the dinner party of a mutual friend—and then their wedding day, their honeymoon, the births of their children, first Daniel, then Michaela, both of whom, as they entered the world, pink and plump and yowling with life, filled him with the most acute sense of his own inadequacy. But they were gifts, his son and his daughter—gifts of flesh and blood and bone, a corporeal bounty—and they'd been given to *him*, Simon Addison, even though he'd done nothing to deserve such luck, and Simon remembers how excited they used to get whenever they saw one of those big searchlight beams sweeping the nighttime sky, and how every once in a while he took them out in their pajamas, in his old Mazda, to find whatever was being promoted, a street fair or a grand opening or something. They never stayed, just turned around and drove back home, but the accomplishment of locating the event, a pot of gold at the end of a rainbow, was always enough to elicit exclamations of joy from his children—was always better, it seemed, than an ice-cream cone or a new toy, or anything they might imagine. Anything at all.

"What about me?" Juliet says. "Can you talk to me about it?" She moves her hand to his stomach, resting it there. "Can you tell me—Lord, I don't know—what exactly happened that day? How you made it out alive?"

What can he say to her? He listens to a rafter ticking in the ceiling.

"You don't have to," she says. "It's hard for me too. We've never discussed it, and I was only thinking—well…"

He knows what's coming. How has she waited so long?

"Did you see him? In the middle of it all? Did you see my husband?"

Simon feels a pressure against his ribs, as though the wind has been knocked out of him. He takes his arm away.

"It makes no difference," Juliet says, "does it? Not anymore." She raises herself up on an elbow. "I'll tell you what I think. I don't think you really knew him." She pulls the sheet up around her waist, shakes her head. "You didn't know who Andrew really was."

Simon grips the neck of the whiskey bottle. "Those men didn't have to die," he says quietly. "None of them did." He takes another long drink, and there it is, thank God: the swift current of inebriation. The feeling he has—the sense of being caught in his own neurotic cycle of regret—bears some semblance to déjà vu. He will end this, he decides, this fling of his, or whatever he's supposed to call it. It will last no longer than today. He sets the bottle on the carpet and reaches beneath the sheet for his boxers, pulling them on. "None of this should have happened."

Juliet lays her head on his chest, lacing her fingers into his, holding his hand as though she'll never let go.

Maddie

When they wake on the fifteenth morning of their trip, still camped at Zephyr Cove, the Corolla is gone. So is Paula Toms, her doll lying abandoned in the campsite's parking space.

Russell gets a fire going and makes them coffee. He and Maddie sip from their hot cups and take stock of the situation, a light dew dripping from the pine needles, mist hanging thinly over the ground. Where has Paula Toms gone with his car? Is she coming back? If not, where is she headed? To Santa Barbara, for real? Or back to the adult-care facility in Duluth? If she even lives in such a place, or in Minnesota at all. She took Russell's keys from an inside pocket of the tent as they slept. How did they not hear the zipper as she opened the flap, or the jangle of the keys, or his car as it started up and pulled away? Maddie feels an odd kinship with her, a fellow thief.

"What now?" Russell says.

"We pack up. We go home." She knuckles some sleep from her eyes. "I'm ready now."

It's the most she's said to him in the past four days. When he returned from the trail on Friday, after Maddie had run off, Russell leaned against the Corolla and ran his hands over his face and said, "If we leave now, we can make it back to Vegas before dark." Paula Toms was picking dandelions a few campsites away, and Maddie couldn't help wondering what would happen to her if they upped and left. Besides, Maddie wasn't ready to go home, not yet. Home was still the very last place she wanted to be, particularly in light of what he'd told her about her father. She likes it here; it's beautiful, peaceful, and she wasn't leaving just because Russell had turned into an unbelievable fucking asshole. She ignored him each time he tried to apologize, and Russell banished himself to the trails, taking several lengthy hikes along the lake. Maddie passed the daylight hours listening to Paula Toms, wading in the bright, cool water with her, sitting with her on an unmowed plot of grass a short distance from their site, taking a halfhearted pleasure in her endless, zany stories, which were distractions, at the very least.

Now, with Paula Toms gone, she really is ready to leave.

•

By late afternoon there's still no sign of her. They eat Chex Mix and peanut-butter sandwiches, chewing in silence, sipping more coffee, which looks as if it's been used to clean a watercolor brush. Irritably, Maddie douses their campfire with her fourth cup of the day. She still isn't talking to him. Only if she has to.

"It's too bad," Russell says, sitting forward in his lawn chair. "I was really beginning to like her." He won't contact the police about the Corolla. It's fifteen years old, he explains, on its last legs, and he paid only a few thousand dollars for it. He'll get next to nothing if he files a claim. "Let her have it. She's in love with that hunk of junk anyway."

He uses the beat-up pay phone at the campground's office to see about a rental. There's a Hertz location a couple of miles away, he says when he gets back to the site. He's arranged for a Kia to be delivered. While he takes apart the tent, Maddie walks down to the cove and sits in the dirt beneath a very old pine tree on the edge of the beach. She needs some time alone before they set off for Las Vegas. The lake is calm, delphinium-blue. Birds cry out and other birds answer, a warm breeze riffling the long-sleeved T-shirt she bought in Ely. Her anger stems not only from what Russell said to her in the woods a few days ago, but also from what he confessed in the tent that night. The collection of poems wasn't a gift from her father. It belongs to Emma, who left it at Maddie's house by mistake. The handwriting is Emma's mother's. Russell hadn't had the heart to tell Maddie the truth; he'd been trying to protect her, or so he insisted. She nearly stormed right out of the tent. But where would she have spent the night? In the Corolla, with Paula Toms? Instead, Maddie took the book from her purse and shoved it as hard as she could into Russell's chest, turning her back to him and crying herself silently to sleep.

How could he allow her to embrace such a hurtful lie? She can't believe she ever found him appealing in any way whatsoever. *What compelled her to kiss him?* She makes a promise to herself: once their trip is over, she will never talk to Russell again.

She watches two guys in their twenties cross the shoreline and then make their way up to where she's sitting. They're short and thin, with short, thin hair, both blond. They wear polo shirts and swim trunks, and give the impression of being identical twins but look nothing alike. Maddie eavesdrops on their conversation as they open out a blanket a few yards away, in the shade of the conifer branches.

"It's a *play*," one of them says. "By Aphra Behn."

"Ben Affleck, you mean."

"No, idiot. Not Ben Affleck. *Aphra Behn*, the English dramatist."

They begin to eat from a bag of kettle corn—probably college students from Reno. She feels the firm, rutty trunk against her back, looking in the other direction now, down the patchy line of trees. Her anger at Russell pales in comparison to her feelings about Emma. Maddie will confront her as soon as she has a chance—she looks forward to it, in fact—but she doesn't trust herself not to spit in Emma's face, not to punch her in the mouth, even though she's never hit anyone in her life. The outrage swims around inside her, jabbing with its long, sawtoothed snout. She met Emma when she was eleven years old, after Russell had been dating her for a couple of months. Russell joined Maddie and her parents for dinner one night at an old casino in North Las Vegas, a place called Jerry's Nugget that advertises its nineteen-sixties kitsch and a fifteen-dollar prime-rib special. It isn't far from Fremont Street, and afterward they stopped by the Bora Bora during one of Emma's breaks. She was so pretty, too pretty, Maddie decided, even then, for a guy like Russell. And Emma was kind as well—Maddie always thought so. Mistakenly, it's turned out.

Somehow these feelings don't extend to Maddie's father. She wants to believe he was a victim, seduced by an attractive woman. He's just as guilty as Emma, of course. Maddie can't help feeling sorry for him, though, in some incomprehensible way. She can't help still loving him.

How much does her mother know? How will Maddie bring up the subject of her father's infidelity? She sifts through her memory for some repressed, overheard argument about it. Her parents, on the whole, seemed perfectly happy. Her father always seemed like a loyal, honest person, and Maddie will always remember him as one.

She looks back to the two blond guys.

"I give zero shits about anything these days," one of them says. "Zero." He makes an O with his forefinger and his thumb, lifting his eyebrows for emphasis. "You can be that way too. All you have to do is make up that neurotic mind of yours."

What explains her inclination to think back on her father in the most complimentary light, despite what she's learned about his past? She knows that most people can recall nothing but the positive about the dead, elevating them to saints. But she feels, all the same, that he deserves his high place in her mind, no matter what offenses he might have committed.

The blond guys are propped on their elbows now, facing each other and holding hands. She hears one of them say, "In any case, I'm sorry I ruined the morning."

"You ruined the morning," the other one says. "You're ruining the afternoon. You'll ruin the evening too. You ruin everything."

They both laugh.

•

When Maddie returns to the site, a royal-blue Kia stands gleaming in the parking space, the doll lying flat on its hood. All the equipment is in the trunk, and Russell is sitting on a tree stump staring at the ground. He stands up in his jeans and his LIVE LONG AND

FESTER T-shirt, which bears a comma-shaped mustard stain along the hem.

"Hey," he says. "Again, I'm really sorry. I never should have said what I said to you, Maddie. We've got a long drive ahead of us. A little conversation might be nice."

She doesn't even look at him.

"The fact is, it's a very serious matter. *Very* serious. We're not the only people it affects, you know. I hope we can talk about it on the way home."

She gets in the Kia with the doll, hugging it tightly to her chest. The hair smells like a dustpan, and Maddie can feel something beneath the doll's pink cardigan. When she unbuttons it, she sees, pinned to the white blouse, the toy sheriff's badge Paula Toms bought at the store in Genoa. A postscript. A charm, perhaps. Maddie forgot about it until just now.

Russell

"A priest and a nun are alone in the sacristy," he says, both his hands on the wheel, the shiny blue hood trained on a heat-cracked stretch of US 95 that seems no wider than a shoelace. "The priest asks the nun if he can kiss her. What does the nun say?"

Maddie stares blankly out her window, twiddling with the doll's plaid dress. They've been on the road for over two hours and she hasn't spoken a word.

"Give up?"

She shoots him a glance, then turns back to the scenery: the big desert floor, pilled like a sweater with bursage and sagebrush; the big brown mountains; big pink clouds in a shell-blue sky.

"'Well, okay,' says the nun. 'Just don't get into the habit.' Get it?"

He's doing his best to get her to talk to him again, telling stories and lousy jokes, asking questions Maddie answers by paying no attention to him at all. He feels like some second-rate vaudevillian, twirling his cane, singing and dancing in his top hat and tails, while the audience looks on in disgruntled silence. He's trying to forget their kiss ever happened. He's comfortable in Maddie's company again—Russell can act naturally around her, sort of—but what does it matter? She turns a deaf ear to everything he says.

They've driven through Yerington and Schurz and the Walker River Indian Reservation, through Hawthorne and Luning, moving smoothly down the western slope of the state. Gordon Lightfoot sings "Carefree Highway" on the only channel Russell can find, an oldies station choked with static. The volume is low but Lightfoot's baritone, combined with the crackling, is giving rise to some unnamed worry—some shapeless, slippery angst that Russell feels in an almost physical way. He turns off the radio; like his television back home, radio has a tendency to set his heart thudding, noise being high on the list of things that can trigger a panic attack.

Suddenly Russell has a vision of Maddie falling from the ledge of a building to a sidewalk far below, cracking open her head. Every so often, when his weed plays havoc with his brain, he startles himself with something like this, a little fantasy of suffering or death involving someone he loves: Emma being kidnapped and raped, for example, or walking obliviously into the path of an oncoming bus. Things he secretly frets about that in all probability will never come to pass. But he hasn't smoked today; he has to get them home. Also, he's trying to keep a level head. Maybe he'll lay off the weed for a while. Russell enjoys days like this, when he isn't dependent on the crutch of intoxication.

They pass a rusted, hoodless Beetle at the side of an old wooden shack. A cone of dust spins like a top. Maddie chews her lip, looking out the windshield now, holding the doll as though it's a small child on her lap. Russell likes the Kia's new-car smell. He'll have to buy himself a car when he gets home, but it won't be a new one—three or four thousand is all he can afford. He's surprised at how little he cares that the woman took off with his Corolla. It bothers him more, maybe, that she left without saying goodbye. He won't tell Maddie the story of the woman's little sister. He's given her enough disappointing news for one week.

"Does it ever bother you," he asks, "that you're an only child? I've been fixated on this lately, how I wish I had a brother or a sister. With your dad gone, and you not talking to me, and with Emma—well, it seems like I don't really have anybody right now. Bit of a bummer, you know?"

He looks at her in time to catch Maddie rolling her eyes, and Russell reaches over and knocks twice on the dashboard.

"I know you don't feel like responding, but I'm going to keep talking anyway," he says, shaking his head. "Emma doesn't have any siblings either, and not that many friends. We rely on each other a little too much, I think. She kind of saved my life, emotionally speaking. If you ask me, we found one another right when we both needed to and we just held on. Neither one of us has ever dared to let the other one go." His throat is dry, and he sips from a bottle of water. "This must be what it's like to filibuster on the floor of the Senate."

He can't keep his mind off Emma, though he's tried and tried. This trip was meant to be an escape—it was supposed to afford him some distance, both literally and figuratively—but how can he avoid thinking about her? He remembers their first date, two weeks after they met at the Bora Bora. The memory always arrives in warm, generous detail. They went to P.F. Chang's for dinner. It was drizzling outside, and they sat by a window in the company of the rain, a stained-glass pendant light hanging low over plastic canisters of darkly colored sauces. At the table next to them, a party of six was celebrating a woman's birthday, and a waiter brought a bowl of ice cream with a sparkler stuck in one of the scoops. The sparkler hissed and sputtered—its smoke held the odor of a spent matchstick—but Russell wasn't bothered. The high spirits were infectious; he felt giddy. During the meal, the drizzle turned into heavy rainfall, and he and Emma argued playfully about which team would win the Super Bowl in the next couple of weeks, the Steelers or the Seahawks (Emma said the Seahawks were going to win, although she couldn't have told him so much as the city they belonged to). Russell was wearing a tie, the only one he owned—he still has no idea why he'd put it on—but he hadn't knotted it properly, and Emma suggested he invest in a clip-on. They laughed with an attentive sincerity, not in that labored, compulsory, first-date sort of way. They ordered several bottles of Tsingtao, and Russell paid the bill, feeling like a gentleman, even though it was more than he could afford. All of a sudden the downpour was indecisive, starting and stopping, and Emma pointed her thumb at the doors and said they might want to make a break for it. It was in that moment, looking at her thumb—short but gracefully thin, bent backward in a manner he found adorable and sexy and exquisite—that Russell fell in love with her. As they got in his old Chevy flatbed, he kissed her, just a peck on the cheek. They ended up at some swanky lounge in Mandalay Bay, where they both felt out of place. And so they left, slightly drunk, and went to Russell's apartment and watched the second half of *Blade Runner* on cable, falling asleep together on his couch.

"I'm kind of glad it's gone," he says now, his mind changing direction. "My Corolla." He plays with the rearview mirror. "Want to know why?"

No answer.

"I'll tell you. It's where I was when he died. At the steering wheel of that car, driving home from work." He pushes at the bridge of his glasses. He means what he's saying. "I couldn't really feel them," he says, "the explosions, as far out as I happened to be. The last one shook the car a little, but I *heard* them, needless to say. Who didn't? And the smoke. All that smoke."

Maddie shifts in her seat.

"If you'll excuse my French, your father was a very decent man who made one very fucked-up mistake. One gigantic, unthinkable mistake. I don't have to tell you how much he loved you." He moves into the fast lane, passing an eighteen-wheeler with Looney Tunes mud flaps. "It drives me crazy that I'll never see him again, in spite of what he did." Russell means it—this too. He hopes it'll open her up. He hopes this will do the trick. "Your dad," he says. "He'll always be the same person to me. You need to understand that."

Russell still misses him—yes—though it stings terribly to acknowledge it. Likewise, Andrew still appears in his thoughts as the only character he's ever played in the story of Russell's life: his very best friend. Nothing can change that, he guesses. With skepticism, and with a kind of relief, he sees through to the hollow core of his own disillusionment. What's the matter with him? Is he some sort of weakling? Some doormat? Does he have any self-respect at all? When a man stabs you in the back by helping himself to the woman you love, you're supposed to despise the son of a bitch until the day you die. And the woman—your girlfriend, *your wife*. You're supposed to kick her to the curb, are you not? Say *adiòs*. Never look back.

"Emma too," Russell says. "I really do need her, more than I want to admit. It's so hard to stop caring about people. You think you can just turn it off after they hurt you, but you can't. News flash, right? Forgiveness is a whole lot easier than holding a grudge. I'm prone to take the easy way out."

He smiles at her—maybe she'll laugh—but Maddie turns her head toward him and says, "Thanks for the advice, Dr. Oz. You should have your own daytime talk show."

Russell sighs, giving up, tuning the radio to an all-news station. They drive by a place called the Area 51 Alien Center, which is nowhere near Area 51 but includes an alien-themed gift shop, along with a gas station, a convenience store, a topless diner, and a brothel, the amenities listed conspicuously on a fluorescent green billboard. Soon the sun disappears from the western horizon, and beyond the headlight beams, beyond the double yellow lines of US 95, is a vast sheet of darkness, white stars twitching in the sky.

Maddie breathes out heavily through her nose, covering her eyes with her hands—crying, Russell realizes. He looks in the rear-view mirror to make sure no one's behind him. As he pulls to the shoulder, he turns off the radio. He turns off the car, a felty darkness swelling up around them, and takes Maddie in his arms. She weeps powerfully against his chest, balling up the sleeve of Russell's shirt. He rests his chin on her head. To the east, a small brush fire burns in the night. Russell didn't notice it when he was driving.

He wonders what Emma's doing right now. Watching television on the couch, eating her ice cream. Working, maybe; he doesn't know her schedule for the month. He hopes she'll be there when he gets home. He'll give her back her father's book, which he's wrapped carefully in his camp towel, preserving its spine, and placed inside his backpack. He thinks of Las Vegas, his city, and it's all he wants right now: to be back there, to be home.

Maddie cries and cries, and Russell rubs the back of her neck. He strokes her hair the way he imagines her father might have when she scraped a knee as a little kid. What has she done with the doll? There it is—on the floor between Maddie's feet. Russell hopes the woman is safe. He pictures her on the beach where her sister drowned (he believes wholeheartedly that the story is true), walking barefoot through the warm brown sand, communing somehow with little Jane, who's drawn her back. He smiles as he thinks of that last conversation with the woman. *Drawn back*, Russell thinks. *Drawn back*. Why are people born, and why do they have to die? Adolescent questions that hound the mind nevertheless.

Why did Emma break his heart?

She didn't mean to—Russell is certain of this. She fell in love. So did Andrew. And then. And then…

It lessens the pain to think this way, to reason with himself. That she might never love Russell with the same intensity doesn't matter to him, not anymore. Pitiful, he knows, but there it is. A large part of him cannot bear the thought of ever seeing Emma again, as much as he misses her. A larger part, if not quite prepared to forgive, is ready to return. He will drive Maddie home and submit himself to her mother's wrath. Then he'll go home to Emma. He'll tell her about the kiss. He'll piece his life back together. He'll have faith, as the woman told him to. He'll say his prayers. He'll try to understand.

Maddie stops crying, and Russell pats her hand. A pristine silence follows: they have the highway to themselves. He watches the flames in the east, and a feeling shoots up in his chest, like a spark thrown off from a fire.

"I've been so angry," she says. She sits up straight, flattens her shoulders against the seat back. "Not just at you. At Emma. At myself, for not paying attention to what was going on."

"Join the club."

"When did you find out it was my dad?"

"It was a feeling. It was always there."

"I've got so many questions I don't even want to ask," Maddie says.

"Of course."

"What about my mom? That, for instance."

"What about her?" Russell says.

She sniffs. "Does she know?"

"I can't answer that." He reaches back and gets a pack of tissues from his backpack. "Here."

Maddie blows her nose, looking out at the fire—saying nothing, as though its presence is a given.

"Either way," Russell says, "it's something we're going to have to talk to her about. Together."

"What happens when you get home? With Emma."

"Conversations," he says, groaning. "Tears and more tears. The whole nine yards. The whole deal."

"For the past four days I've wanted to rip her fucking throat out. Rip her face off." Maddie shakes her head. "All the anger's over now, though, and I just feel...I don't even know what to call it. This numbness. This numb disappointment—like, in life. In what it's turning out to be."

Russell listens, nodding in the dark. The brush fire flares at one end, sweeping upward into the night, yellow flames lashing the sky. He wonders how she feels about her father's role in the affair.

"That anger," he says. "That'll come back. It's okay when it does." He looks at her. "We'll try our best to be right again. It's all we can do. But the anger. That might overstay its welcome."

•

They stop in an old railroad town for a break. US 95 runs directly through it. The prominent structures are a gas station, a bar, a motel, a few boarded-up shops, and a giant broken-down sailboat that's been turned into a restaurant, the bow of which reads "The Desert Lobster Café." The entire hull is buried, the gunwale level with the ground, so that the sun-yellowed boat appears to be sinking evenly into the earth. Across the highway, in the headlight beams, a sign announces:

Mina
Elev 4,540 Pop 155

Another sign says NO EXPLOSIVE-LADEN VEHICLES ALLOWED IN TOWN. Russell lowers his window for a bit of fresh air, wondering about a place where explosive-laden vehicles are such a problem that the citizens have established a prohibition.

The gas station is a brown-brick building with a corrugated roof, its two ancient pumps overgrown with tumbleweeds. "Gasoline—Sundries—Ice Cream" is painted in red above a long window with a cracked pane. They get out and stretch their arms. Mina, Nevada—more remote-seeming, somehow, than the other towns they've visited—is precisely what people mean by the phrase "the middle of nowhere." And speaking of people, where is everyone? The whole place is straight out of some campy horror movie, *Tremors* or *The Texas Chainsaw Massacre*.

Inside, the store is crammed with merchandise, most of it old and faded. Hunting vests and watch caps. Sunglasses and pocket-knives. Zippo lighters and wool rag socks. Only the food items appear to be new. Maddie picks up a magazine from a small wire carousel. Behind the counter, a large bald man in jeans and a Wolf Pack T-shirt comes out from a back room, the ghost of a green tattoo on his lower neck, a cobra bearing its fangs. The man winces with his eyes closed, working a melon-size fist into his gut, sipping from a bottle of Mylanta. Russell pays him and goes back out to fill the tank. He leans against the bumper, feeling good—hopeful. Down the highway a little, in front of the motel, two lighted palms make the shape of a V, growing from the dirt like fingers in a peace sign. The bar is just next door, a stuccoed dive that reminds him of the All or Nothing.

One of the rear tires looks low, so he pulls the Kia to an air compressor and tops it off. When he looks through the store's cracked window, he sees something strange: the cashier is holding Maddie in his arms.

They're standing near the counter, pressed up against a rack of potato chips. At first glance, the scene seems almost tender, as if she's locked in the man's warm embrace—as if he's taken Maddie lovingly from behind and is about to kiss her on the neck. Russell watches as if in a dream. It takes him a moment to discern what's actually happening. As she struggles to free herself, the cashier appears to tighten his grip, one enormous arm wrapped around Maddie's upper body. Russell doesn't move. He needs to take action—he needs to help her, right away—yet he remains where he is, standing beside the air compressor, feeling the same throb of apprehension he felt during the explosions, the same guilty relief (unlike Maddie, he is free, for now, from danger). His eye starts to water. He starts to sweat. Then it feels as though his windpipe is obstructed, and he thinks fleetingly, randomly, of President Bush at Booker Elementary School on the morning of 9/11, of his chief of staff whispering in his ear and the seven long minutes that elapsed before the president stood up and left the classroom, and then Russell yanks open the back door of the Kia, unzips his backpack, and takes out the Ruger.

What is he doing? Is he going to *shoot* the guy?

No, of course he isn't. But given the size of that arm, given the man's tattoo, the long-fanged cobra with the skin of its neck spread into a hood, Russell isn't going in there without a weapon to use as intimidation. He walks quickly into the store with the gun against his leg. The cashier looks at him and says, "She's got a bunch of shit in her pockets, dude!"

Maddie's hands are clenched at her sides, her face the color of a pencil eraser. A dab of spittle clings to her chin. The cashier's eyes open wider when he notices the Ruger, and Russell sees that one eye socket is considerably larger than the other. How did he overlook this when he paid for the tank of gas? If the left socket is an egg, the right is an avocado, and this feature makes the man even more threatening than he already was.

"Hold on there!" the cashier says, and loosens his grip. "You can have whatever you want. The till isn't even locked."

"I've got a permit," Russell tells him. "This isn't a robbery."

He raises his arms to show the man he has no interest in taking anything, but the cashier drops to the floor, bringing Maddie with him—a human shield—cowering like a puppy.

"Just get your hands off her," Russell says, lowering the gun.

"The cops are on their way, so think real hard about what's gonna happen when they get here, bud."

"You called the police?"

"You're hurting me!" Maddie says, managing to wriggle her hand into a pocket of her shorts, a Coleman sewing kit falling to the floor, followed by a roach clip with a feather on the end. Then a mini stapler. Then a blue key ring, shaped like the state of Nevada, that reads "Battle Born" in slanted white letters. "Here's all your crap back!"

"Jesus, Maddie."

Russell starts to wheeze. He wipes his eye, wondering what it would be like to unlock the safety, walk over to the man, and fire a bullet directly into his head. He wants to do it, as frightened as he is. The pain that has mounted over the past eight weeks—the anger, the resentment—he wants to take it all out on him. The cashier is only protecting his store, but he's gone too far, getting physical with Maddie over a pocketful of junk. Russell imagines pulling the trigger, the binary feeling of release and satisfaction: the feeling of crossing over to a place from which there is no return. Ever since he bought the Ruger, this crazy, obsessive part of him—reacting, perhaps, to his chronic nervousness, his timidity—has been itching to shoot at something other than a paper target.

He holds the gun tightly, his finger along the slide, away from the trigger, the way he was shown during his firearms course. They're in the middle of the desert—NRA country, hunters and militiamen—and he's afraid that if he tucks the Ruger into his jeans, or goes outside and puts it back in the Kia, the cashier will grab a gun of his own from behind the counter. He's afraid that another customer is going to show up and escalate the situation into who *knows* what. Most of all, he's afraid of the police, who, unless the man was bluffing, will be here any minute.

"Look," Russell says, "just let her up and we'll call it a truce. I'm asking you nicely."

"I'll let her up when the cops walk in," the man says, bulging his cheeks like he's about to be sick.

"We just want to leave now," Russell tells him. "We just want to go home."

But they can't, of course. They can't just leave. They can't go home. Not yet, not anymore. He feels himself about to weep, and behind his fear, behind everything Russell is thinking at the moment, are the flattening realizations that this is not going to end in their favor, that he and Maddie are in real trouble, that he's been right all along: they never should have left in the first place.

"Please," he says. "I'm giving you my word."

"All right," says the cashier, "fine"—looking queasy, unwell—and just then Russell hears the muffled clunk of a car door slamming, and he turns around to see the patrol car out the window: a navy sedan whose front fenders read STATE TROOPER. The officer emerges quickly, wearing a dark-green uniform with a broad-brimmed hat, the type worn by Dudley Do-Right and Smokey the Bear. He examines the Kia and its license plate, talking into his radio, and in the span of a few seconds, it seems, he's at the door and he's opening it, and by the time it closes behind him everything has gone haywire.

Maddie and the cashier are still on the floor, Russell is still holding the gun, and the officer has drawn his own gun and is shouting at him to drop the weapon and get down on his knees. Maddie is shouting too, and so is the cashier, who's trying to get up. The officer tells him to stay down, stay the fuck down, but the man won't listen. "I've got a condition!" he cries, clutching his stomach, struggling to stand. "An ulcer!" And in the next instant he's bent over and vomiting.

The vomit is everywhere, slapping the linoleum floor like chowder from a ladle, and Maddie scrambles to her feet, the store so cramped that she is more or less in the line of fire now, between Russell and the officer. Instead of getting out of the way in whatever way she can, she makes a clumsy move toward Russell, shouting even louder, something urgent and unintelligible, the officer commanding him for the third or fourth time to drop the weapon and get down on his knees. The cashier continues to vomit, and Russell flinches, kind of jumping to avoid the splatter. The Ruger raising up above his head. A shot ringing out.

•

Though he knows he's been hit, he feels only a warm heaviness as he lies curled up on the floor, where things begin to fuzz out, slow way down. Even the shouting is distorted now, protracted, something from a nightmare. Then he begins to feel something else—a splendorous, aqueous calm. It sweeps through him like a current, like a body of water moving through another body of water, liquid within liquid, his head as airy as a cloud. Then an outburst of pain at the base of Russell's neck, a sudden thudding in his temples. A sugary texture to his lips, the roof of his mouth. The rivaling odors of vomit and blood.

Then darkness. Nothing.

Emma

They have worked out a plan. She will run the roulette table the way she always does. She will spin the wheel, flick the ball along the rim. The ball will jump and settle, and when she turns her head, as a dealer must, to see where it landed, Marcus Bauerkemper will sneak a bet onto the winning number. He knows just how to do it so as not to get caught; he's done it before, he admitted the other night at his church. It's called "past posting," and Emma's been taught to prevent it—to turn her head only slightly, as quickly as she can, keeping an eye on the layout. But she'll pretend not to notice the additional bet. She'll pay him each time. They'll split the winnings fifty-fifty, and if Marcus Bauerkemper is detected by the surveillance team—the "eyes in the sky"—he'll swear he was acting alone.

They have worked out other, future schemes as well, not just for roulette but for blackjack and pai gow poker too—"pinching" and "coloring up," "card marking" and "hole-carding," "card switching"—and Emma keeps remembering the scene from *Casino* in which Robert De Niro has a security guard smash a player's hand with a ball-peen hammer after the man is caught cheating at blackjack.

Two Asian guys in their thirties are chain-smoking at her table. Spin after spin they lose, and before long they stand up abruptly, scowling, and move on. She spots Marcus Bauerkemper near the centerpiece of the Bora Bora: a giant slot machine in a green grass skirt, a life-size coconut at the end of its lever. He walks toward her in the same outfit he was wearing three nights ago, shirtsleeves rolled to his elbows, the string of red beads doubled loosely around his wrist. He appears relaxed and unconcerned—a man of leisure. She thinks of all the money they could make. A thousand or two, safely, in the course of an hour, Emma estimates. She thinks of her Visa bill, imagines signing a check for the pay-off amount, then raising a glass with Russell at the All or Nothing.

When Marcus Bauerkemper takes a seat at her table, though, something shifts inside her. She hates the way she feels right now—weak and unscrupulous and ashamed, a feeling she's grown accustomed to—and Emma straightens up and says, "You must think I'm some kind of dupe."

He cocks his head, folds his hands at his waist. "It was the Lord who made this happen, Emma. It was the Lord who brought us together. Who are we to repudiate His charity?"

"It's time for you to leave."

"Just hold on a second."

Emma feels her face crinkle—she feels so gullible—her change of heart giving way to a stomach-buckling anger. "Do you have any idea what I've been going through lately? Look at yourself. That stupid necklace around your arm. Your stupid shirts. Like you're the Maharishi, or some guru or something."

He looks down at the beads, puzzled. "These are for energy. They're my energy stones."

"Is that church of yours even real? Is that place even legit?"

"I'm very sorry you see it all this way," he says quietly.

Ed Logan is behind her in the pit—watching, Emma knows. "What other way is there to see it? I trusted you."

"Emma. We are merely—"

"I thought you could help me." She feels herself about to break down. "My whole life's in pieces right now, and I thought, on some moronic whim, I guess, that you might help me put it back together."

"We *are* putting it back. Don't you see? *Fate*," Marcus Bauerkemper says in a confidential whisper, pointing into the air. " 'The development of events beyond a person's—' "

"Would you stop it with your definitions? Who talks like that? Try acting like a real human being for a second."

"The Lord has sent us a message."

Emma laughs, shaking her head. Everything about him is ludicrous. Even his name, unwieldy and self-important, invites derision. She can't believe she placed even the slightest credence in this man. *Accept it*, she thinks. *You asked for this.* She's been exploited, and it's no surprise at all; she's given him the green light from the start. Some self-punishing part of her has hoped it would happen, has known all along.

"Thanks for proving to me what an idiot I am," she says.

"I was so nervous the day we met, I have to admit. You're a very appealing woman, Emma. Now, though. We've gotten to know each other in that certain sort of way—the way of fast friends. *Close* friends. We could be a great team, you and I."

She should notify the police. Warn security at least, denying any involvement in his plans. Or maybe she should put the whole thing out of her mind, simply and forever, forgetting she ever heard the name Marcus Bauerkemper. Surely this last course of action is the most prudent.

"Go," she says, glancing over her shoulder at Ed Logan. "Leave now or you'll wish you had. That's a promise."

Marcus Bauerkemper laughs suppliantly.

"Don't come back," Emma tells him, and he shakes his head.

"Jeremiah Seventeen, verse nine," he says, getting up from the table. " 'The heart is deceitful above all things. Who can understand it?' "

•

She clocks out early, telling Ed Logan she isn't feeling well, and leaves the Bora Bora at a little after eight. She drives slowly across the city, in a state of growing discomposure, getting up her nerve. Soon the entrance to Bighorn Heights is just ahead, and Emma worries at the finger grips of the wheel, the subdivision's sign emitting a flat, creamy light. When she turns onto the block, she drives past her usual parking spots and pulls up to the mailbox in front of Andrew's house. The windows are dark, the driveway empty. The outside lights are off, and the small house hunkers eerily in shadow.

It's a crazy idea, a selfish one as well, but she can't put it out of her mind. She will confess to Juliet and ask her forgiveness. Since Andrew's death, Emma has wanted to protect her by keeping her in the dark. Now she just wants to be honest with Juliet about what she did—make a clean breast of it, isn't that the phrase?—then get on with living, whatever the future might hold. Emma won't spend the rest of her days like Marcus Bauerkemper, two-faced and fraudulent. He's right: the heart, above all things, is deceitful. Hers deceived her into leading a double life. Russell knows the truth about her now, and it's time Juliet did too.

Maddie, by virtue of her age, is another matter. What she will know or not know will be up to her mother, though Emma frets that Russell—thoughtlessly, out of anger or hurt—has already said something.

She assumed Juliet would be home at this hour on a Tuesday. Maybe she's in a back room of the house, her Jeep in the garage. Emma gets out and rings the doorbell. No answer. She'll wait in the Civic until Juliet returns. She'll accept the blame and apologize—it has to be done tonight. She's kept Juliet in the dark for too long as it is. In the end, Emma never needed some pastor, some church, to straighten out her life—to save her. She will take responsibility for her own well-being. She will save herself.

Ten minutes later she's staring at her keys, in a clutter on the dashboard, the house key Andrew gave her still on her ring. Why didn't she keep it separate? A senseless oversight, not that it matters anymore. There it is, though, right there, and something comes over her, something potent and irrational, and the next thing she knows she's walking up the driveway, looking around to make sure no one's watching her.

At the side door of the house, she turns the key and steps past a recycling bin into the kitchen, finding the light switch by the toaster. The kitchen looks the same, save for a couple of cabinet doors whose glass is still missing. Emma sits down on one of the stools. What is the point of this? What has made her come into the house, knowing that Juliet could pull up at any moment? *And she will*, Emma thinks. *She will pull up.* It's bound to happen, isn't it?

She stares into the living room, the place where she and Andrew most often made love. She needed to see it, by herself, one last time, she realizes—this need arising, perhaps, from her decision to fess up to Juliet. Another way of sorting things out. She needs to touch the clothes he once wore, sniff his aftershave, wrap the old leather strap of his Timex around her wrist. Emma is ready to put him behind her, she really is, but she needed to say goodbye, and this is the only way, as insufficient as it might be.

His mother's Victrola stands in a corner of the living room, and Emma gets up and runs her fingers along the record player's nicked and faded edges. Andrew and Juliet married young, and he never forgave himself for replacing music with a life of drudgery at a chemical plant. Emma remembers how animated he used to get when he talked about the composers and rock bands he admired most: Mendelssohn and Chopin, Pink Floyd and The Moody Blues. She goes into the dining room, where she took cover during the final explosion. She roams past the entryway and down the hall, into the spare bedroom, the master—each white wall as blank as a canvas—flipping on lights as she goes, half-expecting to hear the crunch of glass from under her shoes. Her feet feel heavy, not entirely free, as though she is wading through a mold of newly poured concrete. She opens the door to the walk-in closet, Andrew's shirts and pants still hanging on a rod. Emma fingers the collar of a striped button-down, the thin wales of his corduroys, memories of her time with him floating on some far, foggy horizon in her head, as though she's plucked them from a dream.

She thinks she hears something, and freezes. From out in the entryway comes the inevitable sound of the front door unlocking and swinging open, and then Juliet calling, "Hello? Hello!"

Emma pulls the closet door closed and flicks off the overhead light, standing stock-still in the darkness. Of course she'll be found; her car is parked out front. How will she explain herself? (How can she be so self-destructive—always?) She hears Juliet say, "Emma? Are you in here?" Emma opens the door slowly, and as she takes a step out, Juliet rounds the corner into the bedroom, brandishing a poker from the fireplace. They both scream.

"What are you doing?" says Juliet, hand on her heart.

"I don't know," Emma says. "I'm sorry. I didn't mean to scare you."

"How'd you get in here? Why are you in my house?"

She feels faint. "I needed to talk to you."

"So you broke in?"

They stare hard at each other. "I have my own…well…" Emma takes her keys from a pocket of her skirt, squinting sheepishly as she holds them up. "I have a key."

Juliet leans the poker against the wall. She draws a breath, folds her arms over her chest. "I guess that shouldn't surprise me."

Emma can feel herself turning gray, feel the pallor rising evenly through her cheeks. She always wondered if Juliet knew about them. Such a frigid person—around Emma, at any rate, almost since they met. How did she find them out? When?

"Juliet—"

"What were you looking for? Why were you in my closet?"

"Nothing. I wasn't looking for anything. I just…I can't really form it into words." She puts her hand to her stomach. "I think I'm feeling a little dizzy."

"I'm going to ask you again what you were doing in my closet, what you're doing in my *house*." Juliet wears jeans, a beaded belt, and a black V-neck T-shirt, her hair in a loose, feathery bun. She tilts her head, smelling like beer. "Did you lose something? Some personal belongings? You didn't want to come knocking when I was home, is that it? Please—tell me what I can help you find."

"I came here to say something," Emma says, pausing. "I came to say I'm sorry."

Juliet sits down on the bed. "He gave you a key," she says, in a kind of awe, as though she's just been shown the solution to some confounding mathematical problem.

"I know this isn't the easiest thing to—"

"What's going on in that little mind of yours, that simple little brain?"

Emma looks at her.

"You think, what, that you can just walk right in whenever you please, with your precious key? That you get to decide when to apologize?" Juliet puts her face in her hands.

"I know you're upset," Emma says, sitting down beside her. "You have every right to be. You should hate me. I don't blame you if you do."

Juliet laughs, rearing her head. "Who do you think you are? Did you think I never knew?"

Emma keeps quiet. She will bear the abuse she deserves. She wants to ask about Russell, about Maddie.

"Look me in the face," Juliet says, and Emma does, and Juliet leans toward her, eyes rounded in anger. "You fucked my husband. *Were* fucking him, however long it went on. God only knows. You walked yourself into my life and you took something you wanted. You stole from me. Understand?" They're side by side at the edge of the bed, and the conversation, despite its severity, its awkwardness, feels suddenly, oddly intimate. "You probably fucked him right in here, knowing Andrew."

Knowing Andrew? "We never—"

"You know what they call women like you? Slutty little whores. You like being called that? A whore?"

They look steadily at one another. Outside, a helicopter passes overhead, the noise of its rotor blades cutting the silence.

"I'm being a bitch," Juliet says, "I know. And guess what? It feels pretty good. It feels just right, given the circumstances." She leans closer. "Do you like remembering him? Do you like thinking about him? You know how I mean." She blinks her eyes, bits of mascara clinging to her lashes. "Of course you do. I bet you're fantasizing about him right now." She reaches up and taps the back of Emma's head. "I bet he's naked up there. I bet you are too."

They keep looking at one another, both of them jumping when the phone rings loudly across the room.

•

He was taken by ambulance—in shock, with hypotension—to a hospital in Hawthorne, where he was admitted to the intensive-care unit and given an IV: penicillin, a blood transfusion, an antitoxin to guard against tetanus. The bullet entered at the front of his right shoulder and didn't exit. He was lucky to be alive; a few inches lower and Russell's lung might have collapsed. For two days he ran a fever. Twice he was questioned by officers from the sheriff's office but was never charged—he'd armed himself legally, in Maddie's defense. After a brief detainment for her own questioning, Maddie had gone home with Juliet in the Jeep, and Russell kept saying how worried he was that she was permanently traumatized. He's lost all feeling in his deltoid, and it's an exertion for him to flex his elbow. The doctor, a short, bearded man with Benjamin Franklin bifocals, explained that surgery to remove the bullet would likely result in further nerve damage, and so it remains lodged beneath Russell's collarbone, where it will stay. When he was released—his temperature back to normal, no signs of infection—a nurse put his arm in a sling and joked that he ought to consider playing the lottery.

He stands in the doorway now holding his backpack, looking unsure what to do with it, like a bellhop bringing luggage to a guest. Emma steps out of her loafers and tosses her keys onto the couch. It seems as though a lifetime has passed since Tuesday, when Juliet received the call from the sheriff's office and they both rushed out of her house, driving separately out to Hawthorne, Juliet speeding ahead, unstoppable, in her Jeep. Russell sets his backpack on the floor and unzips it and takes something out, something wrapped thickly in his purple camp towel. He comes over to her, removing the towel, and hands her her father's book. Emma smiles. When she begins to speak, he kisses her on the lips. She tries a second time to get the words out—to tell him, once again, how sorry she is, how much she missed him, needs him, how frightened she was during his treatment at the hospital—but he won't allow it. Every time Emma opens her mouth he kisses her. There's an urgency to it, and she thanks God for what's happening, feeling an arousal, a great updraft of desire, that is unfamiliar, unexpected.

In bed, in the semidarkness of their room, she props herself on an elbow and leans over him and skims his body with her fingertips, the way he's always done to hers. His shoulder is swathed in bandages, and she's careful to avoid it. She's overjoyed to be so close to him again, though Emma's mind is restless, scuttling to and fro. She keeps asking about his trip, but Russell only shushes her in reply. Where exactly did he and Maddie go? What did they talk about during all that time together? How has he arrived at this point of seeming forgiveness? And what about his car? The one he rented on the road was impounded as evidence, along with that ridiculous gun of his, which Emma can't believe he had with him. (What was he planning on doing with it?) The sheriff's office handed over his backpack—as well as some raggedy-haired doll—the second time he was questioned at the hospital. Russell answered every question the officers asked him, but he's told Emma almost nothing. He isn't ready to talk about the trip, given what he's been through. He needs to rest, and will explain everything, he says, in due time.

For one thing, it hurts him to speak at any length, pain radiating from his injured shoulder. Emma thinks about the impending bill from the hospital, wondering if she should have gone through with Marcus Bauerkemper's scheme after all. How susceptible she was to his trickery—how willing to be tricked. She has an ethical, if not a professional, obligation to report him to the casino, but she doesn't care. She doesn't want to get involved. Besides, Emma can't imagine him ever showing his face at the Bora Bora again.

"Russell," she says.

"I missed you," he tells her. "I didn't want to, but I did."

"I missed you too. A lot."

"Okay."

"I'm glad you're back," Emma says.

"It's pretty hard for me, you know. Being with you like this. I'm trying really hard here."

"I'm so sorry, Russell."

He looks up at her. "You don't have to say it," he says. "Whatever else it is you think you're supposed to say."

She's astounded by her egotism, her foolishness. Who is she to have strayed from a man who is so reliably good to her? He gave her his love, every last bit of it, and Emma brushed it aside as though it meant nothing. If she's learned anything at all in the past several weeks, it's that you don't take love for granted. What kind of person needs to be taught such a thing? *Me*, Emma tells herself. *Whatever kind of person I am.* She has to live with that, the knowledge of her own special brand of ignorance. She almost lost him, and she isn't in the clear just yet.

This is what she's thinking in these moments, stirred by a feeling of intimate attachment to him, unlike anything she's felt for Russell before. She is so grateful for him: her partner, her best friend. The thought washes over her like a shower, and for the first time she regrets that they've never had children together. It was her decision; she was adamant. Her affair with Andrew was one of the reasons, of course, but a larger one was that Emma has never quite seen herself as motherly. (She's too self-centered. She's clumsy sometimes, and forgetful. She values a good night's sleep.) The subject of parenthood has been dead for many years, but what if she revived it? It isn't too late. Women get pregnant in their forties all the time these days. What if Russell entertained the idea? What if she brought it up tonight?

The curtains are drawn back, and through the windows of their bedroom she can see a small half-moon, yellow-gray and patchy, the color of boiled yolk. A bank of gray clouds drifts over it. They're dark as cinders yet thin as chiffon, and behind them the moon is a spectral flicker, like a light bulb loose in its socket.

"You're still you," Russell says, "even after what you did." He touches her arm, her waist. "I'm still me. That's the conclusion I've come to. That's the way I'm thinking about it now."

Emma nods. She starts to cry, and he reaches up and puts his hand to her cheek. Then she's on top of him—Russell inside her, his body against hers—and she wraps him in her arms. They hardly move, absorbing the initial moments.

"Thank you," she whispers, thinking: *You're still my husband. I'm still your wife.*

So unpredictable, life is: a commonplace notion, a cliché, but so be it. Such sorrows life brings to pass, Emma thinks. Such pleasures and surprises.

Who knows what will happen in the morning? Nothing has been resolved. There's been no discussion about the future of their marriage. Emma, for her part, will try her hardest to keep it in one piece, not out of desperation but because Russell is a decent man and she counts herself lucky to have found him, and maybe she has finally, in the time he's been away, fallen in love with him. Maybe it took his absence to change her heart and mind. Maybe it's possible, as people are always saying, to grow to love someone.

Maybe.

Simon

She's given him until mid-July to find another place to live. After his children returned home to the East, Simon broke down and told Rebecca everything. He couldn't help himself, as much as he still values his marriage. He left out Juliet's name, and how he'd come to know her—that her late husband had been an employee of WEPCO, one of the ones who'd been killed—telling his wife only that he'd been unfaithful on multiple occasions with the same woman. Rebecca listened with a closed-mouth glare, folding her arms and turning a frightening shade of purple. When she demanded to know who the woman was, Simon said he'd met her at a bar on one of the nights he'd gone out by himself to see a movie.

Now he's moving out—starting over, he supposes dismally. He spent the Fourth scouring Craigslist and Rent.com, signing a lease a couple of days later on a two-bedroom ranch house in Blue Diamond, a dusty little gypsum town off Route 159, a few miles from Red Rock Canyon. His commute to the gift shop will be a snap; he can ride his bike if he wants to. The rent is nothing, six hundred dollars a month (the house is tiny and smells like a birdcage), and he's begun to worry about his finances. For the time being, he and Rebecca are merely separated: a "trial separation," the arrangement is called. Tricky as it'll be, they're still sharing credit cards and a joint account. But if she divorces him he could end up paying alimony. He could lose every penny he has.

He hasn't spoken to Juliet since the morning they made love in her bedroom, though she's texted him and called. Simon knows he has to contact her; he owes her that much. His shame at having cheated on Rebecca is far too great: he can't get himself to do it.

The idea of the phone call paralyzes him, the feeling of sitting in the open car of a roller coaster, waiting to ascend the first steep slope.

He's packed up the last of his personal effects, and he loads the cardboard boxes into the bed of the pickup. There aren't many. Rebecca can keep whatever she wants; he isn't about to squabble over spatulas or push brooms. She's at the supermarket and will be home soon. Simon hopes to be gone by then. He can't accept the reality of the situation, that he'll have to say goodbye, if only until the next time he sees her.

Lexie, who will remain here, hops around at Simon's ankles, yapping and sneezing. She follows him inside, into the living room, the house as quiet as a chapel, the windows throwing perfect rectangles of light onto the dark crimson carpet, the whole place awash with afternoon warmth. Lexie coils herself at the foot of the couch, and Simon goes into Daniel's old bedroom, the walls still hung with the sports memorabilia of his youth: washed-out posters and fuzzy felt pennants. In Michaela's room the walls are nearly bare, the way she's always had them. It breaks his heart to imagine telling either of his children that he's moved out. Suddenly Simon feels old: a dismaying, vertiginous feeling, as if he's standing at the edge of an extremely high promontory, looking down upon his past.

He walks back to the living room and stares at the framed photographs on the mantelshelf, in one of which the four of them are standing arm in arm beneath the mimosa tree in the front yard. Simon picks it up and studies it, holding the frame so tightly he's afraid the glass might break. Where is he going? What has he done? Everything has changed and he can't see a way to change it back. He thinks about his life since the day of the explosions—some imaginary life, it seems, some life that isn't really his, isn't the one he's supposed to be living.

How easy it is, he decides, to become someone else, a different person entirely. The realization floats inside him like an oil slick, saturating every other thought.

•

He scoops Lexie up in his arms and kisses her on the head, and just as he steps outside Rebecca pulls into the driveway. She gets out of the Taurus in sunglasses, a plaid button-down, a dark denim skirt, looking beautiful, opening the trunk and removing a bag of groceries.

"Let me grab that," he says, but she walks right past him. He unloads the rest of the bags, two in each hand, and carries them into the kitchen.

"Thanks," she says curtly.

"Can we talk for a minute?"

"About what?" Rebecca lifts a carton of milk from one of the bags, places it in the refrigerator.

"The thing is," he says, "I have something to tell you. Something you don't know."

"What else could you possibly have to tell me?"

"This is different."

She squints sharply at him. "I'm listening."

"One of the men who died—during the accident, the explosions. It was my fault."

"What do you mean?"

"I mean I'm the reason he's dead. I mean I could have saved him and I didn't. That maintenance guy. Andrew was his name. I could have stopped and picked him up, but I was too scared to do it. I drove away. I left him there." As he says this Simon feels the guilt let up a bit, as though he's lying at the bottom of a dogpile and one or two people climb off.

"Simon."

"You're the only one who knows."

"I'm not sure what I should say here. What do you want me to say?"

"Nothing. I just needed you to listen, and you've done that, so I'll go ahead and go. I'll get myself out of your life now."

"Wait."

He walks to the kitchen door, resting his hand on the knob, wondering how long it'll be before she moves back home to Livonia. "It's all right," he says. "I'm all right."

He isn't, though—not at the moment, not at all. But he knows he will be. He'll drive to his new home, begin his new life, a life that his very own actions have brought about. It won't be what he had, but it will suffice. He will summon the courage to accept it. Sooner or later he'll call Juliet and…well, who knows?

"It'll all work itself out in the end," Simon says, just to say something, to bring the conversation to a close.

He's thankful that Rebecca returned home from the supermarket before he could leave, thankful for these final moments with her. Thankful, he realizes, for everything that has ever happened to him, for everything that *will* happen, good or bad or otherwise.

"I'm okay," he says. "Really." He nods, forcing a smile. "I'm great."

Maddie

Maddie and her mother are hanging pictures when the doorbell rings. Her mother frowns quizzically, balanced on a stepladder in a corner of the living room, wearing faded black jeans and an old Runnin' Rebels T-shirt, Maddie's father's. "It's about time we got this place looking homey again," her mother said a couple of days ago. "Time we got back on our feet, you and I." Since then, she's made at least three trips to the nearby Hobby Lobby, buying replacement glass for all the frames. She climbs down the ladder as Maddie goes to answer the door.

On the stoop are two policemen in navy-blue uniforms. One has a flattened-out nose, a dense, sculpted mustache. The other is clean-shaven, much younger, wearing a silver necklace and a big black diving watch.

"Hello," the older officer says, a lopsided smile betraying some sort of unease. "You must be Maddie."

She nods as her mother joins her at the door. It's dark outside—a Wednesday evening in July. Beyond the two men Maddie can see the patrol car, parked at an angle to the curb. The streetlight at the edge of the yard throws an orangey glow over the long white hood.

"Mrs. Huntley?" the younger one says.

"That's right," says her mother.

"May we come in?" he asks. "If you don't mind, ma'am. There's something we need to talk to you both about."

In the entryway, the officers introduce themselves, and before Maddie's mother can offer them a seat, before Maddie has even closed the front door, the older one—Officer Anshaw is his name—informs them that her father's body has been found, retrieved a few hours ago from the rubble at the WEPCO site. "By the cleanup crew," he says apologetically, wincing a little, adding that though her father's wallet was still in his pocket, his driver's license intact, the body will have to be identified.

"We're keeping it from the media until then," says the younger of the two—Officer Montgomery. "We know this isn't easy."

Maddie's mother begins to cry. Maddie does too; she can't help it. It's as if her father has died all over again. Her mother embraces her tightly, the four of them crowded in the too-small entryway. Maddie stops herself from imagining what his body looks like after ten long weeks in the blazing summer heat, not to mention whatever fatal injuries he suffered as a result of the explosions. She wonders if his casket will be dug from the ground, if her father—what remains of him, anyway—will be placed inside it, the casket reburied. Even in her mother's arms, she feels a surprising sort of weightlessness, as though she's woken to discover herself in an orbiting spacecraft, or on the surface of the moon. The closure Maddie's been longing for, it's finally here, or some version of it. But the grief, that's here too, still and all: the core-level ache that she knows will never entirely go away, no matter how long she lives or how her life continues to unfold.

"What do you need us to do?" her mother asks, letting go of her. "What happens now?"

"Sure," Officer Montgomery answers. He rotates the diving watch up and down on his forearm, talking quickly about dental X-rays and DNA analysis.

"I just didn't think they would ever…" Maddie's mother says. She rubs her nose, her red-rimmed eyes.

Officer Anshaw lowers his head, staring down at the floor. "Someone will get in touch with you," he says. "Tomorrow would be my guess."

Her mother says nothing. Maddie folds her arms, because she doesn't know what else to do with them. It occurs to her that she hasn't spoken a word since the officers arrived.

"Okay," she says, softly but emphatically—assuming, for the moment, the role of authority figure. "Tomorrow, then. Thank you for coming." She's holding back her tears. "Thank you for letting us know."

•

Half an hour later, Maddie and her mother are sitting at the kitchen counter drinking coffee, reminiscing about her father. They've said little about the discovery of his remains, preferring to focus right now on when he was alive, but for Maddie the development is such a relief that she almost feels ashamed. She sips from her mug. The kitchen window is open and a warm breeze pours in through the screen, rousing a napkin next to the range, the katydids making their nightly refrain. Maddie and her mother are side by side on the stools, bellied up to the counter like patrons at a bar, and Maddie's enjoying it, sitting here in the comfort of the kitchen, recollecting the happy events of their past—the surprise party Maddie's father threw for her mother when she earned her master's in art therapy; the time he had to rent a plumber's snake and spend three days clearing a beach towel from the skimmer drain of their pool, after Maddie had fed the towel into the drain on her sixth birthday; all those nights she and her father spent camping in the backyard, staring up into the white-flowered dogwood, whose branches creak dolefully in the breeze—though it's all she can do not to ask about Emma. Every time she thinks of her father she thinks of Emma as well. It's impossible not to. Maddie and Russell still haven't spoken with her mother about the affair. Maddie hasn't even talked to him since the day he was shot—her mother has forbidden it—but her feelings for him are completely gone. She wonders if they ever really existed.

Her mother takes her hand now and says, "I know you had to get out of here. I know you needed to leave. I've thought about it a lot, and I get it now. I really do. Not that I didn't before, but it's my job as a parent to—"

"I know, Mom. Don't worry."

Maddie's road trip with Russell: she doesn't want to talk about it, not in the least. Her mother has tried once or twice to treat her with therapy, prodding her into sketching scenes from the gas station in Mina—Russell getting shot right in front of her. It was all Maddie's fault. She made the mistake of saying so, licking tears from her lips, during questioning at the sheriff's office in Hawthorne, and now her mother won't stop bringing up the topic of self-forgiveness. Maddie was given a ticket for shoplifting, and the guy from the gas station was released without charge, and the officer is on some sort of leave while the state continues to investigate. After Russell returned home, her mother called him and told him he was lucky she couldn't press charges, that he was a kidnapper, a son of a bitch—that he'd gotten what he deserved. Maddie listened from behind her bedroom door, remembering the way she'd moved toward him as the gun went off—trying to save his life, perhaps, though the movement, she thought, had been involuntary. She remembered her fear in the minutes afterward, her feeling of helplessness as the officer kept shouting and pointing his gun. Her awareness, at the very same time, of the unexpected, the unbelievable. The countless peculiarities of the world.

"I love you, baby," her mother tells her, sipping her coffee. "Your father did too. Very much. More than you'll ever really understand."

"I understand," Maddie says. "I do."

"You couldn't possibly."

•

After her mother has gone to bed, Maddie changes into shorts and a tank top and sets out on a run. It's late, almost midnight. The air is still warm, the sky cloudless, matte-black. Most of the neighbors' windows are dark, but the sidewalk is brightened by the streetlights, that same orangey glow. She hasn't run with any regularity in a fairly long time, and she's out of shape, her leg muscles tightening up already—she's in a little pain. It's a beautiful night, though, and Maddie's reminded of two lines from one of the poems by Sylvia Plath. They float repeatedly through her head:

> The future is a grey seagull
> Tattling in its cat-voice of departure, departure.

She doesn't know why the night reminds her of these lines. Maybe because she wants to delay the time to come, just for now—wants to savor this, the pleasant temperature, the clear black sky, the whispery calm of the block. Maddie misses reading the poems, and makes a mental note to buy her own copy of the book.

When she's out of the subdivision, she turns onto Stephanie Street, then Sunset Road. Before long the streetlights disappear. She should be frightened but she isn't. Under the dim half-moon, the pavement is just visible enough, stretching eastward in the flat, grayish light—the desert all around her, the night sounds of insects.

When she arrives at the WEPCO site she's panting. Maddie stops at the concrete barriers. She can see nothing but silhouettes, and among the piles of rubble are the dark shapes of the heavy-duty vehicles. From what she can tell, not much has changed since her last visit. She expected some kind of activity—floodlights and police tape—but there is nobody here at all.

She lets herself imagine her father's body now, decomposed beyond recognition—tumbling to the bottom of one of the piles, perhaps, like a model of a human figure, like a ventriloquist's dummy, the limbs flopping unnaturally, in a boneless sort of way, the clothes sooty, in tatters. Someone will get in touch with them tomorrow, the officer said. But where is her father right now? Where is his body? The morgue, Maddie assumes, but how did it get there? (In one of those big white bags you always see in the movies? Do they actually use those in real life? Did they haul her father away in a *bag*?)

She leans against one of the barriers, waiting to feel it, that core-level ache. But it's gone for the moment, and suddenly she thinks about Paula Toms, wondering where she is, what she's doing. Maddie wants to run home and call her. She wishes there were a way.

She stretches her quads and her calf muscles, then starts back down Sunset Road. Ahead of her to the west, the Sky Beam on top of the Luxor—the entire vertex of the big glass pyramid, the most powerful beam of light on earth—illuminates the air above the Strip.

She runs along the shoulder, kicking up gravel, remembering the geology book her father bought her when she was five, the pebbles he used to bring home for her from the plant. He gave Maddie other things as well, things he'd find in their yard. Flower petals and fallen leaves. The feather of an Inca dove, the dried-up wing of a swallowtail butterfly. How Maddie cherished them all, arranging them on her windowsill like specimens in a lab. As she got older she had to pretend a far greater enchantment than she felt. She'd grown out of her pebble collection. A whole stage of her life had ended—gone for good, like a balloon whose string had slipped from her grasp—and it filled her with a deep daughterly affection that her father hadn't noticed. She accepted his gifts every time, and maybe, Maddie thinks, the essence of love is nothing more than this: the impulse to give, the willingness to receive, an unstated agreement that binds us together even after death.

She runs faster, the pain in her muscles worse than when she left the house. Maddie welcomes it, knowing that in just a few weeks she'll be back in good shape. (Training for the cross-country season will begin next month, and she'll be ready.) Soon she's sprinting—sprinting toward home—an unsustainable pace. But it feels so good, the simple freedom of it. She's heard that Las Vegas, viewed from outer space, is the brightest place in the world, and the valley flickers in the distance, and before long this dark desert road will give way to the orangely lit streets of Bighorn Heights.

Then the pain in her legs eases off, her breathing slows, and what is it she's feeling now? Some kind of euphoria, not just mental but physical as well, something like the weightlessness she felt as her mother held her in her arms, when the officers delivered their news. Is it the runner's high, that elusive creature? Maddie's skeptical: she's experienced it only once or twice. But she thinks she might float right off the pavement, right up into the sky, arms and legs pumping like mad, and she runs faster still, with the breeze that blows warmly against her skin, out of one whole stage of her life and into the next. Through the darkness that will open into light.

Acknowledgments

A huge thank you to the National Endowment for the Arts, the Nebraska Arts Council, and the Creighton University Graduate School for generous fellowships—indispensable financial support—during the writing of this novel.

My heartfelt gratitude to the following people for their kindness and help:

David Means, Charles Bock, Ian Stansel, Neil Evans, Nathalie Barrié, and my wife, Seraphim Mullins, for reading early drafts.

Peggy Heck, for information about stiches and tetanus shots; Dr. Erin Linde of Physicians Laboratory Services, Nebraska, for information about the decomposition of human bodies; Jill Rodgers, for Workers' Compensation information; Paul Novak, for information about elementary-school disaster preparedness; Vince Carlson and Nancy Novak, for bartending information; my mother, Marie Mullins, for information about the PEPCON disaster of May 4th, 1988; Officer Suzanne Kessler of the Bellevue Police Department, Nebraska, for law-enforcement information; and Bill Ouren, Deputy Douglas County Attorney, Nebraska, for information about coroners and dead bodies.

Kevin Canty, for awarding an earlier version of this novel second place, in the fiction category, at the Tucson Festival of Books Literary Awards.

Ruth Farrington, John Carlson, and Mary Carlson, for caring for my three children, on many occasions, while I wrote.

John Price, for his fine essay "Man Killed by Pheasant," which inspired one of my favorite scenes in this novel.

My daughter, Zoey Mullins, for two damn-good similes (which I stole like a rogue).

Chris Offutt and Don Waters, for several years of assistance and advice.

Clark Whitehorn, Alrica Goldstein, Sara Hendricksen, and Sara Vélez Mallea of the University of Nevada Press, for their enthusiasm and hard work.

Julie Stevenson of Massie & McQuilkin Literary Agents, for her patience, faith, and editorial guidance.

Lastly—I could not have written this novel without the support and encouragement of my wife or the great, exuberant love of my children. I'm so lucky to have you all.

— D.P.M.

About the Author

David Philip Mullins is the author of *Greetings from Below*, a story collection, which won both the Mary McCarthy Prize in Short Fiction and the International Walter Scott Prize for Short Stories. He is a graduate of the Iowa Writers' Workshop, and his fiction has appeared in *The Yale Review*, *The Massachusetts Review*, *New England Review*, *Cimarron Review*, *Ecotone*, *Fiction*, and *Folio*. He has received a Creative Writing Fellowship from the National Endowment for the Arts, the Dorothy and Granville Hicks Residency in Literature from Yaddo, the Silver  Pen Award from the Nevada Writers Hall of Fame, and an Individual Artist Fellowship in Literature from the Nebraska Arts Council. He is an associate professor of English at Creighton University.